Best New England Crime Stories

Edited by

Christine Bagley
Susan Oleksiw
Leslie Wheeler

Crime Spell Books
Cambridge MA 02138

Crime Spell Books
Cambridge MA 02138
www.crimespellbooks.com

Printed in the USA

ISBN 978-0-9973520-9-2
First Edition

Deadly Nightshade

Contents

Introduction

A s we enter our second year, the editors of Crime Spell Books continue to be gratified by the reception the anthology has received. We are delighted by the new writers we've discovered and continue to admire writers whose work we've read and enjoyed for years. This year's offerings continue the high standard of storytelling and variety in genre.

Several stories are told from the perspective of the guilty party, beginning with the Al Blanchard Short Fiction Award winner. In "The Bookings" by Jason Allison, a man arrested after seven years of living straight contemplates his circumstances, which go from bad to . . . well, he's not sure. Stephen D. Rogers's narrator in "Dead in the Afternoon" knows exactly where he stands and how he got there, and in the end so do we. A young man reflects on the wisdom imparted by his boss, an important figure in the world of crime in "The Impediment" by Bruce Robert Coffin. A psychic is realistic about her work but is unprepared for the consequences in "A Death in New Hampshire" by Jeannette de Beauvoir.

The narrator of "The White Balloon" by Trish Esden is downright creepy in the stalking of his victims. "The Boss of Butler Square" by Sharon Daynard gives an unusual twist to the problem solver in the crime world. The villain is a surprise in the historical mystery "The Gentleman Burglar" by Leslie Wheeler. The reader follows the criminal to the end in "I Would Kill for That House" by Cheryl Marceau.

The supporters of law and order hold their own in a series of tales. The widow and deceased's cop partner solve the man's murder in Kate Flora's "I'll Be There . . ." The small-town police chief in "The Ghost Light" by Ruth McCarty gets some help from her sister. And the police and a DJ solve an unexpected violent death in "Blame It on the Blizzard" by Nikki Knight. A hapless heroine finds her knight in a uniform with a life vest in Christine Bagley's "The Beauport Incident." In Janet Raye Stevens's "Sticky Fingers," the police are assisted by a librarian in this historical tale, and in Edith Maxwell's "The Management of Secrets," the Quaker midwife uncovers the criminal.

Not every crime or criminal fits in the slots allotted for them in our system. The truth finally comes out in Avram Lavinsky's "Playing God," challenging both sides. The guilty party is hard to discern in "One Week in Royal Rajasthan" by Judith Green. The police officer is no match for the woman he arrests in "By the Book" by Tilia Klebenov Jacobs. Regret is not absolution in "Women's Night Out" by Susan Oleksiw.

In three stories justice is achieved outside the legal system. In Hans Copek's "Framed," a man is set up for a charge of murder by his former business partner. The superintendent of Mount Auburn Cemetery in "Clay" by Robin Hazard Ray solves a murder and manages a compassionate justice for the victims. The burglar in "The Perfect Choice" by John R. Clark can't imagine the outcome of his choices. No matter how bleak things seem, however, there is the escape to a better world in "Call Me Mathias" by a.l. Dawson.

This is a rich and rewarding collection of short fiction exploring the various genres, and offering challenging and through-provoking perspectives on crime fiction and the society that has produced it.

Christine Bagley
Susan Oleksiw
Leslie Wheeler

The Bookings

Jason Allison

The lights made him squint. He raised a forearm to shade his eyes. The photographer sighed.

"The camera can't see your face if your hand is in front of it."

Jake lowered his arm.

"Turn to your left."

Jake went right.

"Your other left."

Jesus Christ, why was he so damned nervous? This wasn't a new experience for Jake. But it had been awhile. Six years, ten months, and twenty-one days, to be exact. Almost seven years since he'd walked out of Greenhaven, the max prison upstate. Seven years since he'd been spoken to by a cop or screw or badge of any kind. Seven years of head-down anonymity, gone, like that.

"On the floor to your right's a box marked out by tape. Step into it."

Jake looked to his arresting officer, a near-silent Black guy named Sherman. His head was buried in his phone, his other hand resting on the magazine pouches affixed to his gun belt. The Jake that lived in Greenhaven needed permission from the screws to eat, to shower, to shit. Institutionalization came back quick.

"The box. I need you in it."

The Bookings' photographer was a short white woman with curly hair, librarian's glasses, and a humorless disposition. Jake looked down and saw no tape, only the faint outline of where this mythical box once was, or might have been, before hundreds of thousands of defendants had shuffled into its center so the city could memorialize all who came before an arraignment judge, an arraignment judge who lay, Jake knew, many hours away.

This photo, though, would record how Jake was dressed the night his streak was broken. No. On the night *he* broke his streak. Ownership mattered. His counselor had drilled the concept into him.

Click.

"You're done."

Officer Sherman wiped his nose with the back of his hand, indicated with his head for Jake to step back into the holding room from which he'd been removed. Sherman pushed the door open, reapplied the cuffs that had torqued Jake's wrists since he'd been led from the precinct. The space was cramped, too small for the dozen men occupying it, standing about with their shoulders pinched back, some lost in quiet conversations robbed of the extravagant gestures common to small men who acted big. The kinds of men that filled prisons and precincts. The kind of man Jake had once been, and, now, it seemed, would be again.

"Jake Raskins?"

The skin along the back of Jake's neck pinpricked. A thin white man with a pock-marked face and out-of-style mustache came toward him, weaving through bigger men. Jake was hit by an image of trash bobbing on the ocean, refuse subject to the whims of wind and tides, its destination beyond its control.

"Shit, it is you."

Jake shrugged, his movement limited by the bracelets on his wrists. "Reggie."

"What're the odds, you and me getting pinched, in this town, on the same night? Fucking astronomical. Someone oughta do the math."

That someone would not, could not be Reggie. Numbers had never been his thing. His skills lay elsewhere.

"What can I say," Jake said. "Things happen."

Like adding a one to the temporary tag hanging from Jake's Impala's bumper. All he needed was a few more days to get the ride registered proper. What he got was Officer Sherman, the streak broken.

"That they do," Reggie said, with an ex-con's understanding. He moved close, his eyes flitting left and right. "You got anything going on?"

"No." Best shut this shit down straightaway, Jake thought. "I'm done. Been done a long time."

"Uh huh."

Reggie eyed him skeptically, and Jake knew what was coming. He'd known Reggie his whole life, known a hundred Reggies over the years, associates of Greenhaven Jake. Not friends. Never friends.

"But you're standing here, same as me. So you can't be that done."

Jake said nothing. In the corner, an old crackhead wearing four overcoats squatted, his ratty jeans pulled below skeletal knees. Rear-cuffed, he shat on the floor, sending the rest of the prisoners fleeing to the room's edges, hit by a shockwave of lost humanity.

An expressionless sergeant cracked the door. "Everybody out," he said, without passion or anger, like a man shitting on the floor was a common occurrence.

In places like this, Jake knew, it was.

Reggie slipped into Jake's holding cell just before the attending cop pulled the gate shut. Jake cursed silently. Arrest-to-arraignment times, back when Jake maintained a working knowledge of such subjects, ran between twenty-four and thirty-six hours. Too damned long to spend in a barred cell stuffed with miserable men, an exposed steel toilet, and Reggie fucking Sparks.

Reggie joined Jake on the floor, their backs to the glossy brick wall. The steel cuffs, now removed, had left indentations on both Jake's wrists. He rubbed them absently.

"It's good we hooked up," Reggie said. "Going through's always easier when you know someone. Kills the time."

Jake grunted. He'd killed years in Greenhaven, had no desire to do so again.

"I didn't think you were still in the game," Reggie continued, picking at a purple thumbnail.

"I'm not."

"Of course you're not." Reggie paused. "So what'd they put on you?"

Across from them, a young Mexican kid strained to listen. Every man in this cell had a story, how they came to be in this rancid shitbox. Each hoped they weren't the dumbest guy in the room. Tonight, that title belonged to Jake.

"I changed the expiration date on my temp plates."

"You know that's a felony," Reggie said.

Eight feet away, the Mexican kid stifled a laugh. This version of Jake let it go. Greenhaven Jake wouldn't have been so kind.

"I couldn't take off work to get the car registered," Jake said. "And I needed the car to get to work. It's a no-win."

Reggie nodded. "You're Yossarian."

Jake turned his head. "What?"

"Like in *Catch-22*? Yossarian doesn't want to fly more missions, so he acts crazy, but acting crazy's seen as normal by the generals, so he must be sane. Back up he goes."

Jake blinked at Reggie.

"I did ten months in a treatment center." Reggie made air quotes with his fingers. "Fucking day camp's more like it. Place was a joke."

"You using now?"

"Fuck no. But you ever get pinched with product, say you're addicted. Alternative sentencing, they call it."

"I'll keep that in mind."

Neither spoke for a time.

"What kinda work you doing?" Reggie asked.

"Metal fabrication. Machine parts, tool and die, stamping."

"How's that pay?"

Not nearly enough, and Jake's delay in answering told Reggie so. "It's alright."

In some unseen nearby cell, a fight spun up, the chaos of shouts and cries, of bone on bone, men slamming into walls and steel. Apathetic cops loosed unheeded orders. It sounded like Greenhaven all over again. Jake shut his eyes, wished he could shut his ears.

5

Reggie spoke soft. "You need money, I'm looking for workers."

Down the hall, some cop doused the combatants in pepper spray. Everyone on the floor began to cough.

Jake looked at his left wrist, remembered Officer Sherman had vouchered Jake's imitation G-Shock. Him and Reggie had been separated when the cops emptied the cells, Jake getting bumped to the second floor, Reggie to some hole deeper in the Bookings' first floor. Jake guessed, with some confidence, that eight hours had passed. Cons developed internal clocks, the monotony of institutiona-lization tracking the minutes and hours.

"Scuse me," Jake said to the female cop seated opposite his cell. "You got the time?"

"Yep." The cop flipped a page of her *Us Weekly*, popped her gum.

When it became clear she had no intention of sharing it, Jake wandered to the back of the cell, stepping over the legs and arms of men laid out on the concrete floor. He stared at the wall of gray, punctuated in spots by exposed white where the paint had chipped away. He'd kill for a window, some way to orient himself in this timeless, unchanging, fluorescent-lit world. Prisons had windows, but they cut both ways, offering distraction while reminding those inside of the world from which they'd been removed.

Seven years. The streak broken. Jake breathed deep.

The cell door opened with a metallic grinding. In walked Reggie Sparks.

Shit.

He moved through the cell like a soldier through a mine field, pissed in the toilet, did not flush, sat next to Jake. "So?"

Jake gave him a look like he didn't know what Reggie was talking about. But he did.

"You really a Joe Citizen? Paying taxes, nine-to-five, all that shit?"

"I work nights."

"My point remains."

"Been doing it seven years."

"And look where it got you," Reggie said. "Your boss gonna understand when you don't show for work today? He the compassionate type?"

Jake's wasn't, but Reggie didn't need to know that. Tonight was a blip, an aberration. Seven years, Jake had lived straight. He could do it again, he was pretty sure.

"I'm gonna see the judge," Jake said, more for himself than Reggie, "get released, get my car, and go to work."

"No you won't."

The words came from the Mexican kid who'd been with them downstairs.

"You oughta mind your fucking business, *ese,*" Reggie said.

"Just saying, getting your car, all easy like? Ain't gonna happen."

Reggie began to get up, but Jake stayed him with one hand.

"You got some insight worth sharing?" Jake's voice was even, cold. Shades of Greenhaven Jake.

The kid waved a hand, a guy not seeking a fight, but blundering in, just the same. "I don't mean any offense. I race."

"You race?"

"Street racing. Highway takeovers, that's my thing. Pigs've seized," his eyes drifted, "three rides from me. I'm saying, I been down your road." The kid realized he'd made a pun, smiled.

"I wasn't racing," Jake said. "I fudged my plate."

The kid stood, came over, dropped to a squat. "And that's a felony, like your friend said. But they'll drop that to a misdemeanor, so long as you agree to pay these crazy ass fines. They won't release your car till you do."

The kid was talking Perp 101. Jake should've known all this. Seven years ago, he did. But the streak had robbed him of knowledge he no longer wished to possess. He ran a hand over his jaw. His beard was filling in. Twelve hours now? Fifteen?

"The fines," Jake said. "How much're we talking?"

The kid made a face. "You got a history?"

"Does he," Reggie said.

Jake glared at him, then returned to the kid. "I'm a felon."

"Fifteen hundred?" the kid said. "Maybe two Gs. Ballpark."

Reggie whistled, low and slow. Some first timer made the mistake of flushing the toilet. Thick, brown water bubbled up, flowed over the bowl's lip, onto the floor. The stench was awful, and everyone scrambled to their feet, double-quick. The cell quickly became a lake.

The female cop popped her gum.

"Raskins?"

Hearing his name, Jake woke up. A ragged Timberland boot lay inches from his face, its occupant lying on his side, facing the wall. It smelled something awful.

"Raskins?"

"I'm here."

Jake pushed himself up. The cop slid open the cell door. Next to him was an obvious lawyer, Jake's PD. He followed her into a tiny room containing a frisbee disguised as a table and two molded-plastic chairs, bright orange. The chairs reminded Jake of places he swore he'd never go again, and decided to stand.

"My name's Loretta Baumgartner, your public defender." The heavyset Black woman sat, scanned the open folder in her hand. More folders. "Two felony convictions. Any out of state?"

"No."

"Sex offenses?"

"No."

She flipped a page, then another. "Were you aware someone altered your temporary registration?"

Jake didn't say anything.

Loretta finally looked up at him. The whites of her eyes were lined with red. She got little sleep; inmates suffered from the same affliction. "Did you know someone—"

"I can't afford to fight this," Jake said, cutting her off. "I'll take probation, whatever they want to give me. I need my car. I've got to get to work."

"You work?" Loretta flipped pages fast. "Why'm I here?"

"I've got a job, but I don't make private counsel money."

Loretta stared off into a corner. Jake had seen this before, lawyers running legal math in their heads.

"If I can get them to drop the felony, you'll plead?"

"Will I get my ride back?"

"Once you pay the surcharges. They come with the deal. Nonnegotiable."

Jake rubbed his forehead. His hand smelled foul. "If we drag it out, how long am I looking at?"

"To a disposition? Thirty months. Ish."

Jake shut his eyes again. He needed sleep, but had to get to work.

"You tell me what you want. I work for you." Loretta's exhausted tone implied she wished she didn't.

Jake was quiet for a time. Overhead lights housed in a wire cage buzzed, just loud enough to make their presence known.

"These surcharges," Jake finally said, "how much we talking?"

"The city'll want about $500, but it's the state that gets you. DMV fees are running to four figures these days."

Jake hissed air through gritted teeth.

Loretta flipped Jake's folder closed, set it atop the others, stood up. "I get it. Money's tight, times are hard. Think I'd be doing this work if I wasn't a believer, the good fight, all that? Thing is, registering a car in this state costs a hundred-and-twenty-five dollars. That's not cheap, I'll grant you that, but with one stroke of a Sharpie, you agreed to hand over that number times ten. *That* is insane."

Jake said nothing.

Loretta made for the door, her stack of case folders nestled in one arm. "When we see the judge, you don't say a word unless I tell you to. Got it?"

Jake nodded. His lawyer walked out. The lights kept buzzing.

A rail-thin cop with a gray mustache read off five names, pulled five men from their third-floor cell, marched them to the last stop before the courtroom. Jake had been born in this city. He'd been through the Bookings eight times, had spent close to two cumulative weeks in this hole, still didn't know where the system held females. He wondered if they had it better than the men, decided that was unlikely.

"We gotta be next up," Reggie said.

Jake had tried to grab more sleep, the cells up here larger, emptier, the cops more senior, able to limit the number of prisoners they had to handle. But Jake still couldn't let himself go. Instead, he'd spent hours in that strange, almost-sleep world, eyes closed, senses sharp. He lived that way throughout his forty-four months in Greenhaven, ever alert, never getting more than an hour's fitful rest at a time. He felt that sense of perpetual exhaustion returning. Its arrival terrified him.

"You done any thinking?" Reggie said. "What I mentioned downstairs?"

"Hey," Jake said, "I never asked what you're charged with."

Reggie hesitated at Jake's change of topic. "Molly. They found some in the car."

"Some?"

"Five pills. Personal use."

"Thought you weren't using."

"Alternative sentencing."

"Right."

They lingered there, two idle men, four eyes on the narrow slice of hallway afforded by their position. Jake listened for the sound of heavy brass keys. That clanking sound that presaged a cell's opening, a CO reaching for the next name on his list. Jake hoped his name was called before Reggie wore him down.

"Cause look," Reggie said, his voice low, "I had a runner go down two weeks back. I got roster slots that need filling."

Go down was vague enough to make Jake think Reggie's runner had gotten clipped. Before Reggie could go on, the armored door separating the cell block from the courtroom swung open. The high-pitched metallic squeal cut Jake to the spine. Eight visits over fifteen years, and that door always squeaked. Did COs know about WD-40? How did these people work here?

"That's lunch," a weary voice said.

Prisoners hissed, sighed, and cursed in a half-dozen languages. The judge was taking his—her?—break. Another ninety minutes added to Jake's sentence. He turned from the bars, found a spot on the floor in the back of the cell. Reggie, of course, followed.

"I ain't asking you to do anything other than drive."

Don't ask, Jake told himself. Asking opens the door. Asking is the indicator, of interest, of need. Wait this out. You learned in Greenhaven. Don't ask.

A radio played scratchy Motown.

Don't ask.

Piss flowed into a toilet.

Don't ask.

Two COs complained about mandatory overtime.

Don't ask.

"Where?" Jake asked.

Reggie leaned in close. "The Poconos. Four hours, there and back. Cake."

"I'll think about it," Jake said, intending to do anything but.

That last hour is the worst. Anyone who's ever been through the Bookings knew it. In those final sixty minutes, the mind wanders. You start dreaming of a shower, wondering if you've got food in the fridge, whether or not she'll believe the lie you finally settle on.

Jake had managed to go this long without thinking of Sheila. Officer Sherman had given Jake two calls, two shots Jake didn't take, hoping he'd come up with a story, dress this aberration in the right outfit, make it palatable. Greenhaven Jake would have thought of a dozen lies, not cared if Sheila believed any. But he wasn't that man anymore, hadn't been in nearly seven years.

Seven years. God damn it.

"You got a ride home?" Reggie asked.

Jake didn't.

"One of my boys'll be waiting for me." Reggie let the implied offer hang.

"I'll get a cab."

"Your cop left you your cash?"

Officer Sherman hadn't. He'd invoiced everything Jake had: the watch, an old flip phone, ratty wallet, and fourteen dollars and twenty-two cents. All Jake held now was a photocopied receipt for his own money, and no cabbie was accepting that. "Yeah. I'm good."

"Cool, cool."

Reggie's tone carried one con's acceptance of another's outright lie, because, sometimes, leaving a man a shred of his dignity mattered more than the truth. Still, he eyed Jake sidelong. "I'm just saying, easy work for solid pay. Real money. But you do you." Reggie was shit with numbers, but a born salesman.

Jake said nothing. Truth was, he was beginning to waver. The claustrophobic confines, the fluorescents' unceasing glare, and stinking prisoners laid out either side of Jake had begun to shape his thoughts. The uninitiated might look at Jake's position, at those seven uninterrupted—if not glamorous—years, and wonder why anyone would again consider a life that would no doubt deposit him back here, over and over. But the uninitiated approached the problem wrong. Greenhaven Jake would argue that, since he was going to get pinched again, he ought to make enough money to justify the lost time.

Lost time. Seven years. Gone. And Reggie here, persistent as ever. Jake needed out.

Heavy clattering grew near, and fifteen hanging heads rose as one. A CO in horn-rimmed glasses stared at a clipboard. "Sparks."

Not quite what Jake had been hoping for, but it'd do.

Reggie pushed himself off the concrete floor. He turned, offered Jake his hand. "Want me to wait?"

"Nah." Jake slapped his hand into Reggie's. The man's palm was cold to the touch.

"You sure?"

"Sparks," the CO said. "You can either hang with your boy or see the judge, but not both."

"I'm good."

Reggie nodded, barely. "I'd tell you to hit me up, but I know you won't."

Jake said nothing, and Reggie Sparks followed the CO out of the cell.

Someone in the gallery coughed. A wet, hacking sound, like a lunger.

"Quiet in the courtroom," said a haggard CO, her hands tucked in the armpits of her vest.

The judge, a slight, white woman with silver hair, held eyeglasses just off her face. She read a document, its origin and import unknown to Jake.

"Did the arresting officer observe the defendant alter the registration?" The judge said *dant* so that it rhymed with can't.

Two female assistant district attorneys, straight-out-of-law-school young, huddled, spoke in whispers. Jake stood there, alternating between holding his hands in front of him and behind, the con's endless posture debate. Which made him look innocent? Or, more accurately, less guilty.

"The people cannot answer that question at this time, your honor," one of the prosecutors said.

The judge sighed, glanced heavenward. *Give me strength.*

"However," the prosecutor continued, her voice cracking, "mere possession of the forged instrument, a document issued by a government entity, is, in itself, the sole element listed in the statute."

The judge burped. "Ooof. Ms. Baumgartner?"

"Defense's position remains the same, your honor."

The judge began reading a different form. Jake's attention wandered. Six or seven observers sat in the gallery, mostly women, most carrying infants, rocking and shushing them while waiting for the fathers to see the judge. Purple night filtered through grimy windows. Jake's con clock was off; he'd expected morning.

"Will the people agree to the misdemeanor, with time served?"

Jake returned his attention to prosecutors. Two kids, their ages added together less than Jake's alone. This bothered him more than he'd like to admit.

"The people will, your honor."

"And the defen-*dant*?"

"Say yes," Loretta whispered.

"Yes, your honor."

A pound of the gavel, a stroke of the pen, and it was over. He waited in the gallery for the court clerk to hand him a receipt for his car. $1,354, all in, city, state, and court surcharges. A heavy hit, one Jake couldn't pay. Still, could have been worse. He was free. No pending court dates, no invisible weight hanging over his head. He practically sprinted from the court.

In the lobby, an elderly janitor ran a buffer across the filthy stone floor. A court officer manning the metal detectors fisted a yawn. Jake stepped from the century-old building into the cool, night air, and wondered, not for the first time, how he'd get home.

He could hail a livery, and hope he had forty bucks hidden in his hollowed-out copy of the King James Bible an optimistic nun had given him in Greenhaven. But he'd dipped into that stash Tuesday last, to pay for gas sitting in a car he no longer possessed.

Sheila was another option, though he'd have to find a pay phone and deal with her wrath, her embarrassment. His shame.

He could walk, but he was exhausted. And ten miles on foot, through the dark of night, through a changed city in which Jake was now an outsider, was asking for trouble.

A blacked-out Nissan Maxima rolled to the curb.

"Need a ride?" Reggie sat in the passenger seat, window down, grinning cause he knew Jake did.

"I'm good." Jake heard his lie clear, was certain Reggie did, too.

"Right."

The Nissan idled, the only ride on an empty street. Behind the wheel was a young face, a kid trying to look hard, Jake three decades past, clueless as to the life that lay ahead, how it would break his face and body and soul. The kid gripped the wheel, sneered at Jake.

"Come on," Reggie said. "I'm starving, and so're you. We'll hit a diner, shoot the shit."

Seven years. Seven years dodging the life, only to find himself on an empty street in blackest night, five feet from temptation in a four-door sedan. Jake could turn, walk away, right here. Figure out another option. There was always another option. Except when there wasn't.

"How much to get your ride back?" Reggie asked.

Don't answer. Don't answer. Don't answer.

"Thirteen hundred," Jake said.

"Ouch." Reggie studied himself in the sideview, smoothed his mustache with a thumb and forefinger. "I hook you up, you'll make double that in a day."

Jake stood perfectly still, because any movement would lead him toward the car, what it held. What it offered.

Reggie leaned back, popped open the door behind him. The Nissan's back seat was cavernous, lined in black leather. Jake's eyes were heavy, his stomach empty. He wanted a shower. He needed sleep.

"No obligations," Reggie said. "Just a chat."

Jake glanced left, then right. There wasn't another car on the road. Stop lights cycled green to yellow to red.

"We can consider your options," Reggie said.

This is how it happens, Jake knew well. And that knowledge led to rationalization. Every con's delusion; this time I won't be stupid. Play small ball, don't reach for the big pay day. Grind it out.

"No obligations?" Jake asked. Right there, it was over.

"Course not," Reggie said. "You're a friend."

Of all the lies Reggie spun, that was the most blatant. Men like him and Jake didn't have friends. In their world—in Greenhaven Jake's world—people were tools to be leveraged, cast off when shit got heavy, in that inevitable

17

post-iceberg moment when the hull had ruptured, and water rushed in.

Jake took a step, then another, then another. He climbed in behind Reggie, pulled the door shut. His mind heard the Greenhaven cellblocks locking up after the night's final count. Reggie's new boy rolled off the brake and Jake reset the clock.

Seven years had come and gone.

Dawn would bring day one, the streak anew.

Jake doubted this one would last as long. ❖

I'll Be There . . .

Kate Flora

Maura Kelley was thirty-four, still a vibrant, dark-haired, blue-eyed Irish beauty, when it happened. "It" wasn't the knock on her door by two stricken police officers who struggled as they delivered the news that her husband, and their colleague, Declan Kelley, was dead. "It" wasn't the blur of the wake and funeral and people who seemed to be speaking through a cloud as they offered their sympathy. "It" wasn't the devastating and infuriating fact that the police didn't know who had killed him, only that he hadn't been killed where he was found. "It" wasn't even the moment, in the midst of all the strange and rushed commotion that served as contemporary death rituals, when her body delivered the heartbreaking news she would not be having Declan's baby after all.

"It" was when she was sitting on the couch, alone at last in their dim and silent house, the air still scented with casseroles, funeral flowers, snuffed candles, and people's perfume, and felt a tingle in the air. Something electric, a disturbance in the deadly quiet and a sudden infusion of warmth. It was when Declan's German shepherd, Buddy, who had been lying disconsolate on the floor, watching the door and waiting for a return that would never come, crossed the room and lay down before the place where Declan always sat, and looked up with loving eyes at the space beside her.

Maura was a sensible woman. A nurse. An oldest child and a caretaker. And although—despite all the grief she'd seen through work—losing Declan had made her sadder than she'd ever imagined a person could be, she knew she hadn't lost her grip on reality. She didn't believe in ghosts. Yet when she leaned toward the space beside her, where Declan should have been sitting, she felt his solid bulk and his warmth. She closed her eyes, lowered her head to his invisible shoulder, and let her imagination fill the space with Declan.

"Told you I could never leave you." She felt, rather than heard, his words, as though they moved directly from his mind to hers.

They stayed like that awhile, her head on his shoulder, his face tucked against her head, Buddy in his usual place, lying on Declan's invisible feet. Their little family unit together again.

"I hate making you so sad," he said.

"How could I be anything else? You were my world."

They let silence grow, as they'd often done, but Maura knew Declan wanted to ask her something. She felt the tension she always felt in him when what he had to say was hard, and when he didn't want to ask because it might upset her. His considerate nature had been what first attracted her. Other cops coming into the hospital with victims, or injured bad guys, tended to be pushy, to see the staff as an obstruction to doing their jobs. Declan had been deferential. Polite. He'd asked when he could speak to a patient, rather than demanding. He'd stayed out of their way, watchful but unobtrusive. He'd seen when they needed assistance restraining a violent patient or calming a frightened one. Noticed, and shared her distress, when a small child was abused.

He'd been so considerate and deferential she worried that he'd never ask her out, and when he finally did, she said yes before he'd finished asking. Their first date had been their only date. Since that night, except for their work, they'd rarely been apart. Until Declan was shot.

Maura knew what he wanted to ask. Something that would be hard for her, and something she couldn't do without his help and he couldn't do without hers. The kind of thing a man passionate about justice would ask. She took a deep breath. "You want me to find your killer."

"We need your help, Maura. Yours and Buddy's. They don't know where to look and there's no way I can tell them. But I can tell you."

We. Because even though he was dead, Declan was still a cop. Still a part of the team.

Words poured out as her normally patient husband gave her a mountain of information. There were details and instructions. Street names. Descriptions. Evidence collection techniques. Piling up so fast it made her head spin.

She said, "Stop. Slow down. I don't have your cop's memory or experience. I'll need to write things down."

"Maura, I have to get this out. I don't know how long I can stay."

He started in again.

Her breath caught. He might not stay? She tried not to think about that as she said, "Okay, but let me get some paper."

When she came back with pen and notepad and settled in next to his invisible, yet so real, presence, something else was troubling her. "I'll do whatever you want, Declan, anything so that animal doesn't get away with this. But even if I follow your instructions and find things out, how will I get them to believe me?"

Because this was crazy. Even if she and Buddy followed Declan's instructions and located some evidence or clue, or got Declan's description of his killer, anyone she tried to share it with would think she was crazy. Just a grieving widow trying to engineer what she wished would happen. Telling them Declan's ghost told her would not make her more credible. She pictured herself telling the police sketch artist what Declan had seen.

Impossible.

"This place smells like casserole and too-sweet flowers," he said.

"Yucky, isn't it? But that's what people do. They bring casseroles and flowers. They mean well."

"Be better," she felt his sexy tone, "if they'd brought vodka and cranberry juice." Their favorite drink.

"They didn't want to make me any sadder."

If she closed her eyes, it was like he was really there. She snuggled back into her favorite place between his chin .and his shoulder.

"Maura. Honey. I'd like to stay like this forever. You know I would. But please can I tell you this stuff, just in case?"

"In case . . ." She forced the words out. "You can't come back?"

22

"Yeah. That." He let a few ticks of his grandmother's clock pass before he said, "Get Caleb to help you."

Caleb. Declan's partner. A big, stoic, Black ex-Marine. He hadn't been there the night Declan was shot. He was taking his son to the Emergency Department, leaving Declan to look for an informant who knew something about a fentanyl operation. Partnered instead with Harry DeSouza, a man so lazy he'd taken his sweet time answering Declan's call for help. Who hadn't been there to have Declan's back.

DeSouza hadn't looked too hard when Declan disappeared, either. Just walked a few alleys and then called it in. The search had fallen to other cops, hours later. Cops who'd found Declan's body a mile away.

Maura wondered what the real story was. Whether DeSouza had been involved somehow. She had no one to ask. Although police families were cherished, they were also treated like mushrooms and left in the dark. The theory was it was for their own good. Declan had never agreed.

Now Caleb's son had recovered and Declan was dead and Caleb blamed himself for not being there. She knew that even though Caleb hadn't called or come to see her. Had left immediately after the funeral. She knew why he was avoiding her: because your husband's partner becomes part of your marriage—at least in a good marriage and a good partnership. She and Caleb were both grieving the loss in their own ways. She here alone; Caleb probably hunched over a drink at a cop bar. At least he had company in his grief.

"We had a pact, me and Caleb," Declan said. "Anything happened to one of us, the other wouldn't rest until the bad guy was caught. He'll absolutely believe I came back to tell you this. Likely, he'll be pissed because I didn't come to him instead."

Maura knew that was true. Caleb had a short fuse. He also thought Declan belonged to him. Whatever. Somehow they'd figure out how to do this. She was used to dealing with those in distress who took that distress out on the people around them.

She sat up, poised her pen over the blank sheet of paper, and said, "Go."

He talked. She wrote. She fact-checked. She wrote. Declan was meticulous, as careful as he was in all his reports. "Cops hate to write reports, so they cut corners. My policy is leave nothing out," he always said. "You don't know what may be important later."

Now it was later. And they still didn't know what might be important.

She wrote for what felt like hours, pages of detailed notes, wrote until her hand cramped, forcing herself to write on until Declan said, "That's it."

She set down the pen. She leaned back against him, meaning to snuggle back into her spot. There was nothing to lean against. The space beside her was cold and empty and Buddy had gone back to staring at the door.

Had she dreamed it all? Was that possible?

She looked at the pages of notes. It hadn't been a dream.

After she had a good cry and felt thoroughly wrung out, she called Caleb.

He answered with a flurry of apologies. She brushed them off. No time for that. There was a crime scene out there to be found, and evidence, including blood and a shell casing, to be secured. Tomorrow, the weatherman promised rain. Whatever they could do, they had to do it tonight.

"I need you, Caleb. Right here. Right now."

"Not in the best of . . . shape . . . right now. Uh. Maura. Talk tomorrow?"

Dammit. He'd been drinking. Was he too drunk to help?

"You want to catch whoever shot Declan, don't you?"

"That's a dumbass question, Maura. Pardon my language."

"Then get over here."

She hung up. No way she could explain this over the phone. She had to show him the notes.

Maura turned on the lights so Caleb wouldn't know she'd been sitting in the dark like an idiot. Then she went to the kitchen to see what there might be to eat, staring into the stuffed refrigerator in despair. She wanted something clean and crisp and what she had was enough tuna noddle casserole and lasagna to feed an army. Turning, she saw a fruit basket, the cellophane still intact. She wrestled it off and grabbed an apple. Declan always teased her about liking fruit more than cake. He'd had a serious sweet tooth. Dessert every night. Three or four sugars in his coffee. He never gained an ounce.

She gathered up the soggy tissues that littered the coffee table like fallen clouds. If Caleb was jumpy, as she expected, seeing this would make it worse.

Buddy alerted to the sound of feet coming up the walk, the waggle-eared alert he used when it wasn't Declan but was someone he knew. When she let Caleb in, Buddy was all over him, nosing his pockets for treats and jumping up to give him a big lick.

"Sorry," she said. "He's bereft."

Like Caleb minded. He was giving ear and belly scratches and producing treats from his pocket. "You taking good care of Maura?" he asked the dog. "Taking care of Maura?"

Buddy nodded, as he'd been trained to do. Buddy was Declan's dog, but Maura was part of his pack. He *would* protect her.

Doggie duties over, Caleb turned to her. "So what's this about?"

"Please sit," she said. "And promise you won't act like I'm crazy until you've heard me out."

Maura handed him the notes and sat across from him. He looked at the pages and then back at her. "What's this?"

"Read it. Then we'll talk." He had to see that it was Declan's style. That these were Declan's notes despite the handwriting.

He bent over the pages. Reading. Absorbing. For several long minutes, as her tension grew, there was silence except the rustle of pages and his occasional murmur. An agreement. A question. When he finally set them down and looked up, his eyes were wide. "This is one hundred percent Declan," he said. "But Declan's dead. Where did you get these?"

"He dictated and I wrote them down."

"The hell you did, Maura. Declan was gone when we found him. There was no dying declaration, never mind this." His glare was a cop's glare, like she was trying to put something over on him.

She sank back into the cushions. This was the moment when he opted in or out. She had to make him believe.

"I know this sounds crazy, but . . ."

26

No. She shouldn't start that way, giving him the out that she was crazy. "Look, Declan's ghost or his spirit, or whatever you want to call it . . . he came to me. Said he had things to tell me. Things that would help find his killer. He made me write them down." She gestured toward the papers. "He said you would understand this was his work, not just something his grieving Maura thought up. He said you'd help."

Caleb sat tight-lipped, looking like he wanted to flee, and would if she were anyone but his partner's widow.

"Caleb. He says there's evidence out there. Evidence we can find if we look for it now. Evidence that may be lost if it rains tomorrow."

No response.

"Look. I can go out there by myself. Buddy and I. We can follow his instructions and find where he was killed. Maybe find that shell casing. Buddy is trained to find evidence. But if *we* do it, we won't have any credibility. We won't have access to a lab to test . . ."

She faltered. Grabbed a breath. "His blood. Get ballistics. You're his partner. You do have that credibility. It would be perfectly plausible you'd be out searching for where he was killed. Believable that you'd find evidence."

Caleb sat still as a stone. Declan had been so sure that Caleb would come through for him. And now this.

Maura grabbed a tissue, dabbing at the tears rolling down her face. These days, tears came even when she didn't know she was crying. She had plenty to cry about. But this, which mattered so much? Had Declan been wrong about his partner?

"Caleb. You can't blow me off about this. You can't let him down."

Still Caleb sat.

27

Maura felt despair wash over her. The expression was a cliché, yet that was how it felt. Like something dark and visceral was swallowing her up. Like she was drowning. The darkness in the room seemed to deepen, and the sickly scent of food and flowers thickened like invisible hands were filling the room with more unwanted food and more flowers. She wondered if she was going to be sick.

Then she felt it. That same electric charge she'd felt before.

Some of the darkness lifted.

Declan said, "I never thought he'd blow you off like this. Never. Guess I'll have to step in."

She leaned back against the sofa, her eyes on Caleb. Watching Caleb's set face and rigid posture. Wondering if Declan could communicate with Caleb the way he could with her. Feeling a twinge of jealousy that this might not belong only to her.

Under other circumstances, Caleb's look of goosed surprise would have been comical. He sat up straighter, dragging a huge hand over his shiny, shaven skull, and stared at her suspiciously, like it was something she was doing. Then he fell back against the cushions with an exhaled, "I'll be damned!"

He listened thoughtfully, then picked up her pages of notes, jotting some of his own as he read. He said, "Cell phone?" and made a note about that. Then he jumped to his feet. "We've got to go," he said. "You, me, and Buddy. Let's . . ." He hesitated. "Maura, you can't go dressed like that."

Maura had no idea what she was wearing, or even whether she was dressed at all. What did it matter? But under Caleb's disapproving gaze, she looked down. Black dress. Black stockings, black shoes. Perfectly proper for a new widow.

"Go change into something you can prowl down dirty alleys in," he said. "Jeans. A sweatshirt. Sensible shoes."

She headed for the bedroom.

"Maura, wait. This involves a murderer who's gone to great lengths to avoid being caught. You shouldn't do this. It's not safe."

"I damned well am doing this," she said. "This is my business like nothing in the world has ever been. You aren't charging out there like some white knight and leaving the little woman behind." She stormed into the bedroom and changed. Grabbed the purse that held her gun and her pepper spray. Declan always wanted her to be prepared.

Caleb was waiting with her coat, Buddy already on his leash. She stuffed Declan's notes in her purse, grabbed some of Buddy's favorite treats and his police vest, and off they went.

They took Caleb's car, which was stocked with the gear they'd need, and after a few false tries, found the right alley. It wasn't easy. That neighborhood had alleys behind most of the buildings running parallel to the streets, a maze of sheds, parked cars, abandoned cars, dumpsters, and discarded furniture.

The day had turned dark and cold. Maura shivered despite her warm coat. She'd never seen Caleb in action before. It was a revelation. Despite her years with Declan, her notions of investigation were influenced by TV. Once they'd found the right alley, she was all for charging down it with her flashlight. Caleb said one word, "Wait," and began a systematic search.

Things Declan had said over the years came back to her. "You'd think Caleb's too impatient to be a detective, but all that herky jerky bustle of his? Put him in an interview

29

room or at a crime scene, and he goes into slo-mo. Man's got all the time in the world. Others might rush by, looking for the big score. Not Caleb. He'll search inch by inch and hour by hour."

That was how Declan was, too. No wonder they'd been good partners.

Maura could be that way, too. But here she had no patience. She needed to do something.

Buddy shared her impatience. Once she'd put on his vest and he knew he was going to work, he tugged at his leash and whined as they waited for Caleb's instructions. After a few minutes, he seemed to remember they were there.

"Okay," he said. "Buddy is trained to do evidence searches. You give him the command, "G. U. N." He spelled it out for her. "Then stay close and watch him. You'll know if he finds something because he'll lie down."

Maura nodded. She and Declan and Buddy had played the evidence game many times. Hide something—a bullet, a spent shell, a piece of cloth with gunshot residue, a discarded glove, even a handgun—then give Buddy the command to find it. Declan and Buddy would wait while she hid it, and then Buddy would find it. Every time. No matter how well she hid it. "He's cheating, you know," Declan would say. "He just follows your scent." To make the game harder, they'd get someone else to hide evidence, and then the three of them would go and find it.

Watching Declan and Buddy working together was like watching man and dog become one. She could only hope that tonight Buddy would be willing to form a woman-and-dog team.

"Buddy could find a needle in a haystack," Declan always said.

Tonight, Maura fervently wished that was true, because this was no game. While Caleb continued his meticulous search for the spot where Declan was shot, searching the cold, dark ground for signs of blood, she bent over Buddy, undid the leash, and said, "Find gun."

For all his straining and impatience, once he was off-leash and working, he calmed down and went to work. Maura followed with her flashlight, watching him closely for signs he'd detected a scent. Step-by-step down the dank-smelling alley, redolent of trash and decay, Buddy meticulously checked out everything they passed. Once, twice, three times he paused, checked and rechecked. Each time, her heart jumped. Each time, he moved on.

Suddenly, just as Maura had let her attention wander and was looking back down the alley at Caleb's slow-moving pool of light, Buddy gave a sharp bark and lay down, pointing to an overstuffed chair leaking stuffing through gaping holes in the seat.

"Caleb," she called. "He's got something."

"Hold on. Don't touch anything. You aren't wearing gloves," he said.

Maura praised Buddy and gave him treats. She thought she could sense Declan in the alley. Thought Buddy could sense him, too.

Caleb appeared, snapping on gloves. She focused her light on the chair as he began probing the chair's innards, his face concentrated as he explored, muttering, "Come on. Come on. Dammit. Give me something."

It seemed like an hour had passed before he muttered, "Dammit, I can't find it," and pulled his hands out. As he moved, there was a small, metallic plink. She focused her beam onto the ground beneath the chair, where a shell casing gleamed in the light.

31

Instead of scooping it up, as she'd expected, he set down a small yellow marker. "We'll leave this for the crime scene guys. I'm going to keep searching the alley, working backward from this chair. Why don't you see what else Buddy can find."

"Like what?"

"Like maybe, if he didn't expect us to find this shell, or this location—which would have been the case without those notes—the killer might have tossed his gun?"

She didn't much like his tone. Too much like he was talking to an idiot. But she wasn't here for herself. She was here so Declan's killer would be found. She looked at Buddy, then down the dark stretch of alley to a lit street in the distance. This place was so creepy.

She took the time to snap a couple pictures of the chair and the shell casing with its little yellow triangle.

"On second thought." Caleb scooped up the little evidence triangle, and stuck it in his pocket. "Maybe the bad guy will come back for that shell."

Maura felt uneasy. She hoped he didn't mean tonight, while they were here. She wanted him to grab that shell casing. Put it in his pocket. But he was the cop, not her. "Okay, Buddy. Let's go. Go find the gun."

Buddy looked at the shell casing and then back at her, as if he was saying, "I already did that." Then, in a gesture almost human, he shrugged and continued down the alley. Ears up, alert as he worked the space from side to side, checking and rejecting possibilities. They were nearly at the end where the alley met the street when Buddy stopped beside an overflowing dumpster, sniffed, and then stood up on his hind legs, front legs against the side, sniffing, moving, sniffing, and finally, with a sharp bark, lying down. She stared at the dog, amazed he could pick out a particular smell from that fetid mess.

Declan said searching dumpsters was the nastiest part of the job.

"Buddy's got something," she called, turning toward Caleb. But Caleb wasn't there.

"Caleb?" she called.

No answer. Everything behind her was dark. There was no sign of Caleb or his flashlight. Instinct told her not to call again.

Her heart beat faster. What if the killer had come back to tie up a few loose ends—find that spent shell and retrieve the murder weapon—and stumbled on them doing their little independent investigation? An anxious, suspicious part of her even briefly thought, *What if Caleb was somehow involved?* She just as quickly dismissed it.

She didn't care how stupid it made her look, she needed help and she needed it now. She wasn't a macho cop. She was a sad, scared woman alone in a dark alley. She moved to the far side of the dumpster, away from where she'd last seen Caleb, and called 911. When dispatch answered, she gave her name, her location, said she was being stalked by a man with a gun, and asked for help. Before dispatch could tell her to stay on the line, she disconnected. She couldn't hold her gun, her dog, and a phone.

She felt a sudden patch of warmth. Declan said, "That's my girl."

"Now what do I do?" Maura whispered. "Where's Caleb? Is he okay?"

No answer. She wanted to yell that he couldn't keep coming and going like that. It made her crazy. But it was also crazy to yell at a ghost. Crazy, at this moment, to yell at all.

Something was very wrong.

Beside her, Buddy was anxious to get back to his find. She grabbed his collar and pulled him closer, giving him the command to be still. Even in the dark, she knew he was giving her one of his skeptical canine looks.

Time passed. She got colder. Even in the cold, the dumpster reeked. If help was really coming, it must have been coming from Siberia. And there was no sign of Caleb.

Maura was scared. She wanted to go home. Wished she'd brought her own car instead of relying on Caleb. Where the heck was he? He wouldn't have abandoned her, would he? What if something had happened to him? What if he needed help? There didn't seem to be any help coming.

She wanted to stick her head around the corner of the dumpster and see what was going on. She started forward.

Declan said, "Wait."

A second later, there were quiet footsteps and Caleb slipped around the corner. She brought her gun up. He put a finger to his lips.

They waited together in the smelly darkness, the metal dumpster cold against her shoulder, Buddy's warmth heavy against her leg. Her fear had put him on full alert.

In the stillness, she could hear other footsteps coming toward them, and see the bouncing yellow cone of a flashlight beam.

Buddy tensed.

Caleb put himself between Maura and what was coming.

There was a thud, and a muffled curse. Then the sound of something being dragged. A dull metallic sound as something bumped against the dumpster, and then heavy breathing and a clang that reverberated through the alley as someone threw up the dumpster's heavy lid.

A loud "Oh shit!" and a wave of expletives as the man surveyed the mound of smelly trash. A moment of silence, then the rustle of plastic and the clank of cans and glass as heavy bags of trash were dumped on the ground. The falling bags were accompanied by a sotto voce commentary of "Jesus. Fuck. Where the hell. Where the hell. Fuck!"

Then a triumphant "There you are!" and footsteps as the searcher stepped down from whatever he was standing on, and began searching through one of the bags.

Maura was getting dizzy from holding her breath, and her hand on Buddy's collar was cramping. She shifted, and Caleb's hand went up, warning her to stay still.

A leather jacket creaked as the searcher straightened up. She imagined he had found the gun and was tucking it away. Then movement as whoever it was came toward them. As he passed the end of the dumpster, Caleb stepped out.

"Police officer, put your hands up where I can see them," he said.

In response, the man shoved Caleb and began to run.

"Get him, Buddy," Maura said, and let him go.

Declan used to say a dog can be scarier than a man with a gun. Buddy was a big, bite-trained German shepherd. By the time she and Caleb got there, the man was screaming, "Get him off me! Get him off me!"

Maura ordered Buddy off while Caleb searched the man and cuffed him. And suddenly, they were surrounded by police.

"Harry DeSouza," Caleb said, "you have the right to remain silent."

She knew Caleb wanted to work that crime scene, but he insisted on taking her home. On the ride back, Caleb said, "DeSouza was the fucker Declan's informant was gonna talk about. Up to his ass in that fentanyl operation. Guy's such a macho asshole . . . excuse my language, Maura, it's gonna sting that he was taken down by a dog."

Maura stepped on her anger. At least they'd gotten the guy. That would make Declan rest easier. "Taken down by a dog and a ghost," she said. "I'm hoping that ghost will stick around."

"Think of the crimes we could solve," Caleb said. "Oh, and I apologize. I told the responding officers to hold off. I hope you weren't too scared."

But Maura wasn't thinking about solving crimes or about backup that was slow to arrive. She was hoping Declan would be around for awhile for her sake, not Caleb's. She'd take Declan's invisible shoulder over any one in the real world.

They did the rest of the drive in silence. ❖

Call Me Mathias

a.l. Dawson

The Outsider adjusted his binoculars. The ash in the air sometimes made it difficult to see, but with every turn of the lens the shadowy figures below him became clearer. Three junior sweepers were there. One stood, the other two sat at his feet. *Hadn't ever seen them at the edge of the park before. Not a good sign.* All the local outsiders had been removed, but he escaped. Did they know he was hiding in the forest?

The sweepers didn't seem to be in any rush. If they were coming for him, they would probably wait until dusk before they acted. He shifted his position in the nook of the oak tree to get a better view. The other two sat cross-legged on the ground with their eyes focused on the standing figure. They were dressed in standard black leather outfits and oxygen helmets. The one standing took off his helmet and glanced in the direction of the forest where the Outsider hid.

The Outsider stiffened. He knew that face. It was three months ago, on the eve of the Day of Reckoning. The junior sweeper brigade had roamed the school corridors and stopped anyone who fit the profile of an outsider. They had grabbed him as he rounded the corridor and shoved him up against a locker. Their leader, the Junior Commander, had been the former student council president, but now he was a different kind of big man on campus. The kind that kicked him in the groin and laughed while he writhed in pain. The kind that took away his name and used red indelible ink to write *Outsider* across his forehead. That had been the last time he had seen him. Until now.

He needed to think but not here. The Outsider made his way down the branches. On the ground, the ash and fog were worse. The three junior sweepers now appeared as ghostly forms from another world.

The Junior Commander finished what he had to say to the recruits. He was pretty new himself. Who would have thought a week ago he was about to lead his first burn? The nation's leader preached to the country, "It's BC time." He liked that, the time to burn and cleanse. Too many people didn't get it. Like, the roundups of outsiders or the cleansing of the cities from top to bottom. On and on the bitching went. For the Junior Commander it was all about new opportunities, and those who could see that would make out fine.

As Junior Commander, he had to impress this idea upon the two under his charge. They looked to him for orders. They seemed hungry to learn so he'd feed them what they needed to know.

"Okay, before we do anything today take out your phones and tap the BC App."

The recruits stood up and fumbled with their belts before retrieving their phones. There was silence for a few seconds before the voice of the nation's leader boomed out over the phone speakers. "Burn for the future, burn for the nation. Cleanse the diseased cities, cleanse the outsiders. This is your sacred duty."

The Junior Commander tapped the app shut, and the recruits did the same.

"Remember those words."

Both recruits nodded and stomped their boots on the ground.

"All right. Let's burn the hell out of the park grass."

One of the recruits asked, "Sir, what about the forest?"

"Not yet. We wait at the tree line. If we do our job right, the senior sweepers will join us to burn the trees. It's enough for us to clear out the grass before they get here. Understood?"

Two heads moved up and down as one.

The second recruit said, "One more question, sir. Do you think there are any outsiders in the woods?"

The Junior Commander responded, "We can only hope." A broad smile spread over his face. The other two mimicked his grin.

"Time to burn. Helmets on."

With the ash hanging in the air the forest remained in preternatural twilight. After months of living in the forest, the Outsider knew how to move quickly in near darkness. It took him only five minutes to travel from the oak tree to the abandoned field station he called home. As he approached the clearing, the gray stone structure came into view. Others might just see a derelict hunk of stone, but to him it was his fortress and sanctuary.

He entered the combination to the lock on the metal door. Once inside he plopped down on a folding chair.

Sleeping bag on a yoga mat, a wooden crate for a nightstand, and that pretty much did it for interior design. A small window with metal bars provided the only light.

The Outsider stretched his legs and sighed. He hadn't thought the sweepers would have come to the park so soon. He had to think through his escape plan. The sweepers were about to burn the park and then the forest. His heart began to race. At sixteen he'd thought he could take care of himself. Now he felt like he was about to pee in his pants.

He took out a photograph from his back pocket. All the others were on his phone, and that was no good to him. The sweepers tracked outsiders through their phones. The photo was from another life. It reminded him he was a real person with a real name before the regime registered him as Outsider #351. He walked over to the barred window so he could see the faded image better. There he was with his parents on the beach in happier times. Before his father had died. Before the Day of Reckoning, when the sweepers took away his mother.

The waking nightmare kicked in. Mom giving him a seed pouch and saying, "Hide in the attic." Her terror as the sweepers hauled her away. The fear that paralyzed him as he hid in the attic and did nothing. The Outsider wiped the perspiration from his forehead and took a swig from his water bottle. He had to focus. He'd spent enough time wondering if he could have helped her. *Can't do that now. Focus.*

He placed his hand over the pouch hanging from his neck. He jiggled it, and the sound of the seeds calmed him. He could at least save the seeds. First, though, he had to save himself.

Back to the plan. He'd already checked out the sewer grate at the far end of the park forest. His father had once told him that some of the old sewer tunnels went for miles beneath the streets leading eventually to the city limits. Maybe that was the way he would find other outsiders and not have to hide who he was anymore. His dad also had told him never to go there alone because the sewers were dangerous. He said he'd go with him one day and they'd explore together, but that day never came.

The Outsider stood up. He checked his backpack to see if the essentials were there: flashlight, jar of peanut butter, Ritz crackers, and water bottle. He bent down and rolled up his sleeping bag and tied it to his backpack. He picked up the crowbar next to the door. *Can't forget that.* He took one more look at the cracked stone walls that had kept him safe. He sighed and stepped out into a cloud of smoke.

Once the sweepers made it to the edge of the forest, the Junior Commander raised a clenched fist and said, "Flames out. Helmets off. Take a deep breath, boys."

Both recruits breathed deeply and coughed their lungs out. The Junior Commander bent over in a spasm of laughter.

"You two have a long way to go if you're going to make full sweeper grade. You gotta toughen up and take in a little charcoal now and again. That's who we are. We burn, and we show pride. The first thing we do after a good burn is take those helmets off and get a few ins and outs with those lungs of yours. Took me awhile, but I got the hang of it. I live for it now. You will too one day."

The Junior Commander saw himself as a teacher. He had to admit they'd done well for their first burn. Charred the entire park right up to the forest line in less than two hours. Easy stuff, but still, they did good.

"The senior sweepers should be here within the hour. Sit your butts down. Just don't burn another hole in your rear end. I'm going in to get a burn sample."

The Junior Commander unhooked his burn gauge. It could burrow into the thickest tree trunk and get a good temperature reading. Sweepers couldn't just be cowboys and wave their flame throwers left and right. They needed proper data to do the job right.

He left his flame-thrower pack on the ground and headed toward an oak ten yards into the forest. As he squatted down and inserted the point of the burn gauge into the tree trunk, a shadow enveloped him.

The stench in the air was unbearable. The Outsider pulled the bandana over his mouth and nose. It was impossible to see more than a few feet into the park. What he could see was an undulating carpet of charcoal. Not a speck of green grass left. *Sweepers*. The forest would be next. *Gotta move fast.*

He walked near the oak where he had last seen the junior sweepers, but he didn't see the crouched figure on the ground. He stopped in the nick of time. *Him.* The Junior Commander looked up, and for a moment they stared at each other without saying a word.

Then the Junior Commander uttered, "You." He reached for the freedom baton on his belt, but the Outsider kicked the baton out of the sweeper's hand before he had a chance to pull the trigger. Those things could hit you with an electric charge and inflict serious damage.

He'd never stood up to a sweeper before. Always hid, always ran. For the briefest moment he felt different. Something more than an outsider.

It didn't last. The Junior Commander was already on his feet. He snorted like a feral beast ready to charge.

The Outsider did what he knew how to do best. He ran deeper into the forest. He cut left and right among the trees, not bothering to look back. He doubted the Junior Commander would follow him this far. Still, he ran because fear was what had kept him alive all these months. When he stopped ten minutes later and caught his breath, he realized he'd felt more than fear in his encounter with the sweeper. Whatever it was it wasn't a bad feeling at all.

The Junior Commander got to his feet just as the two recruits entered the forest.

"Sir, where are you?"

"Over here."

By the time the recruits found him he'd recovered the freedom baton.

"Commander, are you okay? We heard voices and—"

The Junior Commander cut him off. "Yeah, yeah. There were three outsiders, but I chased them away. They ran back into the forest."

The recruits stared into the darkness of the trees.

As if he could read their minds, the Junior Commander said, "Don't worry. We'll light up that cesspool and burn them out once the senior brigades arrive. Let's get back to our gear."

Seconds later they emerged into the twilight mist of the freshly burned park. The Junior Commander told himself. *This didn't happen.* He repeated it over and over again. It had worked for him in the past, and he could tell it was working now.

It took a few minutes to reach the sewer grate. The Outsider figured he had maybe an hour at the most before they started to burn the forest. No time to feel sorry for himself. A close call with the Junior Sweeper. *Too close.* Next time he might not be so lucky. He had to leave if he wanted to still be alive by the end of the day.

He took the crowbar in both hands and gave the rusted lock a few good whacks. The grate creaked open to a view of a sewer tunnel that was about five feet in height. He bent down and entered a pitch-black world.

The Outsider took out his flashlight and waved it in an arc. The tunnel's darkness seemed to overwhelm the beam of light. He couldn't see much beyond fifteen feet. What he could see were bits and pieces of brick fallen from the curved walls of the tunnel and water dripping from cracks in the ceiling.

He tightened the straps of his backpack and took a deep breath of the stale air. He stepped into the void. The silence and blackness wrapped tighter around him the further he walked.

The Outsider thought about his father's warning. He told himself there were no alternatives. Just focus on his goal. Get to the edge of the city proper and find an opening to the street. Then, maybe, just maybe, he could find other outsiders. The chance to be someone else gave him hope.

As he rounded a bend, a yellow vapor wafted out of the blackness. The taste of sulfur coated his tongue, and the acrid air burned his lungs. The Outsider dropped his flashlight. He pulled his bandana over his face, but he couldn't stop the coughing.

He searched for the flashlight. Its beam created zigzag shadows that danced across the sides of the tunnel. He reached for the flashlight but took hold of something soft and fleshy. He recoiled at the touch and dropped the dead rat on the ground. As he grabbed the flashlight, he saw hundreds of dead rats piled up in front of him. *The fumes.* He had to go back.

The light improved the closer he got to the sewer opening. So did the air. The yellow cloud seemed to go no further than the dead rats. The regime must've poisoned the air in the tunnels to prevent people like him leaving the city.

He took off his bandana when he reached the opening. The air was not tunnel air, but it still wasn't good. A wave of sadness swept through every pore of his body. His hand went to the pouch around his neck. He jiggled the seeds that would never be planted and wiped away a tear mixed with the ash on his cheek.

The sound of drumbeats pulsated through the scorched air. The veteran sweepers had arrived, and their numbers filled the park. The Senior Commander stood with his arm wrapped around the Junior Commander. They both turned and faced the twenty rows of sweepers. The Senior Commander raised his arm up and clenched his fist. The drumbeats stopped.

With arms akimbo the Senior Commander called out. "Sweepers. What day is it?"

Hundreds of voices shouted, "Wednesday!"

He paused for a second and then called, "What do we do on this day?"

The hundreds responded, "Burn!"

"Why do we do this?"

The hundreds called out even louder, "To cleanse!"

The Senior and Junior Commanders then sat down on their knees and folded their hands in silent prayer. The hundreds did the same.

45

After a minute of silence, the Senior Commander stood up and faced the forest. The Junior Commander picked up the Senior Commander's helmet and placed it over his head and adjusted the oxygen filter. The Junior Commander next picked up the flame-thrower kit and attached it to the Senior Commander's back. A roar of approval erupted from the hundreds. In choreographed movements all the sweepers turned to their assigned partner and did the same.

Silence descended upon the hundreds as they turned their heads to the right. Two drummers entered from the side of the park and walked to the front of the line. Their drumming was slow and rhythmic but grew louder and faster the closer they got to the Senior and Junior Commanders. Behind them a sweeper dragged an emaciated, old man. The drummers stopped beating their drums once they came face to face with the Senior Commander.

Silence descended again. Only the cries of the old man could be heard by sweepers in the first two rows. No one flinched. The hundreds waited for what would come next. The Senior Commander looked down at the crouched figure. In the blink of an eye, the Senior Commander turned on his flame-thrower and aimed. The old man lit up in orange flame.

The Senior Commander spoke through the voice regulator on his helmet. "Sacred missions demand a sacrifice of the diseased. Burn and cleanse those that hide in this pestilent forest."

With flame-throwers pointed upward the hundreds pressed their triggers. Blue flames lit up the haze hovering over the park.

The Senior and Junior Commander aimed their flame-throwers toward the forest and moved forward. The hundreds followed, except for the drummers, who stepped aside, careful not to step on the burning man. They then resumed a steady beat that didn't let up.

The Outsider stopped running once he heard the drums. That meant the sweepers had finished their prayers for the burn. They most likely had sacrificed an outsider, and now they would enter the forest. Flames, heat, smoke, and death would follow.

He picked up his pace. As he fled to the remotest corner of the park forest, he thought back to the confrontation with the Junior Commander. He'd feared dying right then and there. He always lived with fear, but this time something else happened when he saw the Junior Commander groveling on the ground. Tree branches rubbed and snapped against his body as he ran. Each snap of a branch crystalized a thought he was trying to grasp. He stopped suddenly. It came to him. He would hold on to the thought, even if he had to die.

By the time the Outsider reached the ancient maple the first stages of the burn had begun. He dropped his backpack on the ground. He gripped the pouch around his neck and jumped up to a low hanging branch. He climbed from branch to branch until he stopped halfway up. This is the place he wanted to be when the end came.

It didn't take long for the heat and smoke to reach him. He pulled the moistened bandana over his face. He heard animals run through the underbrush. Trees started to crack and buckle under the flames and heat. *Death will be soon.*

The Outsider found it hard to stay awake. His thoughts drifted. Then a voice slapped him in the face.

"You! I see you. Payback time."

The voice came from the base of the tree. *Him.* The Junior Commander's words had a staccato quality as he spoke through the helmet regulator, but it was definitely him.

"You're toast, Outsider." The Junior Commander laughed at his choice of words.

The Outsider had a hard time keeping a clear head but managed to shout down, "Call me Mathias!"

The last thing the Junior Commander saw was a figure dropping like a brick through the branches.

The next morning the ancient maple was the last tree left standing. The clean-up crew had to lift one of the maple's charred branches off the Junior Commander's remains. Two of the crew gasped at the sight of the body. Two others fought back the urge to vomit.

One of the crew said, "Nothing much left. Are we sure it's—"

The crew leader cut him off. "We're sure. See the insignia on his suit."

The other crew members strained to see it. A red-and-white lightning bolt was partly visible on a sleeve.

"I'll bet he'll get a Line of Duty commendation."

The crew leader said, "For sure. He was the Senior Commander's favorite. Okay, let's bag what we can."

Embers glowed like a thousand red eyes across the ash-covered ground. This burn had been hotter than most. Even the crew's suits failed to keep out some of the heat. They hurried to finish their job.

As they lifted up the body bag, another one said, "Say, where's his helmet? That thing never burns."

The crew leader snapped, "Seriously? We're out of here."

The little one let go of her mother's hands. She ran a few steps and stopped in her tracks. The head of a giant black bug peered out of the sewer opening. The child pointed to it.

Her parents wondered what she had seen. Then they saw it. A figure with a black helmet climbed up onto the deserted street. The woman shouted, "Sweeper! Run!"

The woman went to pull the little one away. Then she hesitated. The boy/man took off the helmet. His clothes hung like rags. His face was covered with grime and ash.

She shouted back to the others, "Hold on. I think he's one of us. Just look at him. Thin as a rake. That's no sweeper."

The boy/man wobbled. He collapsed in the middle of the street. The woman and the little one approached him.

The woman said, "My name's Yvonne. This is my daughter Emma. Here, take a few mouthfuls."

Yvonne handed him the water bottle. He forced himself not to drink too much.

Yvonne said, "We need to go. There's a place outside the city where others are like us. Do you want to join us?"

He nodded and did his best to smile.

Emma touched the pouch hanging around his neck. She stepped back and asked, "What's your name?"

He shook his head. "Name?"

Emma looked into his eyes and said, "You have a name, don't you?"

He uttered, "Yes, yes, I do. It's Mathias. Call me Mathias."

Emma took Mathias's hand and led him away from the fire and ash. ❖

Dead in the Afternoon

Stephen D. Rogers

A bartender walks into a bar. Punches in, checks the beer was restocked last night, and begins cutting fruit.

Tony put down his pen. Picked up his rye and sipped.

Glanced over at the bartender, who'd been wiping the same glass ever since Tony walked into the bar. He considered asking how much longer it would be until the stain was scrubbed away, but thought better of it.

The bartender nodded toward Tony's notebook. "What are you writing?"

"Jokes."

"You a comic or something?"

"I'm a journalist."

"Those still exist?"

Tony grinned. "So maybe I'm the joke."

"I ever read anything you've written?"

As if Tony could answer that. "I write for *The Journal*. Local politics." He indicated the notebook. "I dabble with comedy to keep my mind nimble."

The bartender pointed, rag dangling from his fingers. "Local politics? Now there's your joke."

"A local politician walks into a bar."

"He says, 'I'm going to make sure you can't make a living.' "

"A local politician walks into a bar, hands the bartender a citation, and waits for a free drink."

The bartender laughed. "I don't say this often, but maybe you should quit your day job."

Tony raised his rye and drank half of his double. Put down his glass and recorded the joke. Added, "A tennis ball walks into a bar. Bartender looks up, says, 'We don't serve your kind.' " Tony drew a line through the words.

The bartender resumed wiping the glass. "I had a guy in here once. Dead in the afternoon, like now. He also drank rye, and not many people do, at least not here."

Tony studied the bartender. "Aha. Your hair's different. Right?"

"I switched to contacts."

"That must be it, then. I didn't recognize you."

"Maybe you had a few before you came in."

"Not today." Tony cupped his glass. "Medicinal only."

"A doctor walks into a bar."

"A funeral director walks into a bar."

"An embalmer walks into a bar."

"An embalmer walks into a bar, asks for a stiff drink."

The bartender smiled. Recommenced polishing the glass.

Tony finished his rye, cracked his lips. "A cop walks into a bar. Produces a picture and asks, 'You recognize this guy?' "

"The bartender says, 'He looks familiar.' "

"The prosecutor asks, 'Did you serve him?' "

"The bartender says, 'I was just doing my job.' "

The bartender raised the glass to the light and rotated it, creating sparkle that reflected in the mirror behind the bar.

Tony wriggled on his stool. "You know the word *tender* has several meanings. You can tend to something, such as a bar."

"Imagine that."

"*To tender* is present something: to tender payment, to tender your resignation. You can tender an offer. The tender can be the payment offered." Tony paused. "A tender can be a ship, or a train car that carries fuel and water."

"Chicken tenders."

"I already ate lunch, but thanks. But, yes, a tender can be a strip of chicken. If you want, you can tenderize the entire chicken."

"Tenderize by bashing it with a mallet."

Tony smiled. "Irony."

"Irony walks into a bar."

"Oooh. I'm going to have to think on that one."

The bartender continued polishing the glass. "Let me know when you figure it out. Or would you put it in the paper?"

"A journalist writes about other people. A person who keeps a journal writes about himself."

"Maybe a journalist writes a story about himself."

Tony placed a bar napkin over his empty glass. "Conflict of interest."

"But maybe it's in his best interest. Maybe it lets him get things off his chest."

"That is where it sits, you know. The knowledge. The thing."

"I do know."

Tony pulled the napkin off the glass and onto the bar. Anchored the white square with one hand while he brushed the layers flat. "I think I'm ready for another."

"You sure?"

"I'd ask what's the worst that could happen, but we already know the answer to that."

"A ghost walks into a bar."

Tony drew a ragged breath. "Yeah."

"*Tender* also means to be kind. To be forgiving."

Tony tapped the rim of his glass, saying nothing.

"To treat someone with tenderness." The bartender lifted the bottle out of the well and poured. "Doing a kindness can be a way to pay forward, to pay back."

"Irony walks into a bar."

"The bartender asks—"

Tony raised a finger. "Maybe for once the bartender listens."

"That's all bartenders ever do. Maybe this bartender needs to get something off his own chest."

"The irony."

The bartender dropped the bottle into the well with a clang. "You got to hear a jury say, 'Not guilty.' I was never even charged."

"A jury walks into a bar."

"There are only eleven open stools."

Tony struggled to find a punchline. "A judge walks into a bar. Says, 'I thought I passed it.' "

"A drunk walks into a bar."

"That's a surprise?"

"It's a surprise when he testified he'd sworn off drinking."

"Maybe just not forever."

"He implied otherwise."

"A bartender walks into a courtroom. Walks up to the stand."

"I was subpoenaed."

"You hung around afterward."

"I needed to see the woman's family."

Tony covered his eyes. "I can't stop seeing them."

"What really happened that day?"

"Something on the other side of the street caught my eye. I don't remember what. That's when she stepped out of her car."

"Did you see her?"

Tony winced. "I heard the impact."

"Irony walks into a bar."

"You just keep repeating that, and maybe eventually I'll be able to finish the thought."

"The joke."

Tony cupped his hands, formed a ball that he mimicked turning one way and then the other before tossing it into an imaginary basket. "A joke is self-contained, self-extinguishing. You get to the end, and it's over."

"You know what I think?"

Tony raised his hand. "A mind reader walks into a bar. Turns around and searches for another bar."

He pulled over his notebook and recorded the joke. Joke? Thought? Sentence?

Through blurry eyes he tried to read his own writing.

Failed. ❖

Playing God

Avram Lavinsky

Present Day
Stan Kaplan didn't need to open the letter to know the two words printed on the folded page within. Or to know that it was the last. He placed it under his arm with the sales circulars and the insurance offers. He swung shut the coppery door to mailbox 3B, removed his key, and started back up the stairs.

Alone in his apartment, he inserted a pinky under the top flap and tore open the hand-addressed envelope. He withdrew the letter, folded it, and placed it in his hip pocket. He tossed the envelope and all the other mail into the recycling bin under the kitchen sink.

In the living room, at the side table his wife had picked out when they first moved in, he reached for his favorite picture of them together, the one from the boardwalk at Coney Island. He had one arm over her shoulder and the other extended beyond the edge of the image to hold his phone. They both wore dark sunglasses. Behind them stretched a three-tiered railing of metal pipe and beyond that, endless water, and beyond that, endless sky. He ran a forefinger over the top of the silvery frame, feeling the tight grain of the combed metal and displacing a layer of dust that swirled up into the light from the nearby window like a tiny solar flare. He lifted the photo and pressed his wife's image to his lips.

He left the apartment, pulled the door closed behind him, and checked the knob to make sure he'd locked it, half laughing at the absurdity of this particular habit in his current situation. He took the empty elevator to the fifteenth floor.

The steel stairs to the roof clanged under his Nikes. He leaned into the push bar, and with a clack, the fire door unlatched. Somewhere below, the honk of a horn echoed between the buildings. He squinted against the sunshine and made his way across the asphalt surface to the hip-high brick parapet capped with rounded masonry. He stepped up onto it. Teetering, he closed his eyes.

Eight Years Ago

Aviva Kirchner hugged the round plastic hamper to her body and made her way to one of four washing machines lining the back wall of the basement laundry room. She flipped up the lid of the washer and hoisted the rim of the hamper toward the opening.

Paul, her husband of less than a year, clomped down the stairs barefoot behind her with the other hamper, the wooden runners groaning beneath his weight.

Aviva's body stiffened. She coaxed out the last remaining item from the hamper, a yellow pillowcase, flinging it into the washer with a flick of her slender wrist.

She set the hamper down and, with the back of her forearm, swept a few stray strands of wavy black hair back from her brow.

Paul crouched to keep from banging his head on one of the naked bulbs at the center of the ceiling, its stark light revealing curtains of churning motes thick with lint. He dropped the second hamper and gave it a shove. It skidded briefly on the concrete floor behind Aviva.

She flinched at the sound but didn't turn to look. She poured a cap of detergent and a smaller cap of fabric softener into the machine. She wound the dial and pulled the knob outward. It clicked, and the sound of running water drowned out the bull-like breathing of her husband at her back.

A sudden movement in the shadow along the wall in front of her caused Aviva to freeze where she stood. She could make out the outline of Paul's raised arm angled toward her head.

The bullet tore through the gray matter of her brain, destroying the centers for processing sound before the soundwaves from the report ever reached her ears. Her arm shot out awkwardly as her chest and shoulders crashed onto the edge of the washing machine. Her knees struck the floor, and she folded backward over her legs.

It struck Paul that she looked like a magician's assistant, one of those female contortionists somehow crammed into one half of an ornate box, ready for the giant buzz saw blade to pass down the center line and cut her in two.

He thought about cutting her up. It seemed to him that she had something more coming to her. Even now, she seemed to defy him, to bait him. He searched her open eyes for remorse at what she'd caused but found only the white gleam of the light bulb overhead.

The expanding pool of blood beneath her head ebbed toward his bare feet. He turned and clomped back up the stairs to finish the job, emitting faint wheezes of self-pity each time he exhaled.

Eight Years Ago

Rabbi Eron Danovitch had worked as a chaplain with the New York City Police Department for just under two years when he got the call. A detective named Fitzgerald with the Thirteenth Precinct requested that Danovitch join her to comfort the Roth family as she notified them of the loss of their only daughter, Aviva Roth Kirchner, in what appeared to be a murder-suicide perpetrated by her husband.

Danovitch had just traveled back from working the burial of a retired sergeant in Yonkers as part of his duties with the Ceremonial Unit. Detective Fitzgerald picked him up at One Police Plaza, and they made good time heading uptown on First Avenue. They entered Stuyvesant Town at Eighteenth Street and parked in a loading zone.

Luckily, Detective Fitzgerald knew her way around the looping access roads and the dozens of identical brick buildings. They followed a curving path past a row of basketball courts on one side and climbed a few cement stairs to enter a vestibule.

Detective Fitzgerald found the intercom button with the name Roth beside it in faded ink and held it down. "NYPD. We need a word with the Roth family."

After a few awkward seconds, a buzzer sounded, and the door unlatched.

The two stepped into the lobby. The elevator's outer door, a weighty metal slab painted candy-apple red, had a small rectangular window crisscrossed with wire in a diamond pattern like the fire doors in schools. They pulled it open and stepped in. The detective pressed the eighth-floor button, and the slowest elevator in New York jerked to life, inching its way upward.

When they finally reached apartment 8E, Fitzgerald rapped on the door three times. She unclipped the badge from her belt as footsteps crescendoed inside and then stopped. She raised the badge to chin level. The peephole darkened. The door opened a few inches, and the chain snapped taut.

Even with only one quarter of the woman's face visible, Fitzgerald and Danovitch could see the terror in her expression.

"Mrs. Roth. I'm Detective Fitzgerald. This is Rabbi Danovitch. He's a police chaplain. Could we come in please?"

Not for the first time, Danovitch contemplated his own presence as a portent to the family of the victim. As if a solemn-faced New York City detective in a suit at your door didn't confirm your worst nightmare, here stood an NYPD chaplain to erase any remaining hope.

The door swung inward, and a woman regarded them from the narrow entrance hall. Petite and slender to the point of frailty, she had an oaky complexion and a lined face that still bore traces of beauty beneath the cumulative effect of troubled years.

Her expression the rabbi understood well. She knew. But she couldn't let herself believe. Not yet.

"We'd like to come in and sit down, please," said the detective.

The three walked the walk of the condemned down the narrow entrance hall into the living room. From a photo atop the lid of a baby grand piano, a much younger and supremely radiant Mrs. Roth beamed at them, a swaddled baby resting a tiny head on her shoulder. In the next frame, a daughter in mid stride, her black cap and gown accentuating skin fairer than her mother's, though she shared the same radiant smile, accepted a handshake and a high school diploma from a waiting school principal in a more ornate gown of regal violet. In the next, the same young woman held a bridal bouquet, still looking girlish in a simple white veil and wedding gown, her petite frame dwarfed by the bear of a man in the tuxedo next to her, the edge of a paisley-pattern vest showing across his massive chest.

Mrs. Roth motioned with an unsteady hand toward a couch and drifted to the far end of it. Detective Fitzgerald waited to see her sit prior to seating herself. Danovitch sat on a wooden chair with a spindled back facing them both.

An ancient woman in a gossamer robe drifted into the room from another narrow hall on the other side.

"Mama," said Mrs. Roth, a forced calm in her voice, "they're from the police."

"What has happened?" The older woman had an Eastern European accent Danovitch couldn't quite place.

Danovitch welcomed her presence. They needed the bereaved mother to have company. Per protocol, they wouldn't have left her alone without at least seeing to some arrangements with a family member or a neighbor.

A stifling sense of helplessness gnawed at him, a sense of a greater pain soon to follow, the way a tickle in the back of the throat portends the entire illness to come. Perhaps it was the nature of a murder-suicide. The perpetrator had put himself well beyond the reach of law enforcement. No justice. Not in this world, and Danovitch's religion did not place great faith in any other.

Fitzgerald leveled a mournful smile at the grandmother. "Why don't you sit and join us as well, please."

The grandmother slowly wilted into an armchair.

"I'm sorry," said Fitzgerald, "but Aviva Roth Kirchner and her husband, Paul, were both killed this morning."

Present Day

As the only Unitarian Minister in the unit, Deacon Eugene Bradley responded to more calls than any of New York's other twelve police chaplains. He couldn't avoid it. His was the faith that welcomed all faiths, and so he remained dispatch's second choice to comfort citizens of any denomination.

Emotionally drained from four different bereaved families that day, he felt ill-prepared for the conflict on the twelfth floor of the building on the Upper East Side.

Along with the two detectives from the Nineteenth Precinct, he had been prepared to notify and comfort the jumper's niece, who lived nine floors above her deceased uncle in an apartment with impressive views of the East River and Roosevelt Island.

But it turned out she not only knew about her uncle's death; she had strong opinions about it.

"I'm not buying it!" Her eyes flashed a challenge behind the glassy layer of tears. "He wouldn't."

"He wasn't depressed?" The senior detective, a guy named Van Tyne, had a basso voice that any clergyman would die for.

"It's winter in New York. Everybody's depressed. I just don't believe he'd do that to himself."

"We did find a note in his pocket," said the detective. "A bit mysterious."

"Of course, you did. Let me guess. It said, 'Zero days.' "

Van Tyne shared a wide-eyed glance with the chubby-cheeked junior detective, Pearson, or maybe Paulson. Bradley hadn't quite gotten his name.

"We only called you people about those letters around a hundred times. I knew something like this would happen."

"Are you saying your uncle received threatening letters, and you notified the police?"

"Probably a couple thousand of them."

"A couple thousand threatening letters?" Van Tyne's gray eyebrows rose until the creases in his forehead turned to taut bands.

"Not like you're picturing. My uncle got one letter every day from the same sender."

"Every day. One threatening letter?"

"Judge for yourself." The niece marched off and returned a moment later with a shoebox. "We have nine or ten boxes full."

Van Tyne placed the box on a side table next to a photo of the victim. He pulled a pair of blue latex gloves from the inside pocket of his jacket, and stretched them over his hands.

Removing the lid, he took one letter from the pile within and inspected it while Deacon Bradley and the junior detective looked on. No return address. The American Flag Forever stamp had a postmark that read "NEW YORK NY 10001" in letters along the perimeter of an inky circle around the date.

He removed a folded piece of printer paper from the envelope. In block letters at the center was the message, "31 Days." Nothing more. The half circle of the capital *D* in "Days" had a wide horseshoe shape. The lowercase *a* had a distinctive hook at the lower right.

He placed the letter back in its envelope and took up another. Same forever stamp. Same zip code on the postmark. He opened it. It read "24 Days." The *D* and the *a* had the same telltale features.

"So it was some kind of countdown?"

"He told me that at first, they counted up. I can't imagine why." She pressed her lips together in thought for a moment. "Sometimes I felt like he knew more than he was telling me. Then last year they started counting down. That's when he got nervous. But the cops kept telling us to bug off."

"It's not their fault." Shaking his head, the junior detective cut in for the first time. "The letters aren't really threats. There's no crime there."

"That's what *they* told us. We sent one to a lab. It took two months and six hundred bucks. Nothing."

"No prints? No DNA?" asked Van Tyne.

"Nope. And now somebody pushed him off that roof. I just know it."

"Tell me why you're so sure," said Van Tyne.

"Like you said. It was a countdown. And today's day zero."

Eight Years Ago
It had been the grandmother's request. Once she had learned that Aviva's body couldn't possibly be released for burial within twenty-four hours in keeping with Jewish custom, she had begged Danovitch to say a mourner's *kaddish* at her granddaughter's side, so the rabbi found himself back in the

passenger seat of Detective Fitzgerald's unmarked Dodge sedan, heading to the forensic lab.

"Probably would have been easier to walk." The detective waved the back of her hand at a yellow taxi that cut her off with only inches to spare.

The Office of the Chief Medical Examiner of New York was tucked behind Bellevue Hospital on East Twenty-sixth Street. Miraculously, they found a legal parking spot on Twenty-fifth. They strode past students with an assortment of facial piercings outside a Hunter College dormitory. At the office's main entrance, Danovitch followed Detective Fitzgerald to the stainless-steel awning and into the rhythmic vacuum of a revolving door.

For all the graveside prayers Danovitch had offered, he'd never encountered any place like the autopsy room of the Forensic Biology Lab. It struck him as part hospital, part butcher shop, with the row of rolling stainless-steel tables and the clocklike hanging scales.

Fitzgerald, seemingly unphased, passed Danovitch a mask and a folded plastic apron. He gladly donned both.

The horrid smell of rotting flesh mingled with acrid detergents. The first body he encountered soured his stomach. He had never known a human corpse could bloat to that degree: the eyes swollen shut, the tongue seeming to occupy all of the open mouth.

It dawned on Danovitch that he knew nothing of death. Perhaps his entire life's journey in search of spiritual understanding had been no more than a desperate flight from the indignity and insignificance that lay so starkly before him on that table.

He recognized the naked woman on the fourth table: Aviva Roth Kirchner, no longer childlike but still beautiful, her skin porcelain-white except for a faint bluish band along her side that darkened toward the metallic surface of the table.

Just beyond her, the naked corpse of Paul Kirchner appeared monstrously large by comparison. With a week's grizzle on his cheeks, he had a predatory look even in death. Beneath his thick body hair, dark blue lines marbled his skin. His privates seemed absurdly thick, and Danovitch wondered if some strange postmortem physiology caused changes of that nature. Each of his thighs looked heavier than both of Aviva's combined.

In that moment, Danovitch hated his own maleness, the hormones coursing through him with all the impulses they could bring. He hated his own feeble attempts to provide hope and comfort while the Paul Kirchners of the world leveraged despair and pain every day to hoard away the only currency they knew. Power. All for Power. Most of all, he hated the criminal justice system so unable to do anything about it.

As Detective Fitzgerald launched into a technical discussion with a medical examiner, Danovitch walked to Aviva's side and angled himself so that he did not have to view her murderer.

He rocked back and forth gently at the waist as he prayed, moving within the familiar rhythm of the mourner's *kaddish* he had uttered a thousand times, pronouncing the words in Hebrew but considering the English meaning as he did. He rattled off the litany of adjectives describing his God, *glorified and celebrated, lauded and praised, acclaimed and honored, extolled and exalted.* In all his life, he had never felt such futility in those words.

Seven Years Ago

A young patrol officer pulled the yellow police tape taut and tied the end to an alternate-side-parking sign. Catching sight of Rabbi Danovitch in uniform, he put the roll of tape under his arm and saluted him.

Further down the block, next to a double-parked box truck, a detective near retirement age took notes as a man in a navy-blue freight service uniform spoke. The detective gave Danovitch an abbreviated salute, the pen still in his hand.

Danovitch saluted and approached the patrol officer.

"Afternoon, Rabbi," said the officer. "That's the husband over there wearing out the pavement."

He gestured toward a fair-skinned man pacing between the stoops of two brownstones, a bag of some kind clutched in one shaking hand. "His name's Kaplan, Stan Kaplan. Said he tried to grab her by the shoulder but ended up with a handful of her scarf."

Beyond a crouching investigator, a woman lay sprawled in the middle of the side street. Long waves of hair vanished in a pool of blood nearly as dark as the asphalt. The unnatural angles of her limbs brought to mind a tangled marionette.

"The trucker already admitted he was on his phone." The officer eyed the man in the freight service uniform. "He never even saw her until he climbed out." He shook his head. "She was only twenty-four. Two years younger than *my* wife."

As Danovitch approached the husband with measured steps, he realized that what he had mistaken for a bag was actually the wife's scarf as the officer had said, silky, with a gold and black pattern. He couldn't blame the husband for clinging to it.

"Mr. Kaplan. I'm Rabbi Danovitch. I'm an NYPD chaplain."

Kaplan stopped short and stared at the six-pointed star at the top of Danovitch's badge. "You're a rabbi?"

"Yes"

"Why are you here?"

"The officers noticed you and your wife are Jewish and asked me to help in any way I can."

"I don't think anybody can help. I don't know . . . I'm just so . . . angry."

"It's okay to be angry."

Kaplan rubbed the scarf across his cheek with a shaking hand.

After a few seconds of silence, Danovitch went on. "It's normal. Anyone would be." Danovitch gestured at the trucker.

"I'm not angry with *him*," said Kaplan.

Danovitch waited for Kaplan to continue. When he didn't, he asked, "Who are you angry with?"

Kaplan seemed about to speak but then compressed his lips tightly.

"It's alright. You can tell me. Whatever it is."

"I'm angry with *me*," Kaplan said in a squelched tremor.

"You tried," said Danovitch. "You're only human."

Kaplan said nothing.

"You weren't behind that wheel."

Kaplan raised his eyes to Danovitch's. "You don't understand." He drew back the corner of his mouth into a snarl. "I pushed her."

The words sent a jolt through Danovitch's midsection.

"We argued. She had her finger in my face. I batted it away." Kaplan's eyes, bloodshot at the edges, searched the rabbi's. "Then we had our hands on each other. And I did. I pushed her. Right into the street." Kaplan's face seemed to develop strange contours around the brow ridge and cheekbones. It seemed to undulate, defying three-dimensional logic like an Escher lithograph.

Danovitch cleared his throat, his voice sputtering. "You . . . didn't tell the responding officer or the detective that."

Kaplan shook his head. "I couldn't do it."

His voice seemed to crackle, as if funneling through a bullhorn at Danovitch's ear. In fact, all the sounds on the cordoned-off side street seemed to ring in Danovitch's brain at once, the cooing of the pigeons absurdly loud, the groan of a truck downshifting on the avenue nearly deafening.

"I'm not even sure why I told you," said Kaplan. "You said I could tell you anything. I just . . . believed you, I guess."

Danovitch chose his next words carefully. "Are you going to tell *them*?" He glanced at the patrol officer and the detective, feeling their eyes drift momentarily toward him.

"I don't want to spend the rest of my life in jail." The sibilant consonants of Kaplan's words continued to hiss and distort in Danovitch's ears. "Guess you'll be telling them anyway."

Danovitch exhaled to steady himself. "I can't. Not if you don't want me to. What you tell me is privileged."

Harsh metallic clicks, painfully loud, pierced Danovitch's consciousness. The truck driver had turned his back to the detective, who was slapping the cuffs onto the man's wrists.

"Mr. Kaplan," said Danovitch, his voice drawn thin, "I can't tell you what you should and should not say. I can only ask that you think of *that man* as you make your decision."

Present Day
Deacon Bradley's living room still smelled of polyurethane. With the help of a rented sander, he and his wife, Elaine, had restored the parquet floor to gleaming glory in November. With the room finally reassembled, Bradley was admiring the holiday cards spread out on the hearth.

In the photos, all the children of their friends seemed to have turned into young adults overnight. It made him feel old. He noticed how many of his police friends sent pictures with kids but no spouse. Some years, divorce seemed to rampage through the police force like a plague.

He picked up one nondenominational card. No picture, but the words "Joy and Light" stretched out across the front, embossed in a metallic rose-red. He checked the back. "Happy Holidays" was printed in a shiny pine-green, and below that the hand-printed name, Eron Danovitch.

Bradley went to set the card down, but something made him stop. A closer look at the name gave him a prickly sensation in his spine. The half circle of the capital *D* in Danovitch went past the vertical line in a wide horseshoe shape. The lowercase *a* had a distinctive hook at the lower right.

Present Day
The two men met in a coffee shop, but with the weather so unseasonably warm, they got their coffees to go and crossed the street to stroll Prospect Park. Danovitch inquired politely

69

about Bradley's wife, Elaine, and they both lamented the injury-plagued Brooklyn Nets.

They found a bench overlooking the lake, and after a long silence, Bradley said, "That one case. It just seems like you haven't been the same since. You know the one."

"The Kirchner case." Danovitch's mouth took on a sour twist. "I think if it hadn't been that one, it would have been the next or the one after that. I don't know if another case will ever shock me like that one did, but they all haunt you, you know?"

Bradley struggled to choose his next words. "Eron, I know you did something . . . from the handwriting on your holiday card . . . and I need you to explain it to me."

A swelling breeze caused branches along the water's edge to sway, their inky reflections strobing across the rippling surface.

"I've always known I'd have to explain it to someone eventually," said Danovitch, his face betraying nothing. "I certainly never thought it would be you, but I'm glad it is." He sipped his coffee. His eyes narrowed against the sunlight as they scanned the silvery shimmer along the expanse of the lake.

"I know," said Bradley, "you would never push anyone off a roof," his tone a little less certain than he had intended.

"Nah," said Danovitch, exhaling, a brittleness creeping into his voice. "Not with my hands anyway."

Bradley said nothing.

"I'm not going to sugarcoat it for you," said Danovitch. "I did what I had to do. You can do what you have to do as well. I don't care who you tell about it."

"What you *had* to do?" said Bradley. "I found the file on the Kaplan woman's death. All you *had* to do was comfort Stan, the bereaved husband. Anonymous letters? Why would you play mind games with him for seven years?"

"I think it started before I even met him. Like you said, maybe that Kirchner case changed me. Did you hear much about it?"

"Not the particulars, no."

"The husband shot his wife in the back of the head in their basement. Then he walked upstairs and shot himself. She wanted out. One of those 'if I can't have her, nobody can deals.' " Danovitch winced stiffly.

"The family asked me to go say a *kaddish* by the bodies. I go to the autopsy room, and they're both laid out naked on tables, side by side, not six feet apart. She looked like a kid. Whole life ahead of her. He looked like a rhino. Probably three times her weight. Ball sack like a breadbasket.

"So I'm saying the *kaddish*, line after line about the greatness of God, and I knew, for the first time, why my people have been repeating those words for all these centuries. It's not because God is great. It's because we are so freaking small. We are so ungodly."

On a tree branch at the side of the lake, a hawk shifted with a brief beating of wings. White feathers with gray bands flashed and then disappeared behind the pine needles.

"Kaplan told me he killed his wife," said Danovitch. "He told me he pushed her in front of that box truck. He wouldn't tell anyone else though. So I couldn't either. He let the trucker take the fall for it. They cuffed him and took him away right in front of us. Poor bastard didn't even know enough to keep his mouth shut about texting on the road."

"So you thought you'd creep Kaplan out with threatening letters?"

"I don't know. I just wanted to remind him. At first anyway. Every day he walked free was another day in a cell for that poor trucker. The guy ended up getting the max. Seven years. I sent the first letter the first day he spent in prison."

"So that explains why you counted up at first. But then you started counting down."

"Once the trucker had a release date, I thought maybe I could at least get Kaplan thinking by counting down to it."

"You think he even got that? That he even understood what the letters meant?"

"I didn't care what he understood. Or maybe I did. It's not like the trucker would ever come after him. He's a gentle soul. I visited him at Rikers. He wasn't cut out for the place. But if Kaplan happened to think the guy knew what he'd done and meant to settle the score, that would have suited me fine."

"But why bother keeping the secret of his confession if you're going to disregard your oath and torture the man?"

For the first time, Bradley saw anger smoldering in Danovitch's face. "I didn't torture anybody. The only person torturing someone was Kaplan torturing that trucker. He got beat down multiple times in that prison yard and God knows what else indoors. He had a wife that left him and a daughter whose first communion he just missed. Kaplan took everything from him."

"We all feel it," said Bradley. "We all get angry at the injustice. If it started getting the better of you, you could have come to someone on the unit. You could have come to me. We could have talked about it."

"I know."

72

"Only Kaplan, right? No others?"

"One daily letter campaign is about all I can handle."

"You wouldn't ever do anything like this again, would you?"

"I don't know. When I heard Kaplan killed himself, my outrage kind of drained. Maybe not my disgust. Now I just feel disgusted with myself too."

Bradley pointed a finger into the air as if trying to prove some theorem on an invisible whiteboard. "If you knew he would kill himself, if you pulled his strings to make him do it, then that's way over the line. Like the homicide detectives say, nobody gets to play God."

"Then I guess you'll have to report me."

"Not this conversation. I'm on the job. This is privileged."

"But you recognized my handwriting from my holiday card. Nothing stopping you from sharing that info. You have to. Can't impede the investigation. No choice."

"I just . . ." Bradley's shoulders caved, his face suddenly weary. "I just love the Chaplains Unit. I love the PD. I can't do it. I can't spread all that shame."

Danovitch sipped his lukewarm coffee and scanned the trees for the hawk but saw only the gently swaying clusters of pine needles. "I guess we all play God once in a while, some just a little more mercifully than others." ❖

Clay

Robin Hazard Ray

You're not meaning to put them *there*, are you, sir?" As he spoke, Barney Ross blocked the door to the office of his employer, Sumner Bascomb, the superintendent of Mount Auburn Cemetery. Though the superintendent was descended from the Anglo-Saxon merchant class of Boston while Barney Ross was a survivor of the Irish famine—one in collar and tie, one in a dirty canvas coat—they generally understood and trusted one another. But the arrival of the girl victims from the West End of Boston had thrown them into new territory. The girls' dead bodies in cheap, charity coffins were now stowed in the cemetery's Receiving Tomb, awaiting burial later this March.

"It's a pity," Bascomb said, "but it can't be helped. Not a dime from the family. The Diocese won't bury them. It's only philanthropy that allows us to take them at all. Where else can we put them?"

Ross backed out into the open air and looked away. "But, sir," he said. "The clay."

A feeling of shame crept over them both: Bascomb felt it. Ross on the part of the Catholic world that had failed to take in its lost sheep; the superintendent on the part of an elite cemetery that could do no better for its poor cases than a dank hole.

"I know," said Bascomb. "The clay."

One wouldn't think it would make a difference. The terrain of Mount Auburn Cemetery was shaped by the collapse of glacial ice at the end of its reign over New England. For hundreds, perhaps thousands of years, the decaying glaciers wept their waters over the land, pulsing out layers of boulders, pebbles, and sand. In places, though, the long seep of tiny, waterborne rock particles fused into clay. Clay that never warmed in the summer but kept its cold heart. Clay that stuck to a man's boots like sin.

It was absurd, really. Earth was earth, ashes were ashes. When a coffin went down, the mourners were offered a trowel of earth with which to acknowledge the impending decay. What did it matter whether the trowel flung sand or clay?

But it did matter. Digging in sand: brisk, clean, and light. Digging in clay: clammy, sticky, airless. Lowering into clay: one just prayed there would not be a sucking sound when the box met the bottom. The ropes were cloyed with the stuff upon retrieval. Burying in clay: the dreadful splotch when the clay was replaced, shovel by shovel. It was undignified; it was mean. No respectable family would stand for it.

No wonder Barney Ross was upset.

"I'll look into it," said Bascomb finally. "Perhaps there's something we can do."

75

Later that day, having got some paperwork organized, the superintendent stopped by the Harvard library, which was not far from Mount Auburn. There he went through back issues of the Boston papers, looking for all reports on the case of Katherine "Kitty" Kelly and Martina "Tiny" Alvarez. The newspapers had printed every sensational detail and contradictory fact but Bascomb could piece together the sequence of events.

On the last day of February in this year of 18—, a suspicious landlady in the West End of Boston had knocked on the door of Kitty's tenement room. A neighbor had complained of foot traffic to the girl's room in the middle of the night, cries of an indecent nature, and finally no stirrings at the hour when Kitty should have been off to work. Kitty was a reliable employee at the "small fines" counter at a dry-goods emporium, so this was unusual. The landlady's knock and voice met with no response.

When the landlady used her pass key on the door, a scene of horror awaited. Kitty lay on the floor, half-dressed, cold and dead. On the bed three feet away lay another young woman, also half-dressed and barely clinging to life. An empty vial of arsenic was discovered. A doctor was sent for, then the police. The press hounds were not far behind; for a week, the papers were full of speculation and titillated awe.

A name had been attached to the surviving young woman: Martina Alvarez, known as Tiny. A husband had been found: James Kelly, a reporter who worked now and again for this paper or that.

The *Evening Dispatch* ran a long, sympathetic report on the husband. The Kellys were both newly married and newly separated. James, who was older than his wife by a decade, recounted their courtship and marriage, with little explanation of their separation. "I have only ever sought to reconcile with Kitty, whom I continue to love and cherish," he told the *Dispatch*. "I am heartbroken by her death."

The doctor who had been called to the scene testified that the cause of Kitty's death was arsenic; the empty vial was exhibited. While the doctor was on the stand, a message reached the presiding judge that Tiny Alvarez too had died. The doctor opined that, barring other evidence, he was inclined to consider it a suicide pact.

A waiter from a local hotel came forward as a witness. He testified that Kitty and Tiny had eaten at the hotel on the night in question. Both had seemed in fine spirits, celebrating a birthday. They had oysters, soup, chops, and two glasses of port wine apiece. Yes, he had seen them together before; no, not often. He did not remember their ever being accompanied by a man or men. He wondered where the girls had got the money for such a feast, but it was not his business so long as the bill was covered.

The landlady testified that Tiny was a known acquaintance of Kitty's, that she came and went frequently. She, the landlady, did not know anything of Kitty's marriage or husband; she had never seen him until today in court. It was not her habit to poke into the private affairs of her tenants, as long as the neighbors did not complain.

Kitty's mother, surname O'Sullivan, had been sought but not discovered. She was a widow from New Brunswick, it was learned; Kitty was her only surviving child. The mother worked as a polisher in the jewelry trade. She usually worshipped at the Church of the Holy Cross, but had not been seen for some weeks. The *Transcript* speculated that she had gone back to Canada, though no one could say for sure.

In the days after the court inquiry, the *Transcript* reported that no one knew anything of Tiny's origins or occupation, and that no family had come forward to claim the deceased.

Two dead girls. No note. The presiding judge took the doctor's suggestion of a suicide pact and gaveled the two women into perdition.

Bascomb had read the reports at the time but forgot them as other business arose. Then, two days ago, the cemetery president had forwarded a letter from the coroner of the City of Boston, who was an old friend. The city had custody of the bodies, which needed burying. The Archdiocese of Boston demurred, citing their suicides. James Kelly had not claimed his wife's body. No one had even inquired about the Alvarez girl. The cemetery president had directed Bascomb to locate an inexpensive spot within the grounds where the girls could be buried, suggesting a location along the western wall.

Where the soil was clay.

Having reread the newspaper reports, Bascomb lingered in thought. Only when a bell rang to signal the library's closing did the superintendent stir.

In Harvard Square, he caught the trolley that ran into Boston. The newspapers had furnished the names and addresses of everyone pertinent to the Kelly-Alvarez case, so he had no difficulty finding the tenement in which Kitty and Tiny had met their ends. It was a hulking, five-story brick building that occupied a corner. There were two entrances, one on each street; he picked one at random.

The outer door, which was unlocked, gave onto a dismal entryway. Its plaster walls were green with damp and smudged with generations of fingermarks. Names of residents were written in a dozen different hands above numbered mail slots. No. 42 bore a relatively fresh slip of paper reading "Kelly."

He trudged up the unswept stairs, with the smells of waste and poor dinners washing past him. Rats had left their traces. A whiff of carbolic at the third floor was a downright pleasure compared to the organic odors it tried to correct.

On the landing of the fourth floor, a black-haired woman was marching back and forth with a screaming infant. She stopped when she saw Bascomb and, in a language he did not understand, demanded to know his business. The infant stopped crying long enough to stare at him, then started up again with redoubled energy. An unshaven man in a grimy shirt and suspenders came out from a doorway and looked Bascomb over dubiously.

"Who are you, then?" the Irishman wanted to know. He added a few soft words to his wife in a different language. As she and the infant retreated into their room, two curious children of three or four came out, moving to clutch their father's trousers on either side. They too stared at Bascomb as though he were a form of life they had never seen before.

"I'm sorry to bother you," said the superintendent. He handed over his card. The Irishman glanced at it before handing it back.

"This about the girls again? Thought we'd done with that."

"We're getting ready to bury them on Friday," said Bascomb. "But there were one or two things I wanted to find out. Did you know either of them?"

"Aye, we knew Kitty all right. Nice girl. A bit fancy."

"Did she seem . . . well, did the suicide verdict seem correct to you?"

His interlocutor looked aside. "Wouldn't have thought it, but you never know. We've had four in the building since last year. Not counting them girls."

"Suicides?" The man nodded. "Tell me, did you know the mother or the husband at all?"

"Never met the mother. I think they weren't on grand terms. As to the husband, I never knew there was one till he showed up here to claim her things. I put her down as . . . like I said, a bit fancy. Gay, like. But nothing against her at all," he hastened to add. "The kiddies adored her." He placed one rough hand on each of the twins' heads and petted them gently. They pulled closer to his legs and roughed their hair on his trousers.

"Is the room open?"

"Aye. No one wants it. It's just over there," said the man, nodding his head toward the end of the hall.

"Thank you, Mister, ah?"

"Ryan."

"Mr. Ryan," said Bascomb. "If you wish to come, the funeral is set for ten in the morning." Then he felt foolish. How was a man like this going to find the time and car fare to come to a funeral on a week day, at a cemetery that was five miles away? Yet the invitation had warmed Ryan, who extended his hand.

"Thanks for giving her a decent burial," he said. Then turning to hide his face, he herded his children inside.

Bascomb hesitated at the door of Kitty Kelly's room. He knocked, more to delay going in than in expectation of a reply. Then he turned the dented metal knob and entered.

The light leaking in from the street was just enough for him to find a candle stub on a dirty plate. He lit it and looked around. As he did so, a tabby cat came in the door. It nosed his ankle with a proprietary air.

For furniture, the room contained only an iron bedstead with a stained mattress folded at its head, a bentwood chair, and a dresser, on top of which were a pitcher and basin. On the wall was a plain crucifix, slightly off its axis, a coat hook, and a mirror whose backing was deteriorating. How a girl could make herself presentable enough to sell "small fines"—lace handkerchiefs and the like—with only such equipment was more than Bascomb could imagine. Perhaps other items had been pilfered by now.

He was vaguely ashamed of having come, for what did he expect to discover? He moved to snuff the candle. Then he remembered the cat.

Where could it have gone? He looked around. A slight noise emanated from under the bed, an arrhythmic ticking sound. He bent down to look.

The tabby was stretched out with its white belly uppermost, energetically batting at a shred of cardboard lodged in the bed springs. It started in terror at Bascomb's appearance and bolted for the door.

Painfully—for Bascomb was not getting any younger—the superintendent knelt and peered under the bed. He dislodged the strip of cardboard with which the cat had been occupied and stood to bring it over to the candle.

It was a second-class steamship ticket, fully paid, for Katherine Kelly and Martina Alvarez to go to Barbados via Bermuda. The date of their planned departure was the very day they had been discovered unresponsive in this room.

Bascomb found supper at a hotel near the Boston State House and then turned his steps toward the address given for Kitty's husband, James Kelly. His lodging, though not luxurious, was several steps above what Kitty had been living in as regarded cleanliness. A sort of keeper at the door asked his business before sending him up to the third floor.

As he reached Kelly's room, out of breath, voices could be heard behind the door. A woman laughed as Bascomb knocked on the door. There was a cheerful cry— "Well, Harry, it's about time!"—and the door was flung open.

She was a messy girl, with hair draggled and a freckled face that must have been cute in childhood. Now it was flushed with liquor, to judge by the empty bottle in her hand. Seeing Bascomb, she drew back.

"Jim," she said flatly, "visitor for you."

James Kelly had by now come behind her. He pulled her arm with steady but not violent force so that she staggered backward and bounced awkwardly onto an unmade bed.

"Who are you?" Kelly asked in a low voice. He was enormously tall, practically a giant, with liver-colored lips and straight black hair beginning to recede. He had on a good shirt but no collar. Under better conditions, the superintendent guessed he could be handsome.

"Pardon me," said Bascomb, offering his card with half a smile. "I'm the superintendent of Mount Auburn Cemetery where we will be interring Mrs. Kelly on Friday. As you are the next of kin, I need to trouble you for a signature." He extracted a form from his pocket and handed it to Kelly. "It's not a bill."

Kitty's husband shot him a mistrustful glance as he unfolded the paper. "Give me a minute," he said and shut the door in Bascomb's face. A minute later, when the door reopened, Kelly had snapped a collar into place and run a comb through his hair.

"Forgive my manners," said Kelly tonelessly. "I haven't any space here. Could I meet you at the Surrey in five minutes?" Bascomb nodded and took his leave. On his way down the stairs, he passed a portly man with a plaid coat coming up, carrying a string bag of brown bottles. Harry, he guessed.

The Surrey was half a block away. Though it was the sort of place you would not want your mother to see you entering, it was not bad of its type. It stank of spilled beer and the sawdust on the floor was getting tired after a long day, but the tables were clear and fairly clean. Bascomb took a seat, ordered a whiskey, and waited.

It was not five minutes, more like twenty when he saw Kelly in the door. He had on a smart coat and a necktie in addition to his collar, and his expression had assumed some character. As he sat down opposite the superintendent, Bascomb was unsure whether the glint in his eye reflected anger, embarrassment, or calculation. Kelly cast his eyes down after he ordered a beer from the waiter.

"I . . . I miss my wife very much," he said after a long pause. He took the paperwork from his coat pocket and slid it across the table. Bascomb glanced at the signature— large, practiced, educated—before tucking it away. "I only ever wished to reconcile with her and live again as man and wife. I'm glad that the funeral has been arranged."

Bascomb nodded, appreciating Kelly's deft use of the passive voice: "has been arranged." Must be the journalistic training, he thought. "We have not been able to find a next-of-kin for Miss Alvarez," he said. "The court allows us to bury her regardless, but I don't suppose you have any information on that point."

Kelly moved his shoulders as though working out a kink in his neck. "Afraid not. My wife's company after we separated was . . . no longer my concern."

Their conversation was broken by a vagrant woman in a kerchief who approached their table with outstretched hand. The waiter intercepted her and hustled her off, but Kelly took the opportunity to escape. He threw a dime on the table, mumbled an excuse, and left.

A fog had descended during the time Bascomb had patronized the Surrey. The damp air felt pleasant after the stifling saloon. As he started off toward the trolley, he spied his business card crumpled and discarded on the walkway.

Good for Kitty, he thought. She got away from him. Kelly had not even asked when the burial was.

The next few days were busy ones for the superintendent. The late winter was harvesting another sheaf of pneumonia and consumption victims. On Wednesday he was at his desk sorting through the day's transactions—burial plot purchases, memorial installations, even one request for a disinterment—when there came a knock at his door.

"Come in, please," he said without looking up. He signed and blotted his paper before rising to meet his visitor. Only with a quick effort did he keep from gaping.

It was the vagrant woman from the Surrey. She was wearing the same shapeless coat and the same bright kerchief over her hair. Now that he looked at her full in the face, he saw brown eyes that, though rheumy and dimmed with age, were fired with purpose.

She approached his desk, holding a calling card—dirty and creased—outstretched in her hand. "That you, sir?"

It was indeed his card, picked up, he guessed, from outside the Surrey on that foggy night. "Yes, madam," he replied. "Please, won't you sit down."

"You have my Tiny?" The cadence and accent were Caribbean.

"I beg your pardon?"

"My granddaughter Martina. My Tiny."

"Oh, dear me, I apologize," Bascomb stammered. "Yes. Yes, we have her. My deepest . . ."

"I can see her." It was not a question.

"Of course," he said.

It took some minutes for the superintendent to find Barney Ross and the necessary tools.

Snowdrops were stirring in the wind as he escorted Mrs. Forde—for that was her name—toward the Receiving Tomb, where the bodies of Kitty Kelly and Tiny Alvarez lay in wait of their burial. Upon unlocking the heavy iron door, Bascomb spied the matching coffins on adjacent shelves. He winced as he noticed that the name "Alvarez" had been carelessly chalked on the side of the coffin, as one might advertise tripe for sale.

Mrs. Forde waited in the doorway as the two men hefted the girl's coffin to the floor and pried open the lid. Bascomb stepped forward hastily, hoping to shield the old woman from what he saw: the remains lying as though dumped, with one arm stuck under the torso, entirely naked except for a piece of stained toweling thrown carelessly over her midsection. Her dead eyes stared at the side of the coffin; her mouth hung open.

"This is outrageous," he muttered. "How can they have been so . . ."

But Mrs. Forde did not look shocked, nor was she deterred. She fell on her knees beside the coffin, tenderly

85

lifting the cold arms to arrange them, placing her weathered brown hands on her granddaughter's eyes until they stayed closed, tying the jaw closed with a ribbon she took from her pocket, straightening and adjusting the bit of cotton toweling until it looked like a wedding gown on a pale bride. Throughout this process, Bascomb and Ross watched in wordless awe.

As Mrs. Forde worked to prepare the corpse, doing what the coroner—or any human being—should have done, a few things struck the superintendent. Tiny's face had a blue caste to it, something Bascomb had never seen before in many years of observing the dead. A little streak of blood had dried at the corner of her mouth, which her grandmother tenderly wiped away with a handkerchief. Bascomb pondered these things in silence, wondering what it was, exactly, that coroners were paid to do. There were no signs of an autopsy.

At last Mrs. Forde finished to her satisfaction. She made the sign of the cross over the body as tears ran down her face. Then she allowed the men to reseal the coffin and replace it on the shelf. She accepted the superintendent's arm to return to his office.

Bascomb threw some coal into his little stove to warm the room and set about organizing the proper forms. Mrs. Forde sat in silent meditation while he did so. As he set the ink and pen out for her to sign, he offered her a glass of spirits.

She hesitated, looking at the bottle. "My Tiny," she said at last, "she liked that sort of thing, how you call it?"

"Brandy?"

"Yes. Brandy. It went with her new life. We are more folks for the rum." She took a sip and then picked up the pen. "She came here . . . to start over."

86

The papers having been signed in a rough hand, she stood to go, but Bascomb waylaid her. He rummaged in his desk and pulled out the ticket that he had found in Kitty's bedsprings.

"She wanted to come home. She wanted to come back to you, with Kitty," he said. "She did not get the chance." He shook her hand. "I hope I will see you on Friday."

"No," said Mrs. Forde absently, fingering the ticket. "No, I think not."

Bascomb watched her go, then sat back down at his desk. He looked at the residue of brandy in Mrs. Forde's glass. Then he stood and moved over to the wall.

An enormous map of the cemetery hung there, with every lot number and boundary painstakingly drawn. He knew every square foot of Mount Auburn, from its towered high point to its lowest pond. He moved his hand over the map, away from the western wall. The hand stopped at a spot between two grand family plots, both the property of dynasties that had died out.

"That's better," he muttered to himself. He went out to find Barney Ross.

Friday came at last. It was bitterly cold and blustery, as like to January as a March day could be.

But the cemetery knew that spring was coming. The willows waved their long yellow stems, as though sweeping away the debris of winter. Some of the hardier birds were making their first mating calls and hopping around in the shrubs.

The wider of the cemetery's two funerary wagons was harnessed to a pair of horses hired from a local stable.

They were not as elegantly black as the superintendent might have liked but they were stately and well behaved.

With the help of Barney Ross and a couple of gravediggers, Bascomb extracted the coffins of Kitty Kelly and Tiny Alvarez from the Receiving Tomb and loaded them side by side in the wagon, covering them with a gold-fringed drape of black velvet. They drove to the front gate to await any mourners.

To Bascomb's surprise and pleasure, he found Ryan, the Irishman from Kitty's tenement, there with his wife and the three children. They had brought a small but dignified wreath of dried flowers with a ribbon reading "In Memoriam." The superintendent furnished everyone but the baby with an armband of black crape.

To his surprise and consternation, Bascomb also spied the portly man in the plaid coat whom he had passed on the stairs at James Kelly's building. The man called Harry beamed about him as if he were at a seaside resort rather than attending a funeral. He cheerfully accepted an armband.

When it was clear that no one else was coming— neither James Kelly nor Mrs. Forde nor Mrs. O'Sullivan— the funeral party set off, the wagon leading and the mourners following behind.

Ten minutes later, they halted at a vacant spot on a hill that faced the rising sun. The gravediggers had done their work, excavating a deep rectangle and creating a golden mound of sand and pebbles on the turf. Ropes lay at the ready across the grave.

Kitty went in first and then Tiny, as close in death as they were in life. In lieu of clergy, Bascomb recited a prayer and all who had gathered at the graveside said amen, even the little twins, who turned out to be girls.

As the diggers completed their work, the Ryan family took its leave. Barney Ross lingered behind; by prior arrangement, he would be planting drifts of Rugosa roses and creeping myrtle, so that in a few weeks' time no one would know a grave had ever been there. Five dollars each to the gravediggers, supplied by Bascomb, ensured that they would be as silent as the dead themselves.

The superintendent found himself walking back to the gate with Harry. "I'm a bit surprised to see you here, Mister . . ."

"Just call me Harry," said Harry affably. "Thought I'd see 'em off given I was one of the last to see 'em living. Nice girls. Really nice. Can't think why they've done it. Poisoned theirselves, I mean."

"Were you really? On the night of . . ."

"Brought up the birthday present, didn't I? Decent bottle of brandy. Don't mind saying it was a bit better than what I normally supply, if you get my meaning." Harry winked heavily.

"Birthday?"

"So she said. The mum, I mean."

"What mum?"

"Not that I got why I was to deliver it and not her," said Harry, spitting tobacco juice onto a forsythia bush. "Ran into her not half an hour later, just around the corner, like she was waiting for someone. 'Mrs. Kelly-in-law,' says I, seeing as I didn't know her name, though I knew who she was well enough, she was Mrs. Kelly's mum, 'you run up quick you'll have a glass left of it for yourself!' She fairly growled at me! No knowing with people, eh, sir?"

By this time, Bascomb's step had slowed. He tugged irritably at his side whiskers, as though they could help him pull thoughts out of his head. When he looked up again, Harry was waving farewell and hurrying to the gate.

It was too late, Bascomb knew. Too late to raise any kind of fuss about the deaths of two girls who were regarded as disposable and whom the state, the Church, and even Kitty's husband would happily have dumped in a potter's field.

He was probably the only one who knew that, as a jewelry polisher, Mrs. O'Sullivan would have had ready access to cyanide. That cyanide left a blue cast on its victims, such as he had seen in Tiny Alvarez's poor cold face. That its taste was readily disguised by brandy. That Mrs. O'Sullivan was lurking around waiting to remove the evidence after she could be reasonably sure they were dead or dying. It was a deft touch to leave behind an empty vial labeled "arsenic" for the police to find. She had calculated, rightly, that no one would bother with a test.

What her motivation was the superintendent could only guess. The idea of two women being happy together, having a future together, might have been just too much to bear.

When he got back to his office, he took out the cemetery ledger and falsely recorded the gravesite of Katherine Kelly and Martina Alvarez as Lot 28474, up against the western wall. In the clay.

Summer followed spring, and then it was September. Bascomb was working at his desk when an unnaturally tall man folded himself in through the doorframe. It was James Kelly, as sallow and cold as ever, possibly more so. He didn't look well.

In his expressionless voice, Kelly explained that he had been thinking much about his late wife and had determined that, though separated in life, they should be close for eternity. Could the superintendent show him the location of his wife's grave so that he might be buried nearby? He repeated the lines he had trotted out at the Surrey about having had no desire other than reconciliation with Kitty.

Bascomb regarded him with polite neutrality. This was the man who could not be bothered to pay for his wife's burial plot, her coffin, or a decent funeral. This was the man who had not even showed up when someone else had made all the arrangements. This was the man who had not so much as sent a carnation to lay on Kitty's grave.

Thus ran the superintendent's thoughts. But he said, "Certainly, Mr. Kelly. There's a very choice spot quite adjacent to Mrs. Kelly. Over by the western wall." ❖

A Death in New Hampshire

Jeannette de Beauvoir

I'd like to make one thing clear from the start: I never meant to kill anybody. I've been called a lot of things in my time, but murderer was never one of them.

Don't you just *hate* it when that happens?

Let's start with what I really am: a con artist. Even that identification could be a little over the top, because it seems the people who hire me must *know* what I'm doing, understand it's an act. Or I wouldn't get hired for frigging children's birthday parties, you know?

But maybe they think children need to be close to the spirits, too.

Okay. Erase "con artist" and substitute "psychic." There you go. If your mother died and you didn't get to make peace, I'm your psychic-internet connection to her. My world wide web is the domain of the spirits, and it's deep and hard to penetrate.

Sometimes, of course, I don't get to penetrate it at all. That's what I tell people when I just can't get a read. "The veil," I tell them, "is too dark today, too heavy." I feel bad about it. They feel bad about me feeling bad, and recommend me to someone else. No one's ever *not* liked what I had to say, with the exception of one hollow-eyed young man a few months ago who didn't seem pleased to be in contact with his recently deceased wife. A mere blip, however, on the radar screen of my professional life.

I practice out of my brownstone in Boston and the best part of the job—besides the money—is the travel. Yeah, I sometimes end up doing creepy adult Halloween parties in the suburbs, but more often they fly me someplace exotic— the Hamptons, Montréal, Vieques, Barcelona. San Francisco once, too, in spite of what must be a glut on the market out there: perhaps they were more trusting of a nonnative-Californian psychic.

This was one of the nicer invitations: a September weekend at the very luxurious Mount Washington Resort in New Hampshire's White Mountains, a group of friends who'd known each other in college and were having a reunion. If you've never seen this hotel, go look it up online. *The Shining* wasn't filmed here, but it could well have been. The resort is one of the grandest of hotels from an age of extraordinarily grand hotels. What's not to love?

I did as much research as I could ahead of time, of course. That's part of my success. Google is most *definitely* my friend. I looked up everything I could on the hotel and the area. I took the names of my new clients and delved into their past, their time at Yale, their family connections. I own a particularly excellent genealogy program that gives me names and dates connected to clients' ancestors. It's saved my reputation more than once. I remember a skeptic who wanted me to get in touch with someone who was still very much alive. If I didn't do research, I might have fallen right into that one.

So I put in a couple of days' work, packed my bags, and on the Thursday got in my car and headed north. I usually arrive a day before I'm actually needed, so I can get a feel for the place, see what I might be able to use. A place like this, rich with Gilded Age history, was a perfect setting, and I was determined to use it to the fullest.

To get to Mount Washington, you drive, and drive, and drive. Past Conway it starts becoming narrow winding roads, climbing higher and higher into the mountains, with glimpses down into deep gorges and up to bare stone peaks, almost always following the seemingly impossible railroad tracks that were the way the great and the good used to arrive. And then, just as you're convinced you'll see nothing other than ski slopes and cabins huddled against the mountainsides for the rest of your life, the hotel comes into view, reaching out across the landscape, white and brilliant and luxurious. The skies stretching over it are the clearest and cleanest of blues. And you really, truly have to catch your breath: it's a building that is so smug, so very sure of itself.

And for good reason. It was here before any of us, and will outlive us all as well.

I took in a massage at the spa—I have to be relaxed and comfortable in order to do readings, right?—and got the lay of the land, chatted up the personnel about the hotel's history, legends, and resident ghost, and finally got myself an excellent night's sleep.

No premonitions. Not a flicker. Which shows what a fraud I really am.

They started arriving during the late afternoon on Friday. My clients came first: Troy and Ellie Morgan. Troy was president of a private financial institution in Boston; Ellie illustrated children's books—both in their thirties, blooming with success and self-satisfaction. I knew more about them than they probably did about each other. "Ms. Vazquez?"

I smiled. "You can call me Amelia." I was probably going to be the only one in the group with a name that didn't sound like it came straight off the Mayflower.

Ellie looked me over hopefully. I don't do the gold hoop earrings or fluttering scarves some of my colleagues swear by; I wear dark colors, usually wool trousers and a sweater, with a necklace that looks esoteric and is in fact a design created in an after-school program by my friend Sophie's eight-year-old daughter. I look simple, elegant, and expensive.

People like the Morgans think the more they pay for something, the better it is. But showing their investment is appropriate is crucial, and my wardrobe reflects my credentials. I look like someone successful in their world, but the necklace hints at something more, something deeper.

Idiots.

"Everyone should be getting here soon," Troy said. "Why don't you join us for a drink, and we'll talk about the weekend?"

The Rosewood Bar is located behind the Grand Staircase (yeah, they do actually talk that way: you just *know* everything is capitalized) and the wine Troy ordered was spectacular. "So tell me about who else is coming," I urged.

Ellie took up the conversational reins. "Well, there's Marcel and Jennifer," she said. "Marcel we knew at Yale, of course; Jennifer was a couple of years behind all of us."

I needed full names to look them up. "I always send a card to people after the event," I said carefully, taking out a notebook. "Sometimes—well, the best way to phrase it is, someone from the other side sometimes has additional information for one of the participants. I like to be able to pass that message along. It happens more often than you'd think. So if we could include full names and addresses?"

"Of course," said Ellie, nodding eagerly. This was all her idea, I thought. Troy was going along because he went along with whatever Ellie wanted. I'm not a total fraud: at least I can read *people*. "That's Marcel Otis and Jennifer Parker-Otis. Here, I'll write the addresses."

"Texting would be easier," said Troy. He pulled out his phone and clicked away. I took a breath; time to show him who was in control here. "The spirits," I said, "have become harder and harder to reach since the advent of the internet. Messages get twisted and tangled. I will have nothing to do with electronic communication."

Well, except for my website, of course.

Ellie took my notebook and started writing names and addresses. "Then there's Stephanie. Stephanie Harrison. She's an architect, she did that building downtown—which one was it?"

"Don't remember," said her husband. He was focused on the phone, no doubt sending and receiving important texts. I'd look up the building.

"She's here alone," said Ellie. She leaned in closer to me. "Divorced last year, if you can imagine that. We never saw it coming."

I made suitably shocked and supportive noises and she started writing again. "Jason and Chad," she said. "Both in our class at Yale, though of course they weren't a couple then. Chad was dating—what was her name, darling? The one whose father owned all those islands in Greece or Turkey or someplace like that?"

"Don't remember," said Troy again, clicking away.

"Anyway," Ellie said, turning back to me, "they both went on to medical school, and that's when they got together. And now they're married and thinking about adopting a child. Isn't that wonderful?"

"So—seven people total?" I asked.

She looked at me anxiously. "Yes. Is that bad luck, having an uneven number? It's just that we always get together once a year and do *something* together, and we didn't know that Stephanie and Clark had divorced—"

"It's fine," I said soothingly. God, this woman was nervous. I knew she was the only child of a diplomat and her alcoholic husband; the daughter had had a lot of expectations placed on her. The mother was now deceased—thank goodness—and there was plenty of material about her online. If Ellie wanted communication, I could deliver.

"So, the schedule," said Troy, putting down his phone and signaling for another bottle of wine. I'd barely drunk half of my glass; it was their vacation, not mine. "We'll introduce you tonight and maybe have a—what do you call it? Séance?"

I smiled. I call it whatever the client wants it to be called. "Séance always sounds like Ouija boards and crazy old ladies," I said, and watched the relief cross his face. "Let's just say meeting, shall we?"

"First meeting, then," he said. "Right after dinner? Say nine o'clock?"

"You're welcome to join us for dinner, of course," said Ellie quickly.

"Thank you," I said, "but I'm sure you'll have a lot to say to each other. And I'll need some quiet time to prepare." Well, quiet time and my genealogy program, anyway.

"Good," said Troy. "Then tomorrow—well, there's lots going on. We're playing golf . . . I thought we could meet again in the evening, if that works? I think twice is enough, don't you, Ellie?"

Ellie obviously did not. Ellie was clearly hungry for whatever she thought I was bringing to her. "We can have some private talks," I told her, and her face relaxed.

Troy saw that, too. "Fine," he said. "We're in one of the tower suites. See you there at nine."

Room-service dinner, a couple of hours with my laptop, and I was prepared. I waited until ten to the hour and headed up the private staircase to the tower suite. All the towers at the hotel have different staircases with different numbers of steps, designed specifically to confuse ghosts and keep them away.

I wasn't really worried. The ghosts always come for me.

The guests were all sitting around the suite's main area, chatting, laughing. I checked the room as I came in and didn't sense any fear or even nervousness; with some groups, the air shimmers with anxiety, but not this one. Everyone, I saw, was drinking wine, all still dressed for dinner; the main dining room has a strict dress code. When I entered, everyone turned expectant—or amused—faces toward me.

Troy rose, languidly, from one of the chairs. "Ms. Vazquez—Amelia—welcome. Everyone, this is Amelia." He gestured toward the male couple sitting on the loveseat, both very handsome, both wearing suits in different shades of gray. "This is Jason and Chad." Chad stood to shake my hand; Jason waved from his seat.

"This is Stephanie, and of course you know Ellie already." Stephanie was dressed in brilliant red: she was looking to replace the unfortunate Clark. The red-dress effect—it's even called that—is a known psychological phenomenon. In her reading, she'd want to hear about doors opening, a future spreading out in front of her.

I could do that.

Troy was sitting closest to the last couple. "Jennifer and Marcel," he said. Marcel also stood up to shake my hand—and held it a few seconds too long. Jennifer looked like she was assessing my outfit's cost; Marcel looked like he was wondering how to get it off me.

All grist for my mill.

Troy was still playing host. "Would you like a glass of wine? Or water? And where would you like to sit—or do you stand for these things?" He looked around at the semicircle of friends and gave a self-deprecating snort. "Virgin territory for me, I'm afraid. I don't know how these things are run."

"First time I've heard you admit to being virginal about anything, Troy," said Jason, a little archly. Everyone tittered.

"That chair is fine," I said, indicating one without armrests. "A glass of water would be lovely. And perhaps you can lower the lighting a little?"

I sat and looked around at them again, my online searches for their dead people flashing through my mind. Marcel's father had been killed in Iraq. He and Jennifer had a baby who'd died a few hours after birth; I hoped I wouldn't have to go there.

Chad's parents had been on Swissair Flight 111 in 1998, engulfed in flames over Nova Scotia; they'd probably have something to say tonight. I'd done the math: he'd been a child at the time. I wondered who'd raised him.

Stephanie's parents were alive and well, but one of her close friends at Yale had succumbed to the pressure and one night had taken several months' worth of hoarded sleeping pills; they'd been in the same dorm.

That, I decided, was probably enough to go on for this evening. That, and Ellie.

I drank some water and looked around. "Is everyone comfortable? I don't want to be crass—" I smiled "—but no one likes being interrupted, the spirits included, so if you need to visit the lavatory . . . "

Another obedient laugh. This group would be great at a comedy club. "All right," I said. "I'm going to take you through a relaxation exercise. I do this because the spirits need a clear channel. You have to leave your issues outside."

"I thought that's what the wine was for," remarked Jason, grinning and looking around at the others. Ellie's face was pinched.

"Please just do as she says, Jason," she said. "You can make fun of it all later, if you have to."

Jason mimed an incredulous *who, me?* look.

"Okay," I said, taking control back. "Before we do the exercise, I need to know if there's anyone that you particularly want me to ask for."

"They come when called?" Troy was slightly more polite than Jason. Only slightly.

"You'd be surprised," I said. So would I, of course. "Is there anyone?"

Ellie managed not to say anything. Neither did anyone else. I led them more or less successfully through a relaxation sequence, then took a few deep breaths myself. "I'm opening the door now," I said, the words I always use to kick things off. "Is there anyone there who needs to talk to us?"

Silence. I let it stretch out, calculating just how far I could go before someone—Jason, probably—changed the room's dynamics. I gave it a count of thirty before blurting out, "I'm sorry, oh God, I'm so sorry! How horrible!"

My peripheral vision showed a crossfire of startled glances. Stephanie picked up her wine and drank it down in one swallow. "Who is it?"

I didn't answer; I was listening. "Everyone was screaming," I said, my breath coming faster now, more ragged. "There wasn't time for anything. There wasn't time to think about anything but the plane crashing. There wasn't time to think about"—a long pause, and I turned and looked directly at him, as though only at that moment discovering it—"Chad."

Someone gasped. Chad had turned white and was sitting on the edge of the love seat, Jason sitting beside him, forgotten. "Who is it?" he asked.

I'd been reading about his father, a diplomat returning to Geneva after meetings at the UN headquarters in New York. "He says he didn't spend enough time with you," I said. "He wishes he had. He wishes he hadn't been so involved with his work." Pause. "If he'd've known, he would've done things differently."

"Christ," said Chad. Jason had let go of his flippancy and his hand found his husband's. "I hardly remember him."

"He wishes he could tell you he's sorry to have left you alone." Careful, I warned myself. I didn't know who'd raised Chad. "He says that you've become a fine man."

Chad swallowed. "He—he doesn't mind that I'm-" He floundered a bit, looking increasingly agitated, and I let him off the hook. "He says if Jason is your soul mate, then that's what he wants for you, too."

"Christ," he said again, and started crying. "I love you, Dad. Tell him—tell him I love him."

"He knows," I said. "He's watching over you, and he couldn't be prouder. He says—"

"Yes?"

"He says you should go ahead with the baby. He says he'll be glad of a grandchild."

Chad kept crying. Jason was crying now, too. That's me, spreading mirth and merriment wherever I go. Time to move on. "I'm hearing another voice," I said. "It's a woman, a young woman. She died—could she have died at school?"

I never got around to Ellie. Stephanie was too busy drinking in her friend's putative wisdom about moving on, moving forward, eschewing regret. I decided they'd taken all they could. It was time to end the evening.

Everyone was babbling at once, like kids let out of school. Troy was opening more bottles and pouring more wine. Chad and Jason had their heads together, murmuring. Ellie walked me to the door. "Thank you," she said, and hugged me. "Can we meet tomorrow? Early? Just you and me?"

"Of course," I said. She was, after all, the one paying my fee. I headed back to my room, sleepy. Enough research, enough work. There was plenty of time to prepare for the second round, and I could handle Ellie.

The next morning, things went very wrong, very fast.

There was a card from Ellie on a special tray delivered to my room, along with flowers, orange juice, coffee, and an amazing brioche filled with sweet cream. Afterward I decided on a walk to clear my head; the sky was again that brilliant and aching blue that only seems to happen in the mountains. When the elevator stopped of its own accord on the second floor, I got off—why not?—and headed for the staircase.

I'd thought the corridor was empty but when I started down it I saw a woman standing there, gesturing toward me to come to her. I looked behind me in case she was signaling someone else, but I was alone.

The closer I got, the less reliable my vision seemed to be; she was becoming less and less substantial. I wasn't even a few feet away when she disappeared altogether, leaving a shimmer of light in the air behind her.

Okay: nothing wrong here. The psychic sees ghosts. Next thing I'll be looking at the little twin girls at the end of a hallway, right? This hotel was making me fanciful.

I stopped by the concierge desk. "That ghost of yours," I said.

She smiled brightly. "Princess Carolyn," she said, nodding.

I cleared my throat. "She just hangs out in the one room, right? 314?" The widow of the hotel's original owner, Carolyn, had remarried—catching herself a prince, no less—and had been in residence year-round since her death in 1936. An elegant figure strolling into the dining room, some said; others noted lights that went on and off spontaneously. I'd been particularly interested, since I could already foresee an opportunity for a future party-séance—ghosts are, after all, my bread and butter.

"I think she likes to check the whole place out," she said. "Make sure everything's running well, you know? I mean, after all, it was her hotel, once."

Ellie was suddenly at my side. "Amelia! Where have you been? I've been waiting for hours."

I was startled: I'd left my room not that long ago. At eight-thirty? "Around," I said vaguely. "Thanks for the breakfast."

"Are you all right?" she asked, frowning.

"I'm fine." Except for having ghost hallucinations, that is.

"Good. We were going to meet, remember? I wondered . . . it's just . . . my mother . . ."

"Of course," I said. To hell with you, Princess Ghost. I have my own fish to fry, my own spirits to contact. I put a hand to Ellie's elbow, steered her away from the desk. "Her death was difficult?"

She sniffled and hit up her pockets for a tissue. "She was in pain when she died, yeah. It was cancer. And I feel so guilty."

"You didn't give her cancer," I said.

"No, but I disappointed her. She was—she was with the diplomatic corps." A memory riding on a hiccup. "Once, we were in some palace somewhere and they served us sheep's eyes at dinner. She told me to eat everything, but I couldn't. She was so angry." Another sniffle. "And I wouldn't mind so much, you know, if it weren't for seeing her."

"Seeing her?" *There* was a twist I hadn't expected.

She nodded vigorously. "It's why we came here. I made Troy. We were here in the spring, and that's when I saw her."

"Here, as in . . . "

Another nod. "The hotel," she said. "I saw my mother here."

I took a deep breath. "I'm not denying your experience," I said, "but—well, they do say there's a ghost here, you know. A woman."

"Have you talked to her?"

Which one? "No," I said, and then, remembering my professional obligations, added, "not yet."

"I think you should," said Ellie. "I know she didn't love me, but I just want—oh, nothing like what happened with Chad, you know, all that love and approval—just for her to let me go. That's really why we're here now."

I was losing my mind. That, or I'd engaged with Ellie in some sort of ghostly *folie à deux*. Neither alternative was attractive. "I can't always talk to people you want me to talk to," I said. "I can try, but I can't guarantee she'll want to communicate."

"Just try," said Ellie. "Please just try. Listen, I promised to meet Troy on the golf course at eleven—it's almost that now—but in an hour? Just before lunch?" She glanced around her. "Not here, though. And not in the tower."

I'd been thinking the tower would be a very good place indeed, with its safeguards against random ghosts wandering in. "Where, then?"

"Your room? Can we do it in your room?" The anxiety was palpable, stretching across the space between us, singing on mental wires.

"Yes, of course." I said and smiled. "It's not a problem. I'll just go for my walk now, and meet you there in an hour." And maybe figure out how it is I seem to be losing track of time this morning. And why every room I walk into seems to be tilting. Maybe I should just go and lie down. I was suddenly feeling confused about where I was and what I was doing.

Her face lit up. "Thank you."

This woman was seeing things. I was seeing things. It all just went to show how vulnerable we all are to mysteries, to stories, to suggestions. Hell, it was the way I made my living, and even *I'd* fallen prey to it, dreaming of an American princess and imagining she was calling to me. I was hallucinating. That was all.

I shook it all off when I got outside, walking in the sunshine, breathing the clean air. Everything was going to be fine. I'd connect Ellie with the woman she wished her mother had been; I'd have a grand dinner and then do a good solid reading and, tomorrow, I'd go home.

I flipped my card key in front of the reader beside my door and walked in without any premonition and saw the body on the floor and in that moment everything changed.

Troy Morgan, my client. Dead. It's odd how you know, at once. Blood around the place where the right side of his skull was supposed to be; blood on the lamp lying next to it. I was bending over him before I had time to think.

And suddenly behind me, in the doorway, Ellie was there gasping and starting to scream. Hotel security was there too, with her, gruff and self-important, asking me why I'd done it.

"I didn't do anything," I said, still not believing this was happening. "I wasn't even here; this is ridiculous. I didn't do anything."

Ellie, not sniffling at all anymore, said, "You told me you were coming straight up to your room after we talked."

"No, I didn't." I stared at her. "Why—"

"You came straight up," she said, nodding vigorously. "I saw you take the stairs. You said you were going to talk to Troy. He was meeting you. You were going to do a reading. Contact his father." She turned to the security guard, her voice rising. "She killed my husband! She's a con artist who took our money. He confronted her about it, he said he was going to, and she killed him!"

106

"No," I said, but I said it without conviction. I was feeling lost, events moving in a stream past me too quickly to catch hold of, to understand. And I was still dizzy as hell.

"She's been in a trance," Ellie told the security guard. "Last night, communicating with spirits. Today, too." She turned to me. "You saw a ghost this morning," she said.

"I told you that?" I didn't remember telling her any such thing, and right now I had bigger things on my mind. It had just occurred to me it was entirely possible I wasn't going home tomorrow after all.

"You're seeing things. You're doing things you don't remember." She looked at the uniformed guard busily writing everything down. "You can tell the police when they come. I came up here to meet my husband, to ask for our money back, and—this woman—was standing over him, with the lamp in her hand. You'll find her fingerprints on it." Pathos in her voice. "She killed him!"

Gaslight, I thought. She's gaslighting me. How did she know about the ghost? Had I told her, and forgotten? Of course not. I'd gone for a walk. I didn't kill my client. "I didn't kill my client," I said out loud.

"They'll have to take you in for questioning," the security guy said, standing up. "They're on their way now. Don't move, please." He was on his mobile again. I stared at him in horror.

Ellie was close to me, too close, her voice low, almost intimate. "Amelia. Amelia, listen to me. You did a séance last spring for someone called Michael Dutton. Do you remember?"

"The police are on their way," the guard reported.

This isn't happening.

107

Her voice, close to my ear. "You told him his dead wife was looking for him. You said she had unfinished business."

"If you say so," I said. *This isn't happening.*

"No, *you* said so. And Michael took it badly. Up until then, everyone thought her death was an accident. We'd engineered it perfectly, Michael and me. An accidental death for her, an accidental death for Troy, and we'd be free and rich. But you *scared* him." A sharp look. "He killed himself because of you."

"Are you hearing this?" I asked the security officer. He ignored me: he was talking to two of his colleagues crowding into the doorway. "Let's get this whole corridor closed off," he was saying.

The voice in my ear was almost seductive. Almost. "You're a killer, Amelia, one way or another. Couldn't get you for Michael's death," said Ellie, "but it was great, really, how you helped me get rid of Troy today. And of course you'll have plenty of time now to think of all the other lives you may have ruined. Maybe *they'll* start haunting you now."

"I saw your mother," I said quickly, grasping at straws.

"You saw nothing," she said, disgust in her voice. "It was in your brioche this morning." I must have been staring at her stupidly, because she got impatient. "I put ketamine in it, you fool. You thought you'd see ghosts, so you saw ghosts." She smiled. "Fuck my mother. It was only ever a way to get you here."

"You drugged me, and then you killed your husband."

"Well, maybe. Or maybe I drugged you, and *you* killed my husband." Her smile was bright. "I don't think you'll ever know."❖

The Ghost Light

Ruth M. McCarty

Erin Donnelly would have done anything to avoid opening night at the Prosperity Playhouse, if her sister Megan hadn't gotten a role. Not that Erin didn't like plays—she did—but as chief of police she was out-straight busy with the summer tourists. There was no way she could escape it, though, especially since the theater was a rehabbed church sitting directly across the lake from her house—converted by the summer folks who populated Still Water Lake.

Since their mother had passed and her nieces had gone off to college, Erin's sister, Megan, had moped around like a wilted rose. Charlie, Megan's husband, had stopped in at the Prosperity Police Station just three weeks earlier to talk to Erin, to tell her Megan needed something to do and did she have anything she could volunteer for at the station. Erin had nothing, but she had heard that morning they were holding tryouts for *A Stranger Comes to Town*, and Megan had taken theater in high school.

Now, like everything she did, Megan was putting one hundred percent into her role, and because she could sew, she was also the costume designer, frantically assembling costumes for the cast.

"The open dress rehearsal is Friday night, Erin," Megan said. "Charlie and the girls will be there then and Charlie again on Saturday night. I want you there on Saturday. Opening night. Here are two tickets."

"Two tickets? I only need one." Erin noticed a familiar look on Megan's face. "Please don't tell me you're fixing me up again."

"I'm not fixing you up. They're yours to do what you want with. But why don't you ask that guy you work with."

Erin knew whom she meant. Ian McDermott. Her chief deputy. The man she'd been in love with for years but would never admit to. He didn't work with her; he worked for her. And unless one of them left the police force, she wouldn't cross the line.

But she could ask him to the play, couldn't she? Maybe go for a couple of beers at Kick Backs Bar afterward. Erin took the tickets and put them in her pocket.

The week had been typical for July when visitors from away descended on Prosperity, Maine. Motorboat mishaps, drunk and disorderly conduct, and the occasional domestic calls kept the department busy. They had hired seven seasonal officers to work along with their full-time officers and were still short-handed.

A cold front from Canada promised to bring a little relief to the hot and humid weather, but it also meant thunderstorms for Saturday night. Erin hoped it wouldn't keep theatergoers at home. Her sister had been at rehearsals every night and Erin hadn't seen her this happy in a long time.

Ian had smiled when she asked him. She'd mentioned the beers first, then slipped in going to the play. She had rearranged the schedule so they both could have the night off.

Erin had been on call all day Thursday and had spent it at the station catching up with reports. She'd worked a seven-to-seven shift Friday and now sat on her screened-in porch overlooking the lake and the theater across the way. Aching all over, she took a sip of beer and tried to relax. She'd stopped by Romano's on the way home and picked up a pizza for dinner. It would do for tomorrow night too. Hold her over during the play until she could order something at Kick Backs Bar.

Erin must have dozed because she woke to the sound of car doors slamming and motors coming to life across the lake. Dress rehearsal over. She hoped it went well for Megan. Erin had read once that if the dress rehearsal was bad, opening night would be good. She didn't believe it, but Megan would.

She watched as the parking lot cleared out. She knew Megan would be the last one to leave, so she grabbed another beer and watched the lights across the lake. One by one they went out as the actors left. Knowing her sister, she'd press and hang every costume tonight so they'd be ready for tomorrow night's opening, then she would light the ghost light, a bare bulb mounted on a portable stand in the center of the stage, before leaving. Protection from the spirits who might cause mischief.

Erin called Holstein, one of her officers, and asked him to take a ride by the playhouse to check on her sister, then headed inside. The camp she lived in had been winterized and refurbished, but the previous owners hadn't thought to put in air-conditioning, which she wouldn't have done either because it was generally cool on the lake, but on scorching, humid nights like this she could have used it.

Holstein called later and Erin picked up on the second ring. "Donnelly," she said as clear as she could. She hoped Holstein couldn't tell she'd been sleeping.

"Your sister just left," he said. "I'm heading back to the station."

Erin glanced at the clock. It was nearly midnight. "Thanks," she said and ended the call.

Erin awoke at five-thirty to a spectacular sunrise. She hadn't slept well because of the heat. She threw on some clothes, then headed into town for breakfast at Rosie's Diner on Main Street. Even at 6:00 A.M. the place had a line. Erin went around back, knocked on the door, and the dishwasher let her into the kitchen. The owner, who was a man named Pete, not the original Rosie, kept a small table with two chairs off to one side. Erin sat.

Pete came over a few minutes later with a pot of coffee and a couple of mugs. "Hey, Chief. What you up to?"

Gray-haired, jolly, and red-faced, Pete sat down across from her and wiped his brow with his apron.

"Not much, Pete. Looks like another scorcher."

"Yup. Till the storm gets here." *Here* sounded like hee-ah. "You on duty today?"

"Nope. I'm off for the first time in weeks. My sister, Megan, is in the play over at the Prosperity Playhouse. You know, *A Stranger Comes to Town.*"

Pete rolled his eyes. "Gawd. Those strangers from away are the rudest bunch."

Erin took a sip of her coffee. "I take it they've been eating here."

"Yup. Wanting fancy shit like artichoke-spinach something or other. I'm right out straight to be mixing up stuff like that. Damn flatlanders. Especially that Miranda Mansfield."

"I heard she's—" Erin started to say when her phone beeped for an incoming text. She took it out of her pocket, saw it was Megan, and read "Come for breakfast." It surprised her that Megan was up this early.

"I've got to go," she said, then reached into her pocket to pay for the coffee.

Pete waved at her, "It's on me. You can pay next time. When you eat one of my not-so-fancy breakfasts."

Erin heard his deep belly laugh as she closed the door. She texted Megan when she got in the car and headed to her sister's house.

Megan looked a wreck. She led Erin to the kitchen where she already had the table set for two. Placemats, cloth napkins, and all. She poured coffee for both of them, then opened the oven and took out a tray with a ton of French toast and slid a couple on their plates. "I've been keeping these warm for you."

"Charlie going to join us?" Erin asked.

Megan shook her head. "He's driving the girls back to school, then going to Bean's."

"Well, aren't you going to tell me about the dress rehearsal?"

Megan sat down, put her hands over her face, and sobbed. "It was a disaster."

Erin didn't know what to say. "That's good, isn't it?"

Megan raised her eyebrows in a look that reminded Erin of their mother. "Everything went wrong. Miranda's costume went missing. I know I hung it in her dressing room, all pressed and pretty, but it wasn't there. We had to hold up rehearsal while we searched everywhere. And do you know where we finally found it?"

Erin had no idea and shook her head.

"Hanging from the trap door under the stage. Someone's idea of a joke. Miranda was furious."

"Meg, that's terrible. But at least you found it."

"She blamed me." Megan hit the table with her hand. "And Brent laughed."

"Brent?"

"The male lead. I wanted to walk over to the trap door and fall in. They all laughed at me."

"I'm sure they weren't laughing at you."

"Oh, Erin. They were. Then someone moved my prop from where it was supposed to be and I looked like an idiot searching all around for it."

"Did you find out who the prankster was?"

Megan shook her head. "No. But I have a feeling Miranda hid her costume herself. She has to have someone fawning over her constantly and it made me look bad. Like I messed up. She was getting on everyone's nerves this week."

"Oh." Erin figured she'd just let Megan talk.

"I think Brent hates her. I swear he mumbles his lines so she messes hers up."

"Would he have moved your prop though?"

Megan sighed. "I don't think so. He's been really nice to me."

"Trying to make Miranda jealous maybe?"

115

"No. Of course not. I don't know, maybe. Brent is a flirt, but he flirts with everyone. Everything seemed to be going well until last night when Miranda blamed me and the others all laughed. Now I feel like a fool."

Erin took a bite of her French toast. "This is really good."

"Stop trying to make me feel better."

"Just wait, Megan. Tonight will be great."

Her sister finally took a bite of her breakfast. She grunted out, "It is good."

Erin pulled up the theater's website and read a summary of the show. Three couples are stranded at a bed and breakfast in Maine when a late-in-the-season blizzard arrives. The owner and her daughter try to keep the couples entertained—until the electricity goes out and a stranger shows up at the door. A stranger who knows secrets he shouldn't know.

Erin scrolled down to the cast. Miranda Mansfield got top billing as Tiffany Logan: wife of developer Joshua Logan. Pouty, petite and blond, staring out from her head shot, a long list of credits both Broadway and summer stock.

Brent Shelton played her husband, Joshua Logan. A brooding dark look to Miranda's light. A decent list of credits and a great looking guy. No wonder Megan was so upset when he laughed.

She scrolled to Megan Curtis as Heather Emmons: daughter of the proprietor. Her sister's head shot looked pretty good. She must have had one of the local photographers take it for her.

Cassidy Jenkins, one of the founders of the playhouse, was cast as the owner of the B&B and played Megan's character's mother.

116

Erin found herself looking forward to the play after all. And to her date that really wasn't a date. And if it wasn't, why was she having such a hard time deciding what to wear?

Erin told Ian she'd meet him at the playhouse, but he insisted on picking her up. "We'll be going over to Kick Backs and you know how hard it is to park there on a Saturday night."

She was ready at seven. Dressed in jeans and boots and a low-cut jersey. So unlike her uniform. She'd even let her hair loose and applied a little makeup.

It was still light out, but the sky to the north was turning dark and the wind blew waves across the lake. She hoped everyone would be inside the theater before the storm hit. She knew sundown was at 7:45, so at least the doors would be open by then.

Ian came to the door, took one look at her, and whistled. Then laughed. "You clean up pretty good," he said.

You do too, Erin thought. "Let's go. I heard they serve alcohol before the play," she said.

Even though it was early, a crowd had gathered. All hoping to get inside before the storm. Rumbles of thunder in the distance cast a pall over the scene. Erin heard people talking and laughing but everyone seemed to be keeping an eye on the sky. A line had already formed at the steps and down the sidewalk.

Ian ordered a beer for each of them and it came in plastic cups. They tapped them together and took a drink. Erin looked around, just waiting for someone from town to jump to conclusions. She took another drink and was about to say something to Ian when a scream pierced the air. They looked at each other, threw down their glasses, and headed to the door of the playhouse. Another scream. Erin tried the door. Locked. She banged on it. An elderly woman with pale

117

hair and skin finally opened it. Erin and Ian ran past her, following the screams down the unlit aisle.

Megan stood in the center of the stage holding the ghost light, oblivious to the crowd of actors gathering around her. Erin broke through them. A crumpled petite form lay on the floor below, a pool of blood surrounding her head.

She turned to Ian. "Call this in. Then call CID in Portland. Instruct everyone outside the show's not going to go on. Tell them they can go sit in their cars but they are not to leave until we get names and license plates."

Megan seemed to hear Erin's voice and stopped screaming. She looked down at her hand and her white-knuckled grip on the light pole. Smashed glass littered the stage and blood dripped down Megan's hand. Erin could tell she was in shock.

All hell broke loose as Erin heard sirens in the distance, torrential rain on the roof, and lightning lit up the room making Megan look like a scene from a Stephen King novel.

"Megan, you can put that down, now," Erin said.

"What's going on here?" Cassidy Jenkins demanded in a voice that resonated around the theater. "What have you done?" she screamed at Megan.

"I didn't do this. I came out to get the ghost light after everyone went backstage. Miranda was there on the floor, with blood everywhere. I thought it was another prank. That it was fake blood and it was all over her costume. I got mad and picked this up, but I didn't hit her. Erin, you have to believe me. I didn't hit her."

"Don't say any more, Megan. I can't question you. In fact, I don't want any one of my officers questioning you. Portland's police department is sending someone up."

"I know what that means, Erin. Homicide. I know what it means when you call them. You and Dad—"

"Megan, please. Don't say any more." Erin turned to Cassidy Jenkins. "This is a crime scene now."

Cassidy put the back of her hand to her forehead and swayed. "No. This is a disaster. We're ruined."

Brent Shelton mumbled, "Overacting again."

Cassidy smirked and said, "That coming from a two-bit actor."

"Yeah, well, look at my creds. You're lucky I agreed to come to this hellhole of a town."

"We all know you followed Miranda here and I know she turned down your passes."

"What the hell are you talking about?" Brent screamed in Cassidy's face. "I hated working with her. I didn't know she'd been cast when I tried out."

"I heard you ask her out as we were leaving last night. She laughed at you."

"You should get your hearing checked. She was laughing at *you*. You loser."

Cassidy lunged toward him, but Erin held her back. "Enough. Everybody take a seat until the medical examiner gets here to take photos. Then we're all going to the police station where you will be questioned."

Brent glared at Cassidy, then stomped to a seat by the exit.

"Can we get more lights on in here?" Erin asked Cassidy.

"Of course we can." She pivoted and strode up the stairs.

"Wait," Megan yelled. "Don't let her go."

Cassidy froze and turned.

"She's wearing a different costume."

119

"You're crazy. You talentless nobody," Cassidy said. "This is my costume."

"No. It's not." Megan turned to Erin. "The dresses are identical but that's not the one I put out for her. The dress she's wearing has a stain on the lower right-hand corner. She spilled ketchup from her burger on it right before dress rehearsal. She knows you're only supposed to drink water when you're in costume. I got the stain out as best I could after everyone left last night and made sure to put out the other dress for tonight."

Cassidy laughed. "Not only are you a terrible actor, you're also a lousy costume designer."

Megan flinched, but her voice was strong. "She had the other dress on when I came in. There were no stains on it."

Erin knew Megan's attention to details.

"You must be confused. This is the one you put out for me."

"She's lying. She had to change because she killed Miranda Mansfield," Megan said. "We need to find her other costume. It'll be covered in blood."

Cassidy Jenkins tried to walk out past Ian but his bulk blocked the aisle.

Cassidy seemed to crumble, then stood tall and regally looked around at everyone. "Miranda called me a backwoods, no-talent, old hag and we were the same damned age. She got what she deserved."

"Take her away," Erin said to Ian. "I'll meet you at the station after CID interviews Megan."

She turned to her sister. "Good detecting, Megan. Dad would have been proud of you."

Erin watched Ian McDermott leave with a funny feeling in her chest. *Not a date.*

She saw Dr. LeBlanc, the medical examiner, and headed toward him. ❖

Impediment

Bruce Robert Coffin

Julian spent his lunch break sitting in the sparse shade of a mature ironwood tree. The thick slab of sandwich meat was okay, but the bread was stale and crumbled with each bite. Julian enjoyed his work, and was good at it, but he wanted more. Mr. Burton, his boss, had told him more than once that a man should never aspire to be more than he is.

"Let the thinking man make the decisions that keep you employed," Mr. Burton would say. And each time Julian would nod and say, "Okay, boss." Then Burton would lay a firm hand upon Julian's shoulder, smile and say, "There's a good lad." And that would be that. End of conversation.

Maybe Julian wasn't, as he had overheard some of Burton's other employees say, "The brightest bulb on the tree." Perhaps he did suffer from a learning impediment, but Julian wasn't dumb. He knew his worth. He took another bite of his sandwich before washing it down with a swig of warm R.C. Cola.

The air was still and hot. And while it was better than sitting under the burning sun, the shade of the ironwood provided little relief. No breeze to help wick away his sweat. Julian studied the partially dug hole. Five feet was the minimum depth according to Mr. Burton. Any shallower than that and you risked having wild animals digging things up. Things that were better off buried.

"That's the kind of labor you're best suited for, Julian," Mr. Burton would say. "God gave you the strength of a bull. It'd be a sin not to use it."

Julian thought a lot about sins. Men like Mr. Burton talked about things like that whenever they wanted to keep someone in line. He wondered how it was that none of his boss's activities qualified as sins. Julian didn't know what God would have made of Mr. Burton's doings, but he was sure the law might have something to say on the subject.

He waved at a horse fly noisily circling his head. The little buggers could be sneaky, as Julian knew all too well. Buzzing around until you weren't paying attention, then they'd attack, taking a painful bite out of unsuspecting souls. He set the bottle down carefully so as not to spill it, then waited for the fly to land. Eventually it lighted on Julian's sweaty forearm. He waited a tick while the insect got settled, then he slapped down hard with an open palm, ending his tiny tormentor's reign. Julian lifted his hand and grinned as he studied the squashed remnants of the bug. He wondered if killing such a small creature qualified as a sin in the eyes of God. He knew old Mr. Burton would have had some thoughts on the subject. Julian brushed the dead horse fly away and resumed eating his lunch.

He finished his sandwich, then picked up the bottle of cola and took another healthy gulp. It sure is a scorcher today, he thought as he gazed into the cloudless sky. Not the best day to be out digging holes, but a man must earn his rewards, at least that's what Mr. Burton always said. "No free rides for anyone."

Julian wondered how many holes he had dug over the years. Thirty? Forty? It was impossible to keep track. Mr. Burton always said, "Don't think of them as anything but impediments to progress, Julian. That's all they are. Nothing more."

No two ways about it, Julian thought, Mr. Burton was a smart man.

Julian looked down at his black dress shoes and trousers. Caked with desert dust, they looked more brown than black. He had never understood why Mr. Burton insisted that he always wear a suit. It seemed to Julian that a pair of jeans and a T-shirt might be better for digging holes and such.

"You've gotta dress for success, Julian," Mr. Burton always said. "People see what they want to see. Know what I mean?" Julian hadn't known, but he nodded just the same.

Mr. Burton was an educated man. Everybody said so. Educated and wily, whatever that meant. People told Julian he was lucky that someone like Mr. Burton had taken a shine to him. Times were tough, jobs were hard to come by. Mr. Burton told him that he needed a driver, and it just so happened that Julian had a license. He told Julian that he would think about hiring him on a trial basis.

After a while Mr. Burton asked Julian if he was as good at handling himself as he appeared. Julian wasn't sure what that meant until Mr. Burton showed him. They drove to a warehouse just off the strip to see a man who owed Mr. Burton money. That man, Mr. Vincenzo, had a driver too. A big man with a crooked nose. Mr. Burton told Mr. Vincenzo that he had a proposal. He said if Mr. Vincenzo's driver could whoop Julian in a bare-fisted fight, he would square their accounts. Mr. Vincenzo readily agreed. Ten minutes later, as they were leaving, Mr. Burton handed Julian a sawbuck, telling him he'd earned it. Julian had worked for Mr. Burton ever since, doing whatever needed doing.

After he'd finished digging, Julian climbed out of the hole. Clapping his hands together to knock the dust off, he walked to the car and opened the trunk. Mr. Burton stared out at him blankly, a dark hole in the center of his forehead. Julian reached in and grabbed his boss under the arms and pulled him from the trunk like a side of beef. He dragged Mr. Burton to the hole, then dropped him inside.

Julian scooped up a shovelful of dirt from the pile beside the hole, then paused a moment to look down at his boss. He wondered if Mr. Burton was proud of him. No matter. Julian was proud of himself. He had finally overcome his biggest impediment. ❖

The Perfect Choice

John R. Clark

When folks mentioned Dub Harlow, his name was invariably followed by the comment "He knows stuff, if ya get what I mean," and heads would nod. Truth to tell, plenty of locals in and around Bell Falls, Maine, sought Dub out when they couldn't find or fix something. It was how he made a living without holding a regular job or paying taxes. Making real cash money under the table suited him just fine, and he never had a problem paying for things with funds the state and federal governments didn't know about.

Such a lifestyle required that he stay on his toes. That, coupled with spending a lot of free time in libraries, was how Dub "knew stuff." It wasn't rocket science. After all, his parents, God rest their souls, had been teachers. Their constant encouragement to ask questions and read voraciously had been the norm growing up. Unfortunately, the pandemic, coupled with a sorry economy in rural Maine, made getting by more difficult every month, even for a guy who "knew stuff." His property taxes were due the first of

October and his bank account was less than half what he needed to avoid interest or a lien on the property.

Dub was thumbing through the 2021 version of the *Maine Register* at the state library when a listing for a business in South Portland caught his eye. One thing about knowing stuff was treating information like a four-leaf clover: look for oddities. Dub sensed this discovery might be his best in years.

At first, he thought the listing had to be a typo, but his hunch button was telling him it wasn't, so he decided to take a trip south. After all, there was that fancy food store in Portland he loved to visit.

The next afternoon he left that store after stocking up on his guilty pleasures. They'd satisfy a number of cravings and eliminate a couple trips into town where the small grocery store marked everything almost twice what the big box grocery stores charged.

When he got off I-295 and turned onto the main street in South Portland, Dub pulled into a convenience store parking lot and reached behind the seat for his well-used *Delorme Atlas*. GPS was all well and good, but he still went for this resource more often than not. He studied the South Portland city map in the back, looking for Backgammon Street. At first, he couldn't find it, but after pulling out his magnifying glass, he discovered it was a dead-end street, well away from the business part of town.

Even then, it nearly eluded him, necessitating a couple extra turns in order to access the poorly maintained roadway. There was a small black-and-white sign over the door, but it was impossible to read until he'd parked and gotten out of his car. Dub looked around. The building was well maintained, but slightly smaller than his own place and didn't look like a business. Still, the sign matched the listing in the *Maine Register.* "Rent A Centaur," he murmured, walking up the steps and peering inside. *Was this a joke, or a play on the more popular nationwide rental company,* he wondered. Well, he'd driven 130 miles to satisfy his curiosity so he might as well knock.

The door opened before his hand touched it and a very short individual looked out at him. Dub wasn't sure if the person was male or female. For that matter, he wasn't certain it was human.

"If you're here, you must have need for my services, so come in."

The guttural voice sent a chill down Dub's spine, but he followed whatever it was down a hall and into a dimly lit office. He took the seat opposite the desk and waited for some hint of just what the hell he'd gotten himself into. Unease battled his original hunch that this place was going to be of benefit to him in a major way.

"Chances are it will, and no, I don't read minds, but faces are as easy as the weekly comic pages," the entity sitting behind the desk said. "As I said, if you've found me, you can benefit from my services."

"What, exactly, do you do here?" Dub asked, looking more carefully at the figure opposite him.

"I rent or lease mythological beings and creatures for whatever purpose one has in mind. To answer your other question, I'm male and mostly human. If I took one of those DNA tests, the results would come back with a bunch of question marks, but my parents said we were Greek expatriates with some asp and crocodile thrown in, thanks to a very horny and dimwitted many-times-removed great uncle who served in Pharaoh's army longer ago than I care to think about. Anyhow, my appearance made going to school or getting a traditional job impossible, so I became an entrepreneur."

"That's quite interesting, Mr. . . . ." Dub hesitated, not remembering whether the listing in the book mentioned a name.

"Ammon Hotep Falafel, but I prefer to go by Zip, as in zip your lips and we can do business."

"Zip works for me. How many creatures, so to speak, do you have available?" asked Dub, an idea forming in his head.

Zip picked up a list, "a couple golems, a cyclops, half a dozen leprechauns—they're a package deal, very popular around St. Patrick's Day—goblins, a gorgon, a minotaur, a centaur, a satyr who is ungodly popular at bachelorette parties, a griffin, a phoenix, but extra fire insurance coverage is required when renting or leasing him, a basilisk, a hydra, a chimera, a pair of banshees—hearing protection strongly suggested—and Medusa."

"Prices?" asked Dub.

"They vary by entity and length of rental. If you tell me which one you have in mind and how long a rental, I can give you a ballpark figure." Zip passed him the list to help him decide.

Dub stared at it, his mind running through some half-formed ideas. He wasn't getting any younger and had no pension or social security earnings. He was getting healthcare coverage through the state, but since he wasn't looking for work, that would expire at the end of the year. He needed some kind of big score, but it had to be one that didn't involve harming decent people.

He scanned the list again and a plan started coming together. "How effective are the banshees?"

Zip shrugged. "I guess it depends on how ambitious you need to get. I wouldn't try using them to clear out the civic center, but a lady rented them last month to screw up her ex-fiance's wedding at a big fancy church in Brunswick. I didn't ask for details, but she had one hell of a shit-eating grin when she returned them, even tipped them big time."

"How do you tip a banshee?"

"Easy," said Zip. "My creatures might not be human, but they have likes and favorites just as people do. The banshees love horror movies. The woman bought them a copy of the remastered *Exorcist*. I bet they've watched it half a dozen times."

Dub nodded. "Makes sense to me. How late are you open today?"

"Business has been slow and since it's a Wednesday, I don't have anything pending this evening. If you're in the process of putting something together, I can have a late supper. How about any time before seven."

"Sounds fair," said Dub. "I need to hit the local library and check something. I'll call if I can't put something together, but if it looks promising, I'll be back well before seven."

He knew the South Portland Public Library was open until six during the week, so he checked his *Delorme* and followed the city map to the library.

One great feature of Maine libraries was how easy it was to use them even if you weren't a patron. Five minutes after entering the building, Dub was sitting at a public access computer looking at the events calendar covering central Maine for the next month. The event he remembered would happen a week from Friday night, and the location was perfect.

Two hours later, he was headed home, having rented the banshees for two days the following week. The cost was surprisingly reasonable. Zip had given him instructions on handling them, as well as a few suggestions regarding horror films the creatures didn't own.

After putting his groceries away, Dub went out and sat in the upholstered rocker on his front porch. It overlooked a small apple orchard and was where he thought best. He needed to work through any doubts or snags before going to bed because he knew how his mind operated. If he could fall asleep with a gut feeling that he was on the right track, his subconscious would work on details, allowing him to wake up with a solid plan. He had no desire to screw up and spend the winter as a guest of the Somerset County sheriff.

Dub awoke later than usual and lay in bed savoring the feeling of comfort and confidence that accompanied a good plan. He could envision exactly how everything would go, no snags, no unexpected surprises, just a smooth operation.

Over the next couple days, he made several reconnaissance runs while buying new earplugs and the best noise-canceling earphones he could afford. Zip had stressed the importance of blocking out the banshees' cries if he wanted to have any success. Even though his bank account was dipping ever closer to zero, he hit the big box store and bought some of the DVDs Zip suggested.

Friday morning, he gassed up his truck and headed to South Portland. Finding Rent A Centaur was much easier this time and Zip was waiting when he climbed the steps. He expected he'd have to sign some paperwork, but all he needed to do was fork over the rental fee, let Zip remind him how to handle the banshees, and shake hands.

"Here they are." Zip opened a door across from his office and two creatures, looking more like escapees from a Blues Brothers' movie than scary mythological creatures, shambled out. They grunted and pawed Dub on the arm before following him out to the truck.

"They might not speak English too well, but they understand it and catch on quickly," Zip said as he watched them get into the truck. "Fill them in on what you want them to do on your way home. They're pretty low maintenance creatures. Good luck."

It wasn't until he passed through the Gardiner toll before Dub felt comfortable speaking, but once he started explaining what he needed them to do, they gave him their full attention. Even though neither spoke, Dub got the impression they understood exactly what he wanted from them and were eager to cooperate.

He left the interstate just north of Waterville, heading along the Kennebec River until he reached the turn for his place. He and the banshees had three hours to kill before the plan needed to be set in motion. After connecting the DVD player to his big screen TV, he popped in Clive Barker's *Hellraiser,* which immediately captivated the creatures.

Dub went into his bedroom and changed his clothing. He dressed in black, including gloves and a ski mask. When they reached their destination, he would add dark glasses as well as the hearing protection. He returned to the living room and leaned against the wall until the final credits rolled up the screen. The banshees waved their hands at the TV, but were careful not to make any noise.

"Time to roll," Dub said, leading them out to the truck. He went over their part in what was to happen while he drove north to the mill town adjacent to Bell Falls. It was nearly three times larger in population and many there had a far better standard of living than folks in his town. That was one of the reasons he'd selected tonight's target.

The parish hall of Our Lady of Evergreen Grace was just outside of town, nestled between the Catholic church and the river. It was a perfect spot for what he was about to do. The parking lot in front of the church was packed, but the poorly lit area behind the hall was empty, and there was a rutted exit road that led down to an old railroad bed along the river. Dub killed the truck's lights and inched down until it was ten feet from what was now a well-maintained ATV trail. When they were ready to escape, he and the banshees could travel on it until they reached a dirt road a mile down river.

He shut the engine off and waited while the banshees stood beside him. "Up the hill, in the back door and then do your thing as long and loud as you want. Once I'm finished, we come back here and disappear."

The banshees tapped his upper arms, their way of letting him know they were ready.

Dub inserted the earplugs, then donned the headphones. He hoped the combination would block the screams coming first from the banshees and then from the panicked crowd inside. He turned the handle of the rear door, heaving a sigh of relief when it opened noiselessly. He entered, followed by the banshees. The main hall where the super stakes bingo games were being held was right around the corner. He waved the banshees past him and held his breath.

At first, he thought everything was going south, but when he slipped on his sunglasses and poked his head around the corner, he realized two things, the hearing protection was working and utter chaos was happening in the parish hall.

The banshees had split up with one floating along each wall, moving terrified parishioners ahead of them like cowboys herding cattle. They were clearly having fun and savoring their effect on the frightened mass struggling to exit through the front door.

Dub opened the pack slung over his right shoulder and sprinted toward the unattended cash box. It took less than thirty seconds to scoop up the money. The room was almost completely empty now and he took a minute to look around, pleased to see how many pocketbooks had been left behind. He whistled to get the banshees' attention and held up a fancy leather purse.

By the time the three of them exited through the back door, they were loaded down with handbags. "Toss them in the bed," Dub said when they reached the truck. He wasted no time in getting the truck started and swerved onto the ATV trail as soon as his passengers were in the cab. He turned on the parking lights and drove as fast as he dared until they reached the intersection.

"I'm taking my hearing protection off now," he said. "You two did a perfect job and I have a bonus back at the house I think you'll like." He waited until they patted his right arm before removing the headphones and ear plugs.

After the banshees helped him carry all the handbags into his bedroom, Dub picked up a shopping bag and pulled out their bonus. "Zip thought you'd like these," he said as he handed over *The Complete Nightmare on Elm Street* and the first six seasons of *The Walking Dead*, all still in shrink wrap. "The living room is yours until we head back to South Portland tomorrow afternoon. Thank you for a job well done."

He walked to the refrigerator and pulled out a couple beers. One per night was his general rule, but their success called for a bit extra.

He sipped on the first one while counting the cash. It came to just under eight thousand dollars. Better than he expected. It took another three hours to go through all the handbags and netted him another fifteen hundred, plus a stack of debit and credit cards. There were even a handful of rings, pins, and necklaces that might fetch another thousand.

Good thing I know stuff, Dub thought as he wrapped a rubber band around the stack of cards. There was a pawnbroker in Augusta who would be more than happy to take them off his hands without asking any questions. After using the bathroom and making sure the banshees were completely engrossed in onscreen gore, he crawled into bed.

Dub drove the banshees to South Portland the next afternoon, making certain to thank each of them as they were walking up the steps to Rent A Centaur.

Zip gave Dub a fist bump after hearing his tale about the bingo hall. "It sounds like you know what to do with my pets. Call me again when you come up with something you think might require some mythic assistance."

Dub took his time driving home, letting his thoughts drift since traffic on I-295 was light. He knew he needed to come up with something else if he wanted to make ends meet for more than a few months. The cash from the bingo hall would cover his property taxes, insurance, and groceries through the winter, but what then? He certainly didn't want to look for work, given the tanked economy in central Maine, so it was time to "know stuff."

Dub's chance at a big score came by accident. He was returning from an afternoon doing research at a nearby city library and was feeling rather discouraged. Hours of

Deadly Nightshade

scanning newspapers, the *Maine Register*, and a couple local magazines had resulted in a sore butt and eye strain. The magazines had been particularly frustrating. Most of the articles were aimed at rich fools who had come to Maine from away. The ads were even worse, highlighting smiling and artfully wrinkled old folks at fancy retirement communities, or ocean homes priced higher than his town's annual budget.

It was beginning to snow when he drove out of the parking lot. Dub needed something to counteract his foul mood, so he stopped when he saw a shivering figure standing by the side of the road with his thumb out.

"T-t-thanks, I've been trying to catch a ride for at least half an hour. You wouldn't be heading toward Miville, would you?" The man looked to be in his early forties.

"Yup, going right through, so you're in luck. Pretty rough weather to hitch in," Dub said to make conversation. He could tell the man was slightly inebriated, but didn't sense anything hostile about him.

"True, most of the time I ride a Harley, but the bank repossessed it and you know how things are right now," his passenger said. "My brother-in-law's in a gang, well, he calls it a club, but I know better. He offered to get me a membership invite, but I'm not desperate enough to pack a weapon and deal coke like those guys. I'll take heating assistance and food stamps first."

"Smart decision," said Dub, an idea starting to form in his head. "I suppose they do their deals in those rough bars down in Augusta and Waterville."

His passenger laughed bitterly. "No, these outlaws don't bother messing with small deals. They only do five and six figure stuff at their farmhouse." He stopped abruptly.

"Forget I mentioned anything about them, will you? If they ever found out I've shot off my mouth, I'm dead."

Dub remained silent until he pulled into the parking lot beside the convenience store in Miville. "Stay warm and don't worry about what you said. I'm likely to forget it by the time I get home."

"Not," Dub muttered as he drove off. Finding the farmhouse would be challenging, but not impossible. Once he did, he knew exactly which creature he'd need to rent in order to pull off the perfect crime.

Three hours looking at tax maps in the Miville town office gave Dub three possibilities, assuming the gang's farmhouse was in that town. As soon as he got home, he went to his computer and opened the online real time mapping program he subscribed to and typed in the coordinates for the center of Miville.

The second location was the most promising. It was a hundred-year-old farmhouse that looked like extensive renovations had been done not long ago. Fifty acres of fields and woodland surrounded it, and it was accessible only by a long private driveway. Dub opened another browser window and searched for the owner. The tax rolls listed a Samsur Mogiul. Searching that name online led Dub down a series of rabbit holes until he discovered the name was an alias for an ex-con currently incarcerated at the minimum security prison in the next county.

Satisfied he'd found the right target, Dub went to Augusta and browsed around in the big box electronics store, waiting until an eager clerk noticed him. Twenty minutes later, he walked out with a whisper-quiet drone that had a night vision camera and the ability to remain airborne for three hours.

The next part of the plan required patience and constant vigilance. He found a seldom used side road that ended atop a hill overlooking the farm. Loggers had cleared the area, making it a good spot to observe. Dub drove up each afternoon following lunch and parked far enough below the summit so he couldn't be seen from the farmhouse. There was a spot between two remaining fir trees where his camp chair fit nicely. He brought a thermos, a book, and an insulated camouflage blanket.

After several days of observation, Dub was satisfied this was where the bikers dealt drugs. He waited until it was dark enough so his drone wasn't visible before directing it back and forth across the property. He made notes on a clipboard while letting the drone hover, doing his best to sketch the grounds and what he could observe inside the buildings. There was one final thing he needed to know before putting the actual heist in motion.

It took two weeks to get that last bit of information. Cars and bikes filled the parking lot, spilling into the field on Sunday evenings, leading Dub to reckon that must be distribution night. His mind filled with images of big stacks of cash, enough, he hoped, to carry him through a couple winters. He'd grab wallets and firearms, too, but leave the drugs. That was a road he had no intention of traveling.

"Medusa, eh?" Zip said when Dub called him. "You sure you know what you're renting with her?"

"Yup, I'll be prepared when I get there as far as protecting myself from getting stoned. What can you add to what you've already said about her?"

Zip thought for a moment. "Well, she's older than most of the other creatures, so she's seen a lot of history, and every so often boredom sets in and she has to adopt a new persona to keep herself entertained. Right now, she's going through a Valley Girl phase, particularly in terms of her speech and music choices. If you can handle that, you should be fine. When would you need her?"

Dub reserved Medusa for the upcoming Sunday and Monday. He returned to the fancy electronics store, this time buying a premium quality virtual reality headset with a high-definition camera built into the left side. His research led him to believe that the setup would give him necessary protection should he accidentally glance at Medusa when her head was uncovered.

Before leaving Augusta, Dub stopped at a thrift store and bought several large dresses, along with three oversized floppy hats. He wanted to be sure Medusa could conceal her snakes until they were needed.

Dub listened to the weather forecast while driving to South Portland the following Sunday morning. Low clouds and fog would move in later that afternoon, creating perfect conditions for the heist. Getting in was the hard part. If all went as planned, their escape could be as leisurely as they wanted it to be.

Zip greeted him at the door, eager to learn what was going down and how Medusa would be used.

Dub shook off his usual reticence and over a cup of Greek coffee, he laid out what he'd learned and how he expected the night to unfold. "See any red flags?" he asked.

"Nope, this caper sounds pretty tight. Wish I could come along, but someone has to ride herd on these creatures. I'll be eager to hear how it shakes out," Zip said before getting up and going to get Medusa.

"Like, hi, dude, I'm totally awed to meet you." Medusa held out her hand to shake. She was dressed in a tie-died sack dress, oversized sunglasses and a knit hat that covered her ears and the back of her neck.

Dub avoided looking at her directly while shaking hands. He thanked her for agreeing to come along and hurried her out the door.

"Wow, like totally cool," Medusa gushed after Dub explained his plan. "Kinda like we're doing a Bob Dylan to the bad guys."

They went through everything one more time at his house while waiting until it began getting dark. Medusa pulled one of the flowery dresses over her outfit, then took the three hats into the bathroom to try on.

"This is, like, the most awesome one," she gushed as she sashayed into the kitchen.

Dub had to agree that her outfit would distract anyone long enough for her to whip off the hat. "Ready to have some fun?"

He adjusted the virtual reality headset as they approached the guard controlling the access gate at the farm.

The guy barely had time to start speaking before Medusa whipped off her hat while trilling, "Surprise!"

"Jesus," muttered Dub as the thug solidified almost instantly. "That was scary. Necessary, but scary."

"You ain't seen anything yet, dude," Medusa chortled as she put her hat back on.

Dub killed the truck's lights and slowly crept into the field, turning so they would be able to make a quick getaway in case anything went wrong. He led Medusa around to the back of the house where there was a bulkhead he was pretty sure remained unlocked.

"Ready?" he whispered when they reached the top of the stairs leading to the main floor.

Medusa nodded.

Dub opened the door and let her pass while he looked at the floor as she whipped her hat off. When he looked up, he saw they were in the kitchen and two bikers were turning to stone by a small bar in the middle. Fortunately, their change kept them in an upright position.

He motioned Medusa toward the doorway leading to where most of the noise was, again keeping his gaze on the floor as she sailed into the room while warbling "Surprise, everyone."

Dub peeked around the edge of the door frame. Nine more statues were standing around a big pool table covered with stacks of cash and bags of white powder. "Can you go upstairs to make sure we get everyone while I start gathering things?"

Medusa grinned and started up the stairway by the hall closet. She removed her hat when she reached the second floor, moving quietly from room to room, catching three more bikers, before intruding on a naked couple in the throes of passion. She apologized, but it was too late.

There was one more room to check. It was unoccupied, but there was a table beside the bed with five powdery lines on it. Medusa bent over to see what they were, but accidentally inhaled part of the powder. It had an immediate effect, one that startled her so much, she gasped, inhaling the rest. She giggled before turning and going back downstairs.

Dub had gathered all the cash and was working on collecting firearms. "Can you grab their wallets and any rings that didn't get caught in the stone, please. That should do it." He failed to notice Medusa's jitterbug dance as she moved around the room, collecting things including a bag of white powder while his back was turned.

"That went better than I expected," Dub said as he exited the field and headed toward the open gate. "Here, you more than earned this bonus." He handed her a small box containing *The Complete Rolling Stones Collection* on CD.

Medusa ripped the plastic off the box and pulled a case free. "I love this song," she yelled as she put the disc in his player and *Satisfaction* started blasting through the cab.

Her urge to move with the music, fueled by five lines of cocaine, had her so wound up she forgot she was in a confined space. Her left hand hit Dub's face, knocking off the headset.

"Oopsie," she giggled while leaning over to retrieve it, letting her hat tumble off her head.

And. That. Was. The. Last. Thing. Dub. Ever. Saw. ❖

I Would Kill for That House

Cheryl Marceau

The Pacific Northwest fog had burned off hours earlier, and the sea sparkled under the late afternoon sun. Molly held a hand over her eyes to shield them as she looked at a simple midcentury house perched on the rocks, overlooking the cove and the pebbled beach where she stood with her husband. "I would *kill* for that house," she said, sighing.

Steve laughed. "Yeah, that's about what we'd have to do. Location like this? It'd be in the millions. Maybe when we win the lottery."

The past months had devastated Molly. Her mother had been diagnosed with a stealthy cancer that had killed her soon after it was discovered. As the pain took over her body, her mother seemed to take comfort in the knowledge that Molly was pregnant. She'd begun knitting a tiny pink sweater during her chemo sessions as the toxins attacked the cancer in her body, gamely insisting she couldn't wait to give the sweater to her new granddaughter.

Molly was nearly inconsolable when her mother died, but the thought of welcoming her child into the world gave her some respite. She planned to name her baby after the grandmother the child would never know. In hindsight, Molly wondered if she'd tempted fate by giving a name to her unborn baby.

The doctor said the miscarriage was completely outside Molly's control, but Molly blamed herself, certain that her grief for her mother had killed her child. She wanted to crawl into the deepest, darkest place she could find and stay there forever. She couldn't imagine ever again feeling alive.

Then Steve cajoled her into taking this day trip to an island off the Washington coast, and they stumbled across this beautiful beach at a state park. On the far end she spotted the midcentury house that beckoned her with an air of peace and serenity, perched on the rocks overlooking the sheltered sea cove where they stood, surrounded by nothing but dense fir and spruce forest.

The house was all window on the water-facing sides, with more substantial walls toward the back of the house facing the forest. Molly imagined the interior uncluttered and soothing. A massive dock jutted into the water, with a pulley system big enough for a large boat.

The scene before her was perfect for retreating from the world, nothing but sea and rocks and sunlight wherever she looked. She pictured herself stretched out on a chaise facing that view, a cup of tea on the side table and a book in her hand. At sunset, she'd pour a glass of wine and stand on the deck until the magenta sky turned dark violet and a silver moon gleamed overhead. She'd immerse herself in that house and that landscape. The vision filled her with a calm she hadn't felt in months.

"Hon? We should head back. If we miss our ferry, we won't get home tonight," Steve said.

Molly held the house in her gaze as if to burn the image on her brain. "I *would* kill for that house," she whispered to herself.

Late that evening as they climbed into bed, Molly pulled out her laptop.

"Catching up on emails?" Steve asked. "We were only gone for the day. Work can wait."

She'd coped with her pain by burying herself in work. Her job was demanding, as she repeatedly reminded Steve, but the structure and routine also helped her push aside grief. When she wasn't on the job, she found tasks to do at home, barely sitting still long enough to eat a meal. The house was spotless and so uncluttered that it could have been staged for selling. She'd donated or discarded anything that reminded her of the child she'd never know. The ceaseless work was one of the few things she and Steve fought about if it could be called fighting. She'd have welcomed a real battle for the surge of emotional energy that would bring.

"Just for a minute," Molly answered.

Steve craned over to look at the screen perched on Molly's lap.

"Never mind, I'm done," she said, yawning. She closed the computer, set it on her night table, then turned off the bedside lamp. Steve curled up next to her, holding her securely. She believed she loved him, and knew she was loved in return, but that hadn't rescued her from the pain. She needed something else.

When Steve began snoring softly into her ear, she crept out of bed and took her laptop downstairs to the living room, returning to the island's property tax records she'd been studying earlier to figure out who owned the house and what it was worth.

Just having some fun, she told herself.

Daylight filtered through the bamboo shades over the sofa. Molly opened her eyes, chagrined to realize she'd fallen asleep downstairs. Damn, she was probably late for work.

Suddenly she was aware of not being alone. Steve stood in the archway between the living and dining rooms. "Did my snoring keep you awake?"

Molly looked at him with guilty puppy eyes, meant to disarm. "I had trouble sleeping so I decided to do something useful."

"Aw, sweetie, you're gonna work yourself sick. Grab a quick shower while I make us some breakfast."

"I'll be late. Just coffee, thanks. I'll take it in the car with me."

Steve sat next to her. "I've already called your office and told them you'd be in by ten." He wrapped an arm around her. "Now go get that shower and we'll have a real breakfast." He kissed her nose and rubbed her back.

"You take such good care of me," Molly said, looking at Steve as if she might not see him again for a very long time.

"How was your day?" Steve asked as she walked into the kitchen. The smell of red chili and pork wafted from the oven.

"*Carne adovada*, yum! You spoil me. I'll be ready to eat as soon as I get changed." She kissed Steve and went upstairs.

There would not be a repeat of the prior night. Molly felt compelled to hide her research. She didn't want to think about why it mattered that she keep this a secret, but it did. Pulling off her work clothes, she relaxed into cotton sweatpants and sweatshirt, tucking her feet into wool slippers. Dinner and a little TV for Steve's benefit, then she'd disappear back into a world that was rapidly becoming more meaningful than the life she inhabited.

Molly waited until Steve was asleep and tiptoed downstairs to continue what she'd started the night before, scrolling through property records to learn more about the place.

The house was on a point. It had last been sold years ago. There was no road to the house, the only access by boat. That explained the huge boat lift.

She scrolled through the tax records and gasped at the assessment. She'd need a lot of money to pay those taxes.

As if I'd ever really pay these taxes.

What kind of person was the owner? Did he live in the area, would he be likely to use the house much, what would he do if he found an intruder in his house? Questions raced through her mind as she typed the name into the search engine.

There was no recent information about him anywhere.

She double-checked the name and retyped it into the search engine. The only person with that name had died several years earlier. Yet someone was paying the taxes. Maybe the family decided it was simpler to leave the title in his name.

I wonder if they ever go there?

Time for another trip to the island. Steve didn't need to know—she'd tell him she was visiting one of the company offices on business.

The ferry docked and Molly drove off, feeling a little more subdued this time. The Northwest fall had finally settled in, bringing low clouds and soft penetrating rain. She headed to the beach where she'd seen the house before, pulled into trailhead parking, and scrambled into a large backpack, hiking as far along the beach toward the house as she could go. The weather worsened until she was thoroughly soaked and chilled, but it was good to feel her body, cold and wet and *alive*.

She shrugged off the pack and drew out a brand-new inflatable kayak with its paddle and a small manual air pump. In a few minutes the boat was inflated and ready. Molly paddled to the house, looking for any way to climb up to the dock, but the seaweed-covered rocks facing the beach were too slick to offer access. She rounded the point and encountered a forbidding stone face. She wasn't capable of scaling the cliff unassisted, and risked breaking her neck on the jagged rocks or dying of hypothermia in the ocean if she failed.

I'm miserable, but I'm not suicidal.

Returning to the beach, Molly deflated the kayak and hiked back to her car, reaching the ferry dock with enough time to buy a sandwich at the little deli nearby. She stared across the water into the deepening gloom, her heart sinking when the ferry chugged into sight.

"Honey, what happened?" Steve asked, rushing to greet Molly as she walked in. "You're soaked! Go get into something dry."

When she returned from changing clothes and toweling her hair, Steve placed a steaming mug on the coffee table. He planted himself next to her on the couch, cradling another mug in his hands. "How on earth did you get so wet?"

"I must have been in a daze this morning when I left. Forgot my rain gear."

Steve looked at her oddly. "It hardly rained all day."

"I was up north," Molly said, vaguely waving her hand as if to indicate the direction. "Pretty dank day. Good to be home. I hope you saw my text about not holding dinner."

"Are you sure you don't want anything?"

Molly thought she heard a note of reproach in his voice. "I'll be fine, sweetheart. Just fine. I would tell you, wouldn't I?"

Three days later, Molly returned to the island. This time she told Steve she was taking the day off and might do some kayaking, though not where she planned to go.

"You bought a boat?" He seemed pleased she wanted to do something besides work.

"I really need to get some exercise. And the water always soothes me."

"I'll come along. Kayaking sounds great."

"I'll be safe. I have the life jacket, I can swim. You don't need to worry about me."

Steve looked like he wanted to argue but stopped himself. Molly was grateful not to have to tell him she really didn't want his company.

The weather cooperated at last. Excited, Molly drove off the ferry and into town. She'd had an idea about where to glean information about her house's owner.

The door chime sounded as she entered a real estate office on a side street. She'd deliberately chosen a smaller, less elegant office, thinking they might be more likely to bite on her story than more prosperous-looking realtors.

Before she stepped past the threshold, she was greeted by a middle-aged woman with a pencil stuck into her thick curly hair. "Can I help you?"

"I fell in love with a property when I was here on vacation not too long ago. It would be the perfect house for me. My new job lets me telecommute, so I should find a really beautiful place to do it, right?"

Molly sensed the agent calculating. Maybe one of those very highly paid techies? How much commission could she make? "We get new listings all the time. If that place isn't available, I'm sure we'll find your new home in no time," the agent chirped. "So, tell me about this property you love."

"It's out at Hurricane Pass. Midcentury house, overlooking the beach. You know the one?"

The agent's face fell, but she recovered quickly. "I'd love to get that commission. The owner died a while back and the family can't agree on what to do. One of 'em lives on the mainland, a couple hours away. Nice guy, but he can't afford it on his own and he doesn't want to sell. The other two just want to cash out. They both live too far away, no other relatives in the area, no interest in keeping the house."

"Do they ever come back to visit?"

"Not that I've heard. There's a property manager who checks on the place once in awhile, but that's it. Crazy, huh, letting a house like that sit empty?"

"Out of curiosity, what do you think they'd ask for it, if they could ever agree on a price?"

"The comps put it at one and a half mil. It'd be a whole lot more if there was a road." The agent pasted a smile on her face. "Maybe I can show you something else that would meet your needs."

Molly returned to the state park. Midweek, late in the season, the campground was deserted. She chose the campsite closest to the house, setting up her tent and arranging her sleeping bag inside, along with a few items to make the tent appear occupied. Then she shouldered her backpack stuffed with supplies, along with the kayak and pump, and followed the marked hiking trail as far as it would take her toward the house. At some point she'd have to bushwhack through the undergrowth.

She reached a large bend where the trail veered north. From there, she would head west off the trail toward the house. It wasn't very far according to the map, but the woods were dense.

After nearly an hour, during which she stopped often to check her compass, she noticed a change in the light. A few minutes later she emerged into a small clearing. The house was a few yards beyond.

Molly shed her pack and rummaged through a side pocket until she found her Swiss army knife. Her hands trembled as she unfolded the knife and started working it in the lock. It clicked open with a little effort, and she was in.

Holding her breath as if someone might hear her, she scanned the walls but found no alarm system controls next to the back door or the sliders leading to the dock. Her entrance appeared to be undetected. She exhaled with relief as she took in the room.

This was not the elegant midcentury home she'd fantasized. It was an old family beach cottage filled with hand-me-downs and cheap souvenirs—worn furniture, rag rugs, bookcases with large seashells, glass floats, beachy knickknacks. But one glance out the sliding door onto the cove, and the tattiness of the room was replaced with mountains, sea, and forest.

A galley kitchen ran against the back wall of the living room, with a large counter separating the spaces. Off a small hallway behind the kitchen were two bedrooms, linens stripped from the mattresses, and a bathroom.

Hesitantly, Molly turned the kitchen faucet. Water sputtered for a moment, then flowed clear. The refrigerator lit up and she felt chilled air when she opened the door. Odd that the family hadn't turned off the utilities. Maybe they intended to rent it after all.

Carefully she went out onto the dock, checking first through her binoculars to see if anyone was close enough to the beach to see her. The boat lift facing the beach would bring unwanted attention if she tried to lower and raise it, but the steel railing on the ocean side of the dock would hold a rope ladder securely.

Molly huddled in the living room until it grew dark, then dragged couch cushions out to the dock and watched the night fall. The stars dazzled, their number and brilliance unlike anything she'd seen before surrounded by city lights. Her throat ached and tears flowed as she thought about her mother and her child. They lived in the stars now, waiting for her.

She woke up damp and chilly. Fog had once more blanketed the cove. While the mist might shield her from inquisitive eyes, it did nothing for her mood. The hike back to her campsite seemed to take longer than the hike in, and the undergrowth tangled her feet. She worried briefly that her bushwhacked trail would give her away, then shrugged off the concern. In this climate, nothing could stay trampled down for long.

The campsite looked undisturbed, as did her car. On the drive home, she formulated her plan. Shopping was at the top of the list—rope ladder, food, bathroom supplies. And pepper spray for self-defense. Just because she didn't notice anyone spying on her didn't mean that no one knew she was there.

Steve was reading in the living room when she got home. He looked at her coldly. "How was your trip?"

"It was fine. Paddling was nice."

He stood up and tossed his book into the chair. "I expected you to come home last night." His voice was tight, with a tone Molly had never heard before. "Didn't you get my message?"

Molly crossed the room and hugged him, kissing his cheek. "I'm so sorry, sweetheart. I forgot my phone charger and *of course* my phone died. I hate that you worried about me. I camped, got some sleep, did a little hiking and kayaking."

"Honey, is there something you aren't telling me?"

Molly squeezed harder. "You are the only man in my life, if that's what you're worried about. Now, how about I make dinner?"

They talked about Steve's job and the neighbor's new car and the weather forecast. They talked about what movie to stream later. They talked about groceries to pick up. The tension built all through dinner and Molly couldn't bring herself to say anything to ease it.

The following Sunday was cloudy and dark, but dry. Molly told Steve she was off on another business trip and would probably be gone a couple of days.

"Where?"

"Nowhere you'd ever have heard of." She shrugged.

"Where are you staying?"

"I don't know yet. I'll ask folks at the office to suggest a cozy little bed and breakfast. Don't worry, I'll be okay."

"I thought it might be fun to take a day off and meet you somewhere. We could have a mini vacation."

"Tell you what—I'll call late tomorrow and let you know how it looks. A getaway sounds great."

All the way across on the ferry, Molly felt guilty and sad about lying so much to Steve yet exhilarated about what lay ahead. The house's pull on her deepened. It was the only place she'd found peace. Steve always tried to fix what was wrong, but he couldn't fix her pain.

Once more she parked at the campground and set up a decoy campsite. She hiked to the house, let herself in, and unpacked the food she'd brought along with candles and matches, the rope ladder, and some other items. She kept the pepper spray clipped to her belt, where she could reach it quickly if needed.

That evening under cover of dusk and fog, Molly set up the rope ladder on the deck railing and worked her way down to the water's edge. She hammered a metal climbing piton into a crack in the rock face so she could tie the rope ladder more securely, then climbed back up, soaked from the waves crashing against the cliff as the tide pulled the water toward land. With kayak access, she could park for days at the ferry lot on the mainland, take one of the island buses to a good put-in place, and paddle to the house. Once there, she could tie up the kayak to the ladder. No one would give it a second glance.

On Monday, Molly slept and read and tried to meditate. She wrote in a journal she'd bought especially for this new life, which was how she'd begun to think of her time in this house. She studied the changing light on the water, grateful to have found a home. She made tea, cooked dinner, watched the moon rise behind the clouds.

It was perfect, or would have been, had she not promised to call Steve. After struggling with herself for an hour, she still couldn't bear to hear his voice in her house and texted him instead.

Checking in, cell svc lousy here, she wrote. *How was your day?*

The phone rang immediately, Steve's number. She waited for it to stop.

He texted back. *Missing u, where r u staying?*

Miss u 2, luv u. Will try 2 call from work site tomw.

She felt cowardly for lying, but she was fighting for her life.

That night she pulled the couch cushions onto the living room floor next to the large windows and stared out at the darkness until she fell into a deep, dreamless sleep.

By Tuesday morning, Molly began to let down her guard. No one seemed to be aware of her presence. She knew she was trespassing, but she no longer cared. There was something thrilling about staking her claim to her house this way.

As the day drew to a close she relaxed, more peaceful than she'd ever felt since her mother's cancer diagnosis. She poured a glass of wine as night fell. After downing most of it, she felt up to a short conversation with Steve.

He answered on the first ring. She pictured him sitting with the phone in his hand, waiting for her call. "I hope you're on the way home. I'm really missing you," he said.

Molly bit her lip. "Miss you too, sweetie. Sorry I can't head home just yet. I'll need at least another day, probably back on Thursday."

In the ominous silence that followed, she thought she heard a noise behind the house. *Animals?*

"Sweetie? Steve? Are you still there?"

"I'm here." He paused. "Look, Molly, I can't keep doing this." He sounded tense and angry.

"You never complained about my job before."

"It isn't that. It's you shutting me out. Right now, I'm wondering if you're really where you say you are. You told me there wasn't anyone else, and I want to believe you, but you're making it hard."

"It's . . . just . . . I don't know who I am or what I want anymore." She sniffled and wiped her face. She couldn't face a divorce, yet she couldn't contemplate returning to her old life. "I swear there is no one else."

Something jostled the back door.

She froze. Her voice dropped to a whisper. "I have to go."

"But Moll—" She ended the call and grabbed the pepper spray from the counter.

"Who's there?" she called out. "Is someone out there?"

She'd researched island wildlife. No major predators, no creatures capable of breaking in except clever raccoons. The caretaker surely wouldn't come at night, and not through the woods. Would he?

Her heart hammered. She slipped the pepper spray into its holster, then strapped it on and grabbed her backpack. The doorknob rattled, then something or someone shoved the door. Hard.

How long would it take to smash down that door?

Rage mixed with fear. Molly refused to let anyone steal this from her, but she was terrified to confront an unknown threat holding nothing more than pepper spray.

She raced out to the rope ladder, unnerved by negotiating the descent in the dark, her right foot flailing as she searched for the top rung. If she missed, her body would be smashed on the cliff below.

With a crash, the back door flew open. *It* was in the house.

Breathe, dammit!

She gained a foothold just as a large shape silhouetted in the house lights burst through the sliding door and sprinted across the dock.

She yanked the pepper spray from the holster and tried to aim, her hands quaking. The figure was almost upon her.

"Stop right there or I'll shoot!" Her voice shook. Was it enough to frighten off the intruder?

"Molly, wait!"

What?

"Honey, it's me, stop!"

She froze. "Steve?" Impossible. Terror morphed into rage. "How did you find me?"

"I put a tracking app on your phone. I had to know if you were okay."

Fury blinded her. She climbed back up to the dock. "You had *no* right to do that. *None.*"

"I was worried." Steve stepped nearer to the railing. "What's going on? You're trespassing. That isn't like you." He inched closer.

"I mean it, I'll shoot!"

"Please, let's leave. Together. Come home with me tonight and nobody needs to know anything about this. We'll clean up and leave it the way you found it."

"This *is* my home." She continued to point the pepper spray canister at him. "My *home!*" Ice formed in her gut. "Wait, what do you mean, nobody needs to know? Who'd know unless you told them?"

"I mean it, let's just get out of here."

"Answer me, Steve. Would you betray me? *Would you?*"

"Molly, sweetie, this is crazy. What you're doing is illegal. Trespassing, breaking and entering, who knows what else. What if you get caught?" He paused, as if gauging her reaction. "This isn't like you at all. Can we please just clean up and go home?"

Molly stared at him for a long moment. "Okay. Fine. But you're not gonna tell, right?" She fumbled with something below the railing, then looked up at him. "I think I'm stuck. Can you give me a hand?"

He reached the railing and held out an arm to help her up.

The stream of pepper spray hit Steve's face. He howled and lurched forward, losing his balance. As Molly held out the pepper spray, ready to fend off a counterattack, Steve careened toward her. She rolled out of the way and watched as he pitched over the railing. His body bounced against the rocks, splashing as it hit the water.

She scanned the channel below, searching for him, watching the waves pull his lifeless form away from the rocks.

Molly rested on the deck, leaning against the wall, nursing another glass of wine. "Oh, Steve," she whispered, as if he were next to her. "Why didn't you believe me?"

She sipped the wine and stared out at the moon rising over a silvery sea, just as she'd pictured it that day on the beach.

"I *told* you I'd kill for this house." ❖

The Management of Secrets

Edith Maxwell

K eeping a secret can be destructive, at times criminal. Midwife Rose Dodge knew it sometimes was an act of kindness.

Despite this being the first month in a new year in a new century, Rose mused that 1900 didn't seem much different from 1899, at least not here in the northeast corner of Massachusetts. The electric trolley still ran. The government still functioned. The newspapers and the milk were still delivered. And women still needed assistance with their pregnancies and births.

A knocking sounded on her office door, the entrance separate from the family's. It was likely a distraught husband fetching her for his wife's labor. She smiled after she pulled it open to see Police Chief Kevin Donovan, instead. She'd worked closely with him a decade earlier, helping to solve a number of tricky murder cases.

"Kevin, do come in. What a delight to see thee." She stepped back. "That is, unless something is amiss with a member of my family." Her smile slid away, and she brought her hand to her mouth.

"Oh, no, Miss Rose, I've no reports of harm to your beloveds." He moved into her office, holding his hat in his hands. "Would you listen to me, now? I can't help calling you Miss Rose, despite you being a married lady and mother to four babies."

"I don't care a bit. It's rather fun to think of the days when I was a Miss. Sit down and tell me the news."

"Look. I know you gave up detecting when your first wee girl was born, and rightly so. But I'm faced with a case that's got my head in a bother, and it seems to cross paths with your own life in more than one way."

"I hope one of my expectant ladies hasn't been murdered nor is suspected of committing homicide."

"Well, no." He rubbed his round head, his carrot-colored hair now shot through with the silver of a man nearing fifty years. "But there might be a lady with child involved. And one of your Quaker gents, too."

"Goodness. What crime is thee investigating?"

"Seems a good deal of counterfeit bills are circulating in Amesbury of late. This fellow, Thomas Franklin, appears to be connected with the offense."

"He's a fellow member of the Religious Society of Friends, it's true." Rose pictured Tom, a handsome accountant not much older than her thirty-seven years. He was married to a pinched-looking woman named Ida, but they had no children. "How is he connected?"

"Edwin Osgood, the grocer, thinks it was Franklin who used one of the tens for his purchase. Him or his wife."

"Interesting. And who is the pregnant woman?"

"Name's Mrs. Penelope McPherson."

"She's a client of mine, in fact. A recent widow, if memory serves, about halfway through her term."

"Yes, her husband was killed in an accident. He owned the printing company over on Market Street," Kevin said.

"And she owns it now." Rose's thoughts swirled.

"Yes. Why's it so quiet around here, by the way?"

"What?" Rose blinked. "Oh, our nanny, Marie-Fleur, took Davey and Herbie off to play with their cousins. Hattie and Clara are in school. And David is either in his office downtown or seeing patients at the Methodist Hospital."

"Four-year-old twin boys have to be a handful, Miss Rose."

"They are. Thank goodness for Marie-Fleur. She has the patience of one of thy saints. It's never quiet here for long, though, and I expected thy knock to be news of a woman in labor." Rose tapped her desk. "Tell me, where else has this counterfeit money been appearing, and what marks it as fake?"

"It shows up here and there in town, including at the post office. Your Miss Winslow first brought it to our attention."

"Bertie's always had a sharp eye." Rose smiled again. Her irreverent friend had been postmistress for many years. "I'll stop by and see her."

Kevin pulled out a ten-dollar greenback. "As for how you can tell, see here?" He pointed to a spot on the front. "This bill is good. But on the fakes, they didn't get this part of the bison quite right."

Rose nodded. "Is it all denominations?"

"No, just the tens. We've quietly alerted Amesbury merchants to check for the forgeries and asked them to put aside any counterfeits they come across. Somebody's keeping a big secret, and it's not good for anyone." He cleared his throat and stood. "I'd appreciate whatever nosing around you can do, Miss Rose, as long as you stay safe doing it. We can't be having our money system tampered with."

"I'll do what I can. Give my love to the family." She clicked the door shut behind him and leaned against it. She couldn't deny the frisson of excitement at being involved in a case again. She had a rich, full life, with her family and her work. But investigating crimes? She knew she had a gift for it. As long as it didn't interfere with her obligations, she didn't see any reason not to help Kevin in his pursuit. It wasn't as if she'd be in danger from a murderer.

"If it isn't the Quaker midwife, herself," Bertie exclaimed half an hour later from behind the counter of the post office. Bertie's curly blond hair was now mixed with white, but her cheery face remained nearly unlined, and her petite figure was as trim as ever in a crisp shirtwaist and dark skirt.

"Good morning, my friend." Rose glanced around. Only two people waited in line to mail parcels. "Might I have a word with thee in private?"

"Eva, I'll be in my office," Bertie said to her assistant.

"Yes, Miss Winslow."

"What's on your mind, Rosetta?" Bertie asked a moment later, using the nickname she'd invented.

"Kevin has asked me to assist in the matter of the counterfeit money."

"From the sparkle in your eye, I'd say you're delighted to be back in business, so to speak."

"Thee knows me too well. I'm experiencing a bit of a thrill, yes." Rose gave a nod. "He said thee was the first to bring the forgery to the attention of the police. What made thee notice a fake bill?"

"Well, I was counting the day's money on Monday, and something was off about the feel of that ten. Look." Bertie extracted an envelope from her desk drawer and pulled out a ten-dollar bill. "The paper's not quite right. I took a magnifying glass to it and spied the tail of the mighty bison was not the same as on a real tenner. There are other minuscule bits that are wrong." She pointed here and there.

"Today is Sixth Day, so only five days have elapsed. Does thee have any idea who paid with this bill?"

"No, more's the pity, and neither does Eva. We get pretty busy here."

"I won't take any more of thy time. I'm off to visit a lady who owns a printing press, and then to hunt down a fellow Quaker."

"You think Mrs. McPherson might be the culprit?" Bertie arched an eyebrow.

"I pray not. She's carrying her late husband's child. But sometimes the simplest solutions are the correct ones." Rose touched her friend's shoulder. "Thee and Sophie should come to dinner tomorrow. My Davey is mad about the mail. He's forever scribbling on papers, folding them into packets, and pretending to send them. He's crushed if he misses the postman. And Clara, at seven, has already declared she plans to become a lady lawyer like Auntie Sophie."

"I'll ask her. Good luck in your hunt."

Rose pulled open the door to McPherson Printing on Market Street twenty minutes later. The office was warm and busy with a young man leaning over a drawing board and a sturdy matron tying a brown-paper-wrapped parcel with string.

Penelope sat behind a desk writing in a ledger. From the back came the rhythmic clatter of a press, but the noise was muffled by a closed door.

Penelope glanced up. "Why, hello, Mrs. Dodge. What can I do for you?" Her hand strayed to the bulge of her five-month pregnant belly, as if having a midwife walk in had brought her growing baby to mind. Her dark good looks were enhanced by the heightened color of her condition.

"Good morning, Penelope." Rose had thought up an excuse as she'd walked. "I'd like to have cards printed for my sons."

"A child calling card?"

"Yes. The twins are only four, but their sisters have cards, and my little Herbie is a serious sort who would quite like something so formal."

"Please sit down. You'll want something small and simple, I assume?"

"Certainly." Rose sat.

Penelope slid a piece of paper and a pencil across to her. "Write their names clearly."

Rose carefully printed David Allan Dodge and Herbert Wesley Dodge and slid the paper back to Penelope. "Those names make them sound like grown men." She smiled.

"As they will be before long." Penelope checked a big calendar on the wall next to her, its squares filled with what looked to be job descriptions. "The order will be ready in a week's time. We have a number of pieces ahead of yours on the schedule."

"Thee seems to be doing a good business here. Was it terribly difficult learning to run it?" Rose had had only one antenatal visit with Penelope, and they hadn't talked about

165

her work. Her client was only twenty-three. Rose was impressed by her competence.

"I'd worked alongside my husband, so it wasn't hard to take charge of the operation."

Rose leaned forward. "Did thee hear there is counterfeit money circulating in Amesbury? I find the news shocking."

Penelope blinked at the change of topic. "It is. Counterfeiting is a federal offense."

"The government caught Emmanuel Ninger for the crime not that long ago. What would be involved in printing false bills?" Rose didn't have to feign ignorance. Creating fake currency was completely outside her experience. "Don't they take a special type of paper?"

"I believe they do. Beyond that, I wouldn't have the slightest notion how to even begin." She didn't meet Rose's gaze.

Rose expected Penelope might have much more than a slight notion about how to print counterfeit money. The door to the back opened, and the noise level rose considerably. A dark-haired man in a long black apron pushed through and let the door swing shut behind him. Rose's eyes widened. What was Tom Franklin doing working as a printer?

"Penny, do—" he began but halted when he spied Rose. "Mrs. McPherson, I've got a bit of a problem back there."

Penelope flushed as she turned to look at him. The matron lifted her head from her work and gazed from her pretty boss to the handsome printer.

"Hello, Tom." Rose stood. "I didn't know thee worked here."

"Good morning, Rose," he said, his dark brows coming together over striking green eyes. "Yes, I do."

The noon whistle went off outside, signaling a lunch break for the many mill and factory workers downtown.

"I'll be getting along," Rose said. "I thank thee, Penelope, and I'll see thee next week. Good day, Tom." Outside, she glanced back through the window as Penelope disappeared into the back room with Tom.

Holding Hattie's mittened hand, Rose trudged along Whittier Street, through freshly fallen snow, the two blocks to the Friends Meetinghouse on First Day morning. She'd been called to a birth last evening just as a delightful dinner with Bertie, Sophie, and the family had been winding down.

It was the third child for the birthing woman, with a speedy and easy labor and the appearance of a healthy baby girl. This morning Rose had had time for a bite to eat at home, a wash, and a two-hour nap before it was time to leave for worship. David, who usually attended the Unitarian service in Newburyport, opted not to go today. He offered to keep the children with him, but Hattie had insisted on accompanying her mother.

"I like being quiet, Mama," she'd said.

Rose didn't blame her, being eldest of four. It was rarely quiet in their busy home. Rose would have stayed home, herself, except she was now Clerk of the Women's Business Meeting, and today was the day they gathered.

At least the storm had passed quickly. Now sunlight danced off crystals of snow, and the air was crisp and clean.

"Mama, does thee think I should become a doctor or a midwife when I'm older?" Hattie asked.

"Thee will find the path that suits thee. Thee would excel at either occupation."

167

"I think we need more lady doctors."

"We do, at that."

Inside the simple white meetinghouse, Rose slid into a pew on the left side.

"I'm going to go sit with Rosie," Hattie whispered.

Rose smiled and nodded, watching as Hattie nearly skipped to the other side to squeeze in with her cousin, only eight months younger, whom Rose's niece had named for her. Rose shut her eyes.

But, in the stillness, her mind raced back to the case of the counterfeit money, which she had put aside in favor of family yesterday. Were Tom and Penelope secretly working together to illegally print greenbacks? Were they, instead, having an illicit dalliance? Maybe it was both. How could she find out?

She eased her eyes open. Tom and Ida sat across the room under one of the eight-foot-tall windows. Ida, hands folded in her lap and eyes closed, had raised her face to the sun streaming in the opposite window. The light softened her usually tight expression. Tom's eyes flew open as if he'd felt Rose's gaze, and he narrowed them at her. She gave him a little smile before returning to what she'd come here for, an hour of silent prayer and expectant waiting on God.

After the rise of Meeting, Hattie ran up and asked if she could go home with Rosie.

"We're going to go sledding." Hattie's eyes sparkled. "Auntie Faith said she'll bring me home in time for supper."

"Go and have fun." Rose kissed her daughter's head and sent her along, then headed over to the right side of the building as a ponderous creaking began. Friends lowered the partition between the two halves of the meetinghouse to let the women conduct their business independently from the men.

Ida helped Rose move a table into place in front of the facing bench. Rose laid her papers and pen on the table and sat, folding her hands and closing her eyes. She sensed Ida sit next to her. The gradual stilling of the room was something to be savored. Women hurried in and took their places on the pews. Footsteps ceased. Breathing slowed. The men did the same on the other side.

After a few minutes of silent prayer, Rose opened her eyes. "We gather on this First Day of First Month in worship with attention to the women's business of Amesbury Monthly Meeting of Friends. Will our recording clerk please relay the minutes from Twelfth Month?"

Ida read the minutes in her thin voice. The meeting went along, with the women discussing a wedding, hospitality, and a memorial Meeting to honor a Friend who'd died of tuberculosis. At the same time, the low rumble of male timbres drifted through the divider as they conducted their own business.

Ida's bony fingers scribed the minutes. She had dirt under her fingernails, which seemed odd, but perhaps she nurtured plants through the winter on sunny windowsills or in a greenhouse.

In the back of her mind, Rose mused on how much younger and prettier Penelope was than this angular woman who rarely smiled. She remembered how Penelope had flushed at seeing Tom come out from the printing room, and how he'd called her Penny. If he, rather than her late husband, was the father of Penelope's baby, keeping the paternity secret from Ida might grow more difficult in time.

Rose gathered her papers after the meeting was over and turned to Ida. "I saw Tom working at McPherson Printing recently. How long has he been in their employ?"

"He's worked there since Mr. McPherson's soul was released to God in Ninth Month. *She* needed someone." Ida's mouth twisted at the word *she*.

"Tom was an accountant at the Merrimac Hat Factory, wasn't he? That's quite a change in profession."

"He was, but they let him go." She shrugged. "Both our fathers were printers. That's how we met. Tom knows the business."

The silence on the other side of the partition ceased, with boot heels thudding and male voices growing louder.

"The men are finished," Ida said. "I need to get along, Rose. Tom doesn't like his dinner to be late."

Rose nodded, watching her go. She thought she might want to spend some time in the public library tomorrow. How exactly had McPherson died? And why had Tom been fired from the factory?

Stretching out a crick in her neck the next morning, Rose gazed around the cramped little library. John Whittier had been a founding member and had donated many of the original books. But with the growth in the town's industry, so had the population grown. Ground was being broken later this year for a much-needed new building. For now, she had to settle for the small table she'd covered with newspapers from last fall.

She couldn't find a word about Tom's being let go, which didn't surprise her, but the firing itself did. The hat factory employed several hundred men and women and was a thriving business. He must have been negligent in some way to have lost his job.

About Arthur McPherson's death, Rose gleaned a bit more. He was forty-five, considerably older than Penelope. He'd died at the beginning of Ninth Month. His horse was spooked and took the open buggy McPherson was driving down Whittier Hill at such a rate that the conveyance overturned near an outcropping of rock. The driver, alone in the buggy, was dead by the time the ambulance wagon arrived. Details about what had startled the horse and what McPherson was doing atop Whittier Hill were not included.

Rose folded the papers and returned them to their shelf. It was time for a visit to the police station.

"Kevin," she began once she was seated across from the chief in his office. "What does thee know about the circumstances surrounding Arthur McPherson's death?"

"Why, it was a runaway horse."

"But what spooked the steed?" The Grand Hotel sat atop Whittier Hill, which meant all kinds of people came and went in the course of a day. "Did thee investigate who was about at the top of the hill?"

"Not that I know of." Kevin peered at her. "Are you thinking the accident was caused purposeful, like?"

"I don't know."

"I can't believe one of your peaceable Quakers would commit a violent act, Miss Rose."

"Sadly, criminals have been known to exist even among Friends. We are all human, after all. What I do know is that Tom Franklin was fired from his job as an accountant with the Merrimac Hat Factory. His wife, Ida, told me it happened about the time of Arthur McPherson's demise."

"You don't say."

"Tom's now working as a printer for Penelope McPherson. In addition, when I stopped in there on Sixth Day, owner and employee seemed overly familiar."

Kevin whistled. "And the two might have conspired to get Mr. McPherson out of the way. But Franklin's a married man, isn't he?"

She looked at him over her spectacles. "When has that prevented many a male from dallying with women younger and prettier than their wives?"

"True enough."

Should she raise the possibility of who had fathered Penelope's baby? Not now. The only way to know for sure was to ask the mother-to-be.

"Also," she continued, "Tom is an experienced printer. I should think between the two of them, he and Penelope might be thy counterfeiters."

"I need proof, though."

"Indeed. Does thee have men watching the press at night?"

"Not yet, but I'll put someone on it, and have patrolmen canvas the neighborhood, as well," Kevin said. "We're short-handed, or I would have thought of it myself. At least McPherson's is the only printer in town."

"The business appears to be doing well, but perhaps it's not. Creating her own funds might have seemed like a solution to Penelope."

"Or to Tom Franklin, after he was fired. He could be doing it secretly, without Mrs. McPherson's knowledge, in order to support himself and his wife."

Rose glanced at the clock. "I need to be getting home. Thee will see what thee can learn about the horse and buggy accident. I'll have a chat with Penelope."

"With your help, we'll get these criminals shut down. Thank you for agreeing to investigate."

"I'm glad thee came in," Rose said to Penelope at one o'clock that afternoon as the pregnant woman reclined on the examination chaise in Rose's office. "Thee was overdue for a second visit."

"Thank you for your note. I didn't realize I needed to see you again before my labor begins."

Rose had clearly outlined the schedule of care at Penelope's first visit, but she didn't scold her for the lapse. And if Rose was able to learn something about Penelope and Tom, so much the better.

"Thee can pull down thy skirts," Rose said when she was finished measuring and palpating Penelope's belly. She checked her file. "At thy first visit, thee said thy last monthly began on the second of August. Is thee sure?" Rose used conventional day of the week and month names with her clients even though Quakers avoided them so they didn't invoke the memory of gods and emperors.

"I'm pretty sure." Penelope fidgeted with the cuff of her sleeve, not meeting Rose's gaze. "Does it matter?"

"It's rather important to gauge when thee will deliver. The baby seems small for being this far along. Is thee eating enough nourishing foods?"

"Why, yes, I have a hearty appetite."

"If the date is correct, the fetus might be failing to thrive."

Penelope kneaded her hands in her lap, frowning at them. She let out a long breath and raised her face.

"Oh, Mrs. Dodge. I'm in a terrible pickle. You are a wise midwife and correct about my condition. Since Arthur died, I have become intimate with Tom Franklin."

"And the baby is his."

"Yes," she said, her dark eyes brimming. "I know how wrong it is. But I was desperately unhappy with Arthur. He was so old, and he was neither kind nor sweet with me. All he wanted was someone to work for free and to give him an heir." She cradled her belly.

"I do not judge, Penelope. But please be truthful. I suspect thee was intimate with Tom before Arthur's accident."

"Not intimate, but we wanted to be," Penelope whispered. "Please don't tell a soul."

Rose couldn't promise to keep her secret. "Are thee and Tom printing counterfeit bills?"

Penelope gaped. "What? Of course not. Why would I do something like that?"

"Perhaps he is, without thy knowledge." Rose raised her eyebrows. "In secret."

"No." Penelope gave her head a firm shake. "He never would."

Maybe. Or maybe not.

At four o'clock, Rose knocked on the door of Tom and Ida's cottage. She'd enlisted Bertie to drive her down here and wait in her carriage. Rose hadn't let Ida know she was coming.

"Rose?" Ida, frowning, gave a furtive glance over her own shoulder. "What brings thee here?"

"I'd like to talk with thee about a matter that has arisen." Rose patted the satchel she'd brought and held her breath, hoping Ida would assume the visit was about Quaker women's affairs.

"Yes?" Ida didn't budge from the threshold.

"May I come in? It's chilly out here."

Ida swallowed. "Very well. Let's go straight back to the kitchen, and I'll fix tea."

Rose followed her, leaving the door ajar an inch. She slipped off one glove and slid her hand into her cloak pocket as she paused at the door to a study. On a drop-front desk, next to a window bare of curtains, lay pens, paper, a sheet of metal, a magnifying glass on a stand, and various sharp tools. A gas lamp with a clear shade was turned up high.

"Is thee creating art?" Rose strove to keep her voice casual. She stepped into the room.

Ida whirled. "What are thee doing in there?" With two long strides she was at Rose's side.

"Ida, I believe thee is part of Tom's counterfeiting scheme. I'm sure the police will be lenient if thee tells them what he's up to."

"That philandering coward?" Her tone was scornful. "He can barely print, let alone engrave. All he can do is romance that poor girl. I despise the both of them." She grabbed the sharpest of the gravers with one hand and Rose's arm with the other. "No, the operation is mine alone. Pretty soon I'll have enough money to escape this horrid town." She pressed the burin into Rose's neck. "I won't let thee reveal my secret."

Rose took in a deep breath even while feeling the point piercing her skin, even with her heart thudding like a locomotive. She drew out the big metal police whistle and blew with all her might.

Ida cried out. The burin clattered to the floor. She released Rose and clapped her hands to her ears.

Rose kicked the tool away from Ida's reach. She blew again, and once more, as close to Ida's ear as she could get. Ida turned toward the door. Rose stuck out her foot, catching Ida's ankle.

By the time Bertie hurried in, Rose had tied Ida's hands securely behind her. The counterfeiter struggled and swore like a sailor, but Rose kept her knee in the small of Ida's back.

"Looks like you saved the day, Rosetta." Bertie beamed. "You just happened to have a whistle and sturdy twine in your satchel?"

"A midwife is always prepared, Bertie. Might thee find a length of rope to secure her feet and then go find the nearest policeman?"

Kevin himself appeared shortly after Bertie returned with a young patrolman.

"You've done it again, Miss Rose." He and Rose stepped into the parlor to speak. "I knew you would."

"How did thee get here so quickly?"

"I was already on my way. My man found a neighbor who has trouble sleeping. He spied a thin woman going into the printing shop in the dead of night more than once. From the description, it wasn't Mrs. McPherson."

"No. She is naturally rounded and now even more so."

"What put you onto Mrs. Franklin?" he asked.

"She records the minutes for our Quaker women's business meeting. Yesterday I noticed her dirty fingernails and thought perhaps she was a gardener."

"In January?" Kevin's voice rose.

"Some people nurture plants indoors. But this afternoon I saw Penelope McPherson. She protested mightily that Tom would never counterfeit money, and neither would she. I felt she was telling the truth. As I got to thinking, I remembered Ida had told me her father was a printer, and I wondered if Ida's fingernails were stained with ink, not dirt. I thought I'd pay her a visit to find out."

Kevin furrowed his brow. "More rightly, you should have asked us to make that call."

"I believed she'd let me in more readily than a man in uniform. I happened to take a peek into the study and saw her equipment all laid out. She probably kept it secret by shutting it away in the desk each evening before Tom came home, and she must have used his key late at night to print at Penelope's shop. Let's just say she wasn't happy about my discovery."

"I should say not."

"Anyway, all's well that ends well."

He bobbed his head. "By the way, we found a stable boy up at the hotel who saw an eagle swoop down toward McPherson's buggy. That was what spooked the horse."

"I'm glad it wasn't homicide," Rose said.

He peered at her. "Miss Rose, your neck is bloody. She hurt you!" He pulled out a clean handkerchief and handed it to her. "I never meant for you to endanger your person."

"I thank thee." Rose pressed it to her neck. "It seemed she meant to kill me. But it's just a scratch."

Bertie stepped in. "Did you want me to wait longer, Rose, or will our esteemed chief of police be transporting you?"

"I'd be happy to leave now, Bertie, so that I might sup with my brood at home."

As Grover's hoofs clopped up the hill in the gloaming, Rose smiled to herself. She'd solved the case. She'd exposed Ida's criminal secret. And she'd kept herself—and Penelope's secret—safe. ❖

Blame It on the Blizzard

A Jaye Jordan Vermont Radio Mystery

Nikki Knight

You might think climbing up on the WSV roof was the craziest and most dangerous part of my first big blizzard in Vermont. Well, no.

See, I lived. Not everyone did.

It all started with the dirty little secret of live local radio: we're not entirely live, or local, no matter how hard we try. Nobody can afford a staff 24/7 these days, so at least some of the gaps are filled with satellite programming. The old owner brought in third-rate talk shows to move the meters, and not incidentally spew hate. I prefer music, all of the wonderfully squishy adult contemporary goo that I play on my all-request live show.

But satellite music requires a satellite dish and that dish doesn't work very well when it's full of snow. So somebody has to go up on the roof and sweep it.

Since I'm the entire staff—unless you count my tween daughter, Ryan, the informal web master, junior engineer, and occasional phone-answerer—that somebody was me.

If I'd fallen off the roof, the accident report would have listed me as Jaye Jordan Metz, but I only use the Metz from my ex at Ryan's school. And yes, I was in fact born Jacqueline Jordan. People always wonder when a DJ has a "radio" name. Jordanski is the usual guess, since I'm from the Western PA glass country, where there are more pierogies than pizza. But no.

Anyway, that afternoon in January, I put on "Paradise by the Dashboard Light," the eight-minute extravaganza beloved by overnight jocks everywhere, then grabbed my broom, and climbed out Ryan's bedroom window to the fire escape.

Like a lot of folks in town, we live over the store.

The station is in the original owners' old townhouse: studios in the basement bomb shelter, mostly empty offices on the first two floors, and a small apartment on top. It's plenty of space for me, Ryan, and our giant gray cat, Neptune. My pal Rob Archer and his family live next door over his restaurant. Across the street, there are probably a dozen people in apartments overlooking the town plaza, from a sweet pair of sisters in their nineties, to a guy who protests every week that I took away his talk shows, to the Chinese-immigrant couple who run the minimart.

Neptune took one look at me on my way out the window, snorted, and stalked off. He did not approve of this Vermont venture, and the blizzard had done nothing to change his mind.

From the fire escape, there's a tiny ladder up to the roof, and the dish is right at the edge; the guy who wired it in was no fool. Even though I'm just over six feet tall and strong, and had the help of gripper gloves and lug-soled boots, the climb was pretty awful. But I managed to wedge myself into a relatively secure spot near the top of the ladder and hang on for dear life with one hand while sweeping with the other.

And promptly succeeded in knocking six inches of snow right into my face.

It's fair to say I was using most of the FCC's least favorite words as I kept brushing, with the wind trying to pull the broom out of my hand.

It was neither my finest hour, nor the smartest thing I'd ever done, but it wasn't like I had a choice. I'd staked everything on this decrepit excuse for a radio station in hopes of a new start for Ryan and me after her father survived cancer but our marriage didn't. I'd worked in Vermont years ago on my way up, and the old owner offered me a break on the price to get a live, local radio station again. It seemed like a good idea at the time. Whether it was or not, there was no cushy New York DJ job to go back to; my old light music station had gone all-sports and I'm anything but a play-by-play artist.

"I hate <bleep>ing snow!" I yelled as I swept and the sharp little flakes blew back in an unwanted exfoliating facial. "I hate <bleep>ing winter. And I REALLY hate <bleep>ing Vermont!"

Of course, I'm sparing your sensibilities. I didn't spare the blizzard's.

I was almost done when I heard the crack. Startled, I dropped the broom and almost joined it in falling thirty feet to the brick sidewalk.

I tried to tell myself it was just a branch breaking under the weight of snow.

But I'd worked in New York long enough to recognize a gunshot. And I'd been here long enough to know that someone might just want to shoot at me.

MeatLoaf and Ellen Foley were fading away in overwrought nostalgia as I shook the snow off my coat, threw it on one of the guest chairs, and sat back down in the slot, wet and discouraged. There were still chunks of snow in the sleeves of my red fleece, my black hair was soaked, and I didn't even want to think about what that blizzard facial had done to my skin, which is fishbelly pale on a good day.

I was a mess—and I didn't just look like one.

Awfully glad I'd had the sense to wear those gripper gloves, though.

On the climb down, I'd pretty well managed to convince myself that it wasn't a shot, and it *definitely* wasn't aimed at me. Sound is weird in a blizzard, after all, and the pushback I'd gotten over changing from angry white dudes yelling to happy love songs wasn't really dangerous. Was it?

The phone lit up just as I seg'd into the allotted once-nightly playing of "You're the Inspiration." Without the limit, I'd have to play the Chicago classic twice an hour, and you don't have to be a big radio consultant to know that's not good for listenership—or my sanity.

"WSV, what's your request?"

"What the HELL were you doing?"

I didn't have to see my one-time boss and on-air partner—and now neighbor—Rob Archer to know his light blue eyes were glowing and his sharp features tight with concern. When a trained professional squeaks like an angry kid, it's pretty obvious.

"Um, cleaning out the dish. You remember—"

"Of course I remember. But you should have asked me—"

"I'm fine," I said firmly. The absolute last thing I needed was Rob, former DJ, current restaurateur, and proud townie, coming over here and playing Mr. Macho Mountain Man helping the poor single mom. His husband, Tim, is an army veteran and might actually have some useful skills, but that's a whole different conversation.

"When I saw you up there, I went to get my boots."

Since he was yelling about my general recklessness instead of anything specific, I could guess he either hadn't heard the shot, or hadn't realized what it was—and I sure wasn't going to tell him. Rob would probably have continued reading the riot act for awhile anyway if Ryan hadn't appeared in the studio doorway.

"Gotta go," I said quickly. "Kid stuff."

It was the perfect excuse. Rob and Tim are the parents of Ryan's new best pal, Xavier, and well versed in the ways of tweens.

"Okay. We'll talk tomorrow."

Right we will.

"What's up, honey?" I asked my daughter.

"Chief George is upstairs."

A visit from the police chief was no reason for the concern in her pale-green eyes, or the scowl. The chief's wife, Alicia, is a fellow transplanted New Yorker and friend, and he'd been by a few times himself to reassure me after some of the uglier letters and calls about the format change. Not to mention the weekly protests from two guys in bad Revolutionary War gear, complete with muskets that I *hoped* were just props.

I held my daughter's gaze. She still can't put things past me.

"You shouldn't have been on the roof, Ma." Ryan's voice wobbled just a bit. So did my insides. She'd been so strong during her dad's chemo and everything after. What right did I have to scare her, even a little?

Dammit.

"I'm sorry, honey. I'll find a better way next time." I ruffled her dark hair in lieu of a hug. "Get yourself a cocoa after you bring the chief down, okay?"

"Okay."

The studio door closing behind her woke Neptune, who'd been dozing in a warm spot on the old turntable cabinet. He snarled something rude and settled back down, leaving me with a full view of kitty posterior, and no doubt of his opinion.

By the time I fired the vintage Bananarama that a listener wanted to brighten her blizzard and set up the next few requests, the chief was in the little kitchenette outside the studio, chuckling to himself as Ryan concocted her favorite, nutritionally terrifying, double-strength cocoa.

Chief George Orr pretty much filled the space, thanks to his six-foot-three frame and his Maine Ranger parka. The olive-drab coat was the announcement that this was a serious storm. He usually wore a black leather trench, an Indiana Jones fedora, and a carefully low-key expression, because a lot of people aren't expecting to see a magnificent Black man as the top cop in a small Vermont town.

A lot of people aren't very bright.

The chief, who'd ended his twenty-five years at the NYPD as a lieutenant, is probably the sharpest cop I've ever seen. He wasn't just watching Ryan make that cocoa, he was taking in the whole situation at the station, for reasons as yet unknown to me.

We exchanged greetings, and shook.

"What's up?" I asked.

He cut his eyes to Ryan.

"My laptop is in the studio. Do you want to go play Hot Wheels for a while?"

I'm not great at monitoring screen time, but I don't usually share my laptop because all of the station stuff is on it. Even though the thing is probably safer with Ryan than me.

"Really? Cool, Ma!"

It was a big enough treat that she didn't question it and just zipped right past me.

The chief waited until the studio door closed behind her before he asked, "Did you hear a gunshot when you were on the roof?"

"I thought I did."

"Damn." He sighed, shook his head. "So maybe there is something to this."

"What?"

"Got a couple of calls from the plaza about a gunshot. One person mentioned that you almost fell off the roof."

"And you were hoping I'd tell you it was a branch cracking and you could go back to the station and work on that grant application for a new cruiser."

"Something like that."

I shook my head. No more denial. "It sure sounded like a shot to me."

"Any idea where it came from?"

"Not sure—but if you give me a second to hand off, my able assistant will run the board while I show you where I was."

The Chief nodded. "I'd appreciate that."

Ryan was happy to take over for a bit, but less than thrilled by the songs, a long and soggy Celine Dion extravaganza and a one-hit-wonder power ballad from a group that had tried to be Journey and failed miserably. They were both longish, though, and I was glad to clear those two anniversary requests without having to actually hear them.

Still don't like anniversaries. Everything's a little too raw.

I grabbed my damp down coat and followed the chief upstairs. As we passed through the reception area, he pointed to the binoculars I'd left on a side table after my latest trip to the transmitter shack.

"Mind if I grab these?"

"Sure." My uncle Edgar gave them to me as a housewarming gift because Vermont is great for bird watching, not that I had time for a hobby. "I don't think the snowy owl is coming down from the shack, though."

"Not for Blanche."

The female snowy owl, inevitably christened Blanche, had been the biggest excitement in Simpson until the blizzard, and now the gunshot. She had apparently found a nice supply of tasty rodents near the station's transmitter up on Quarry Hill Road, and the whole town was fascinated by her.

Chief George, though, was not on a nature walk now.

"Oh," I said, feeling like an idiot. "The bullet."

He nodded. "But don't be surprised if Alicia borrows these later—we both want to get another good look at her."

"You should. She's amazing."

I stepped through as he held the door.

"All right, so you were up there?" He pointed to the fire escape.

"Yep."

The chief focused the binoculars on the wall of the building.

"What's going on?"

Chief George didn't move, but I turned to see Rob, Tim, and Rob's aunt, Town Clerk Sadie Blacklaw, walking out of the restaurant.

"I *told* you I heard something," Sadie said triumphantly. The snow would not have dared to stick to her ash-blonde hair, though it was making a few inroads on her red parka. She stepped smartly through the small drifts to gaze up at Chief George, leaving Rob and Tim to follow in her wake. "So?"

Only then did he bring down the lenses and look at her. "Looks like we do indeed have a bullet hole."

"*What?*"

If a crowd of only four people can be said to explode in surprise, we did. Even though I knew one of the musket guys lived across the plaza, I hadn't really believed—hadn't wanted to believe—that anyone would seriously try to harm me.

"Maybe it was just a prank," I started. "Just trying to scare me."

Four sets of eyes of varying shades of blue, brown, and amber burned into me.

Chief George scowled. "Nobody's laughing."

"Intent," said Tim, who is an assistant district attorney, "is not an excuse."

"How dare they? Marching around with those stupid guns is one thing, but this?" Sadie looked as if she wanted to march upstairs and beat Howard (or maybe Harold, I had a hard time telling them apart) with his musket.

Rob just shook his head.

Another gust of wind whipped around us all just then, chilling me even more than the realization of what had happened.

The musket guys were especially annoying to me because I'd been a history major in college, even hanging out with some pretty cute Colonial reenactors at one point. They'd been really cool folks. Not like these two mopes, who were upset that they didn't get their daily dose of prejudice.

During my summer of chasing the boys in breeches—none of whom I'd caught, by the way—I'd watched them make bullets, and learned to fire a musket. Not that I expected the skill to come in handy.

But it just might.

Depending on the musket, the range wasn't nearly as long, or as accurate, as a modern rifle, and they didn't fire standard rounds.

"Can I have those binocs, Chief?" I asked, then carefully looked at the wall. "Show me the bullet hole."

He guided my gaze to a spot a couple of feet away from the fire escape.

"I don't think that's from a musket," I said, after taking a good look. "I spent a summer with reenactors, and the old muzzle loaders have round lead bullets and a much shorter range."

"Another gun?" Rob asked. "Or someone *else* after you?"

Thanks, buddy, I needed that.

"It may not be about Jaye at all," Sadie cut in, her voice cool and sensible. "Where do you think that bullet came from?"

The chief took the specs back from me. "Well, if it hit there . . ."

He turned slowly to the building across the street. Stared. Refocused the binoculars. And kept staring.

"Wait a minute!" Sadie followed his gaze. "That's where the Cutter sisters live. Babe and Bette have been fighting like cats and dogs for the last seventy years."

Chief George finally brought down the binoculars and reached for the radio on his belt. "Not anymore."

By the time it was fully dark, the snow had stopped, and it was all over but the cleanup. Chief George was finishing his report, and Tim was tucking in Xavier, very glad that he got to be a dad and not an ADA tonight. Ryan had scammed an extra cookie, and skipped off to bed with Neptune and her latest book, *Marie Curie: Cool Girl of Science.*

In the studio, Rob and Sadie were joining me in a pot of very good coffee and sorting it all out. I finished a break, and hit the Beyonce version of "At Last," a request for the chief from his very understanding wife, who had called to make sure I was okay and order me to stay the <bleep> off the roof in the future.

"Always liked this song," Sadie said with a wistful smile as I turned it down a little so we could talk. "Classic romance."

"Nothing wrong with that," I agreed, taking a sip of my dark roast.

"All right, so what happened?" Rob asked his aunt.

She ran her finger over the top of the coffee mug. "Well, you know Bette and Babe have lived together over what used to be the family furniture store for more than seventy years."

We nodded. Until today, my acquaintance with the Cutter sisters had been limited to their crochet doily booth at craft fairs and their constant complaints to the select board about bicycles on downtown streets. They were feisty, firm, and always stylish in little New England-y outfits, Bette in sweaters and slacks, Babe in skirts and boiled-wool jackets.

I admit I thought they were cute.

Not now.

"So," Sadie began, "Bette came to Town Hall a few weeks ago to check the records on their building, including the zoning and the deed."

Rob's eyes widened.

Mine too. "She was thinking of selling?"

"Very good, kids." Sadie gave us a trace of a smile. "She was indeed. Talked about going on a cruise around the world and then settling somewhere warm."

"And what did Babe think of all of this?" Rob asked.

"Nothing good. Last week at church she buttonholed me and asked me what I knew about Bette's crazy ideas. I suggested she talk to her sister. Those two have been at each other's throats forever, and it just looked like more of the same."

Sadie looked down at her mug.

"You couldn't know," Rob said, patting her hand.

She shrugged it off, took a deep breath. "Should have known something."

What we all knew now was that it looked like Babe had decided to reason with Bette, unfortunately with the help of their daddy's old pistol. I could have told them the safety isn't always reliable on vintage weapons, but it was a little late for that now.

Chief George found Bette dead of a gunshot wound to the chest in the chair by the window, and Babe gone from an apparent heart attack at her feet, weapon still in hand.

It had absolutely nothing to do with me, the radio station, or the musket guys.

I wasn't sure if I should be relieved, or sad, or just stunned.

Rob and Sadie looked like they were going for shock, both gazing down at their coffee as if it were the funeral meats. Which fit pretty well, actually.

"Blame it on the blizzard," I said finally.

They looked at me.

"You're the one who told me when I first came up here, Rob," I reminded him. "Blizzards make people crazy."

"That's true," Sadie allowed. "Ever since there's been winter in Vermont, there's been bad things during blizzards."

"Any other time, they would have talked it out without the pistol," Rob said. "They were feisty, but not crazy."

"Exactly." I took a sip of my coffee. "Am I a very bad person for being glad it wasn't about me?"

"Not at all," Sadie said, obviously glad to move on to someone else's feelings. "One of the most important things in the world is being able to know when something isn't about you."

"Sometimes it's good when it's not," Rob agreed.

Neptune, who'd been dozing and observing from the turntable cabinet, yawned, stretched, and gave us all a glare that reminded us that *everything* is about the kitty.

A few minutes later, I put on a long song (more Chicago, but NOT "You're the Inspiration," thank you!) and walked my guests to the door. Sadie gave me a quick hug and walked out onto the porch.

Just then, there was a high-pitched cry and a flapping sound.

We all stared for a moment as Blanche swept by and took a perch on the roof of Rob's building. She stared back for a moment, assessing us as potential food—or threat. Since we were clearly harmless and not anything she might wish to eat, Blanche made a little snorting noise and took off.

"Well, thank you for being a friend, Blanche," Sadie said, chuckling at her own *Golden Girls* reference as she turned for the little side street where she lived. "I'm going back to my nice hot stove."

"I'll walk you," Rob said. "Just wait a minute."

"Oh, fine." Sadie sighed, but stood, watching the stars.

He turned to me. "Still hate Vermont?"

"You heard that?"

Rob laughed. "The wind wasn't quite loud enough."

"Oh." I drooped, the way tall people do when we're embarrassed.

"It's cool, Jaye. I'd hate everything right about now, too, if I were you."

"Yeah, well, at least we live to fight another day."

"Yep. And next time, just borrow my damn roof rake, will ya?"

"Your . . . what?"

A grin. "Got a roof rake with a twenty-foot extension and a brush that'll knock the snow right out of the dish. Tim and I used to have satellite TV."

"Oh." I could just sweep from the safety of the fire escape. There was a distinct possibility the angels were singing.

191

"Remember, you're part of a town now. We take care of each other."

"Right." I liked that. And most of my new life, now that you mention it. But, sorry, I was never going to like blizzards. ❖

The White Balloon

Trish Esden

Baby dolls, your fathers should have warned you about me. They should have taught you to be good little girls, not to smile at strangers or go into restrooms alone, to stay alert—and, most of all, not to go out after dark.

Especially tonight.

A candlelight vigil for my girls. How can I resist such an invitation? Not honoring them with my presence would be rude. They are my work. My captured treasures.

Warmth flushes my body and I chuckle. You couldn't have created a more perfect night for my return if you tried.

I press my latex-gloved fingers against my lips, tasting them with my tongue as I watch you through my windshield. My teary-eyed sheep. My foolish little morsels, gathering to light your candles and mourn your lost friends. Girls I captured last year. Girls I brought home.

My car door opens without a sound. No rust on hinges, that's important. Even the plastic bag in my coat pocket doesn't crinkle. No sound or smell to give away what it contains: a washcloth dusted with scopolamine—the Devil's Breath for perfect compliance.

Folding my arms across my chest, I hide my gloved hands and study the crowd. Two girls in varsity jackets step out of a school bus. They're too old, worn-in most likely. A younger girl in a puffy vest sits alone on a bench, but her hair is slick and as dark as seaweed. Not right at all.

I move forward, blending in with the crowd, moving closer and closer toward the stage and the speaker's podium. And then I see her. The perfect blond morsel. Young, so sweet, a delectable angel. I stop an arm's length away from her and watch as she untangles a bouquet of white balloons. She's doe-eyed and pale, as if her daddy's kept her locked away in his pantry.

"Darn it," she says, as a balloon escapes.

I hesitate, replaying her voice in my mind. Something about it is familiar. I study her face once more. Yes, of course. Her sister was my first, taken from the Pizza Palace on her birthday, one year ago tonight. I smile at the memory. She was all legs and arms. A feisty thing for sure. She bit through my gloves, her muffled screams hot and wet against my sheathed fingers until the scopolamine took hold. I thought she might win that night. I thought the rush couldn't get any better. But I was wrong. It did.

My body quivers with heat and desire. Yes. Yes. This girl's exactly right. She's the one.

I step in front of her and smile. "Need some help?" I ask.

She shakes her head. Then, in a voice so soft it's clear she's been taught respect, she says, "Thanks for offering, but I'm almost done."

Good girl. You're smarter than your sister. Ten seconds alone behind the stage or in the shadows by my car and you would be mine, just like she was.

Wiping the corners of my mouth, I walk away from her and pick up a program off the stage. Its crisp paper slices through my thin glove and nicks my thumb. That won't do. Time to buy a better brand.

I lick the blood off and wander back into the crowd, staring at the photos across the top of the program.

Three pictures. Three girls. That's how many you think I took. Idiots.

You missed the fourteen-year-old, a runaway come from Texas to Vermont's Northeast Kingdom. She had 911 on speed dial. But that didn't do her any good. I'm faster than that. And the Canadian girl who snuck across the border to visit her ex-boyfriend. She was easy. Barely put up a fight. And the one I found sleeping on the beach, half drugged on meth. She was so eager to please. So ready to come home. That makes six.

The number sends a shiver of pleasure and longing through me. But I can't be foolish. Leave too warm a trail, and they'll catch up with me. That won't do at all. Still, it was a long winter, and the pantry is almost empty.

I slide the program into my pocket behind the plastic bag, and force my legs to carry me back to my car. It would be delicious to take a morsel from here. Delicious and poetic. But I'm not naïve like you, baby dolls. And it's barely nightfall, just twilight actually. Better to wait until the darkness settles to decide where I should take you from. Better to play it safe.

My car door opens without a sound, oiled to perfection, and left unlocked to avoid the slightest click. No noise. No smells. Those are the rules.

195

I settle in behind the steering wheel, listening as trembling voices rise in song.

"Come to me," the teary-eyed sheep sing, "I stand beside you. I'm all around you. And though you feel I'm far away, I'm closer than your breath."

I chuckle. Yes. Yes. I am.

A fainter sound reaches my ear. Ticktick. Ticktick. A pitter-pat like blood dripping into a metal pan, or like a clock or timer, coming from the backseat. But the only things in the rear are the tools of my trade—knives, plyers, rope, and duct tape—organized for ready access and stored in a plumber's workbag.

I glance in the rear-view mirror.

A white balloon rises toward the ceiling.

I blink. Could fate have delivered the quarry to my door? Was life that wondrous?

Bang! The balloon explodes. Red confetti sprays outward like intestines released from a sack. It showers down.

My nose wrinkles at the scent of gasoline.

That's not right. No sounds. No smells. That's important.

Another ticktick.

BOOM!

The explosion throws me backward. Flames erupt. Smoke. Heat. Blinding light engulfing me, crackling all around. Agony rips screams from my mouth. Delicious. Torturous. My consciousness gives way.

Oh, clever baby dolls, your invitation was truly wicked.

A candlelight vigil. For me?

You knew I couldn't resist.❖

Sticky Fingers

Janet Raye Stevens

June 8, 1944

Emily Applegate spent a good part of the morning straightening the bookshelves at the Preston, Massachusetts, public library. Not exactly her responsibility as senior librarian. Her assistant, Marian, could handle the job with equal efficiency, but Emily took great satisfaction in hunting for books misfiled on the wrong shelves and returning them to their proper home.

She picked up the last one on her book cart, the racy historical romance *Forever Amber*, and slid it into place on the fiction shelf, then glanced at the clock. A little after one. Way past time for lunch. Emily's empty belly growled in agreement.

She pushed the wooden cart with the wobbly wheels toward the back room, passing the world map she and Marian had spread across a long table when the war began three years ago. Now dozens of pins studded the map, showing the many places around the world where battles had taken place. Two days ago, she'd added a new pin to mark an area of France called Normandy. A battle that had cost many lives but had established a beachhead, a place to start the invasion of Europe that could hopefully soon lead to an end of this brutal war.

The library's main door opened with a creak of hinges. A burst of warm June air rushed in, followed by the tall, broad-shouldered Seamus Murphy, police sergeant, voracious reader of mysteries, and the man Emily had been walking out with for over a year. Seamus swept off his policeman's cap and caught her eye, his expression serious.

"What brings you here in the middle of the day?" she asked, abandoning the cart and hurrying over to meet him. "Don't tell me. You have to break our dinner date for tonight."

"No, Em." A secretive smile fluttered on his lips. "I wouldn't cancel that in a million years." He shifted, sobering. "I'm here to ask a favor. Actually, Lieutenant Fleming wants a favor. There's been an . . . incident at the college and the lieutenant thinks you can be of help."

"Me? How can I help?"

"He says you have the expertise he needs in a situation like this. Are you free?"

"Am I ever." She flushed with pride and a pinch of ego. By *expertise*, the lieutenant must mean last year, when her curiosity and doggedness had helped break up a spy ring. "I'll just grab my lunch."

Emily ate her tuna salad sandwich and apple on the way to Marlowe College, located on the leafy side of town. She'd never ridden in a police car before and found the journey fascinating, despite the vehicle's uncomfortable front seat and smell of cigars and criminals.

"I thought we'd do something special for dinner tonight," Seamus said. That secretive smile came back. "I made a reservation at Luigi's, where we had our first date."

"That'll be delightful," Emily said, preoccupied. Her brain whirled with speculation about why Lieutenant Fleming had called for her help. Was there another group of spies suspected of passing secrets at the college? Or perhaps a gang of saboteurs?

They reached Marlowe College, a bucolic campus straight out of a Hollywood movie, with its many shade trees, lush green lawns, and red brick buildings speckled with ivy. Seamus eased the car into a parking space in front of the administration building and guided her up a short flight of stone steps. Inside, their footsteps echoed as they walked down a wide corridor and stopped at the office on the end, with *Albert Van Dyke, Dean* painted on the door's beveled glass.

Seamus ushered Emily into a large and ornate room. Paintings, artwork, and sculptures filled every available wall, bookcase, and table top. A thin man in his sixties, wearing a finely tailored blue suit, sat at a big desk cluttered with bronze busts of famous men, scattered papers, and piles of books Emily itched to get a closer look at.

Lieutenant Fleming, a tall, beefy man roughly the same age as Emily and Seamus, midforties, paced the room like a caged lion. He skidded to a stop when he spotted them.

"Miss Applegate, thank you for coming," he said. "I asked you here because Dean Van Dyke is missing a book, and, uh, you know about books."

A thorn of disappointment pricked Emily's ego. Fleming didn't want her for her intuitive knowledge of the criminal underworld. He needed her book knowledge.

"Of course," she said, squaring her shoulders. She'd been a librarian for more than twenty years. If anyone knew more about books than she did, she would like to meet them. "I take it this missing book is valuable, and you want me to confirm that fact?"

"It's not *missing*." The dean leapt up from his chair and pounded his fists on his desk so hard the busts of Charles Darwin and Walt Whitman rattled. "It was *stolen*. How many times do I have to tell you that, you imbecile?" He aimed that vitriol at the lieutenant, then swung a scowl at Emily. "And I don't need you or anyone else to confirm my book is valuable. It's a first edition of Darwin's *The Origin of Species*."

Emily sucked in a breath. "My goodness. An *actual* first edition?"

"Certainly. I would own no other. I picked it up at an auction years ago, when the Depression forced people to sell their treasures for a song. My Darwin is valued at upwards of three thousand dollars, perhaps more."

Seamus whistled and Fleming scoffed. "Why would someone pay that much for a book?" he asked.

Emily stiffened. "Why wouldn't they? Especially a book so important to science and history as Darwin's."

Not what Fleming wanted to hear. His face pinched as tight as a girdle as he took a notepad and pencil from his breast pocket. He heaved a mighty sigh and eyed the dean. "Tell me what happened. When did you notice the book was gone?"

"I stepped out for my usual coffee break at ten. No, let me start earlier. I brought the book in this morning, since I've decided to sell some of my possessions as I ready for retirement. I had an appointment later this afternoon with a seller of rare books who's traveling from Boston to meet me.

I left for my coffee break and the book was right there—" He gestured to an empty spot on his desk. "When I returned a half hour later, it was gone. Someone broke in here while I was out and stole it."

Fleming made a few notes, barely glancing at the space where the book had once been, between a pile of other books and file folders. Emily studied the spot with great interest, taking note of the blob of something sticky on the edge of the desk.

"Do you have any idea who this book thief might be?" Fleming asked.

"I'd put my money on Peter Sturges, the college librarian. He's coveted my Darwin since a faculty party at my home, where he saw it on my bookshelf. I told him I was selling, but he offered such a paltry sum, I turned him down."

Fleming took notes. Or appeared to. He looked bored, as if he'd rather be anywhere but here. "Anyone else you suspect? Someone who was in your office today and saw the book?"

"Miss Capra, my teaching assistant, was here around nine. We met to go over the syllabus for my summer philosophy classes. A silly girl, more dedicated to flirting and mooning over Frank Sinatra than her studies, or rare books. Jack Siletsky was here today too. He's a professor of mathematics." Van Dyke's already stormy expression turned thunderous. "By golly, Siletsky could've stolen my Darwin out of spite. We argued, you see. I denied him tenure *and* a pay raise. Justifiably. The man is a boor who lacks the skills to teach second graders, never mind college students."

Seamus raised his eyebrows. "What about your secretary? I'm sure she's in and out of your office a lot."

"Lavinia?" The dean thought that over a moment, then narrowed his eyes. "Perhaps."

201

Fleming tucked his notepad away. "Thank you, Dean Van Dyke. We'll do everything we can to find your missing—er—stolen book."

On that somewhat insincere promise, they left.

"We should talk to the teaching assistant or the secretary first," Emily said gesturing to their offices, a short way down the hall.

"Not *we*, Miss Applegate," the lieutenant sniffed. "*I* will question the ladies. I asked you here to confirm if the book held any value and you've done so. Time for you to toddle off back to your library. Sergeant?" He nodded at Seamus.

Emily set her chin. "Oh no, lieutenant. You can't get rid of me that easily. What if one of the suspects says something only a librarian will understand? I'm particularly skilled at reading people and picking up on clues you might miss."

"She has a point," Seamus added. "Without Emily's crack sleuthing skills, we never would have discovered that spy ring last year."

The lieutenant's answering smile landed somewhere between patronizing and annoyed. "Very well. But stay out of the way and let *me* ask the questions."

They found the teaching assistant's tiny office empty and the door locked. They had better luck with the dean's secretary, ensconced in a cubbyhole a fraction of the size of her boss's office, with a nameplate reading *Lavinia Wyler* hanging on the door.

A curvy brunette with a Rita Hayworth smolder, Miss Wyler sat in a wooden swivel chair, her slim fingers tapping away at her typewriter keys. V-Mail letters from overseas sat on a corner of her desk in a neat pile, next to several pages of what Emily guessed was the dean's correspondence. His personal correspondence, given the salutation on the top letter, addressed to "my dearest."

Miss Wyler stopped typing and turned their way, eager to help. "A missing book? From his desk?" She batted long eyelashes framing keen blue eyes. "Was that the one with the darling green cover?"

"Yes, dear," the lieutenant said like an indulgent father. "Do you mind telling me where you were this morning, between ten and half past the hour?"

"Not at all. I went to the mailbox outside the student union to mail a letter." She nodded to the stack of V-Mail. "I make it my patriotic duty to write to my special man almost every day."

"Admirable," Lieutenant Fleming said, and after they confirmed that Miss Capra had gone home for the day, they moved on to interview Professor Siletsky.

Emily shaded her eyes from the sun when they stepped outside and headed for the faculty building across the college's grassy quad with its crisscrossing sidewalks. The day was warm, and the few students on campus between spring and summer semesters took advantage of the fine weather, sitting on the ground or wooden benches. Mostly women, Emily noted, since their male counterparts were off to war.

They caught Professor Siletsky leaving his office. A solidly built man no taller than Emily and wearing a sadly outdated pinstriped suit, he ate a chocolate bar and carried a fat satchel that bulged with books. Was one of them the dean's missing tome?

"Lost his precious Darwin, has he?" Siletsky said, polishing off his chocolate and wiping his sticky fingers on his jacket. "Serves him right. He sits in his office flaunting his wealth, while I toil day in and day out for elephant's wages."

Lieutenant Fleming frowned. "What wages?"

"He means he's paid in peanuts," Emily said. "Like an elephant in the circus."

"Yeah, peanuts, and with wages frozen for the war's duration I'm not getting a raise anytime soon. The dean at least could approve my tenure application."

"That makes you angry, doesn't it?" Seamus put in. "Angry enough to . . ."

"You think I'd waste time stealing a book when Van Dyke has more valuable items in that office just waiting to be plucked?"

"Mm-hm," Fleming murmured, making more notes. "Where were you this morning around ten?"

"In my office, and before you ask, no one saw me there, no one can back up my alibi. But let me tell you, I wouldn't be so clumsy as to steal anything in broad daylight. I'd sneak in at night and get it."

Goodness. The man sure was eager to point the finger at himself. If Emily had her druthers, she'd take Siletsky downtown and question him thoroughly, but Lieutenant Fleming simply thanked him for his time and they returned to the quad, heading for the library. The lieutenant set a bruising pace, as if he were General Eisenhower leading the troops across the desert in North Africa. He nearly knocked down several young ladies in his hurry to get to their next suspect and finish this investigation.

At the library, Seamus offered his arm to help Emily climb steps so steep she feared she'd get a nosebleed. Inside, she goggled at the domed ceiling and tall shelves filled with books and resources as vast as the sky above.

A young woman at the front desk directed them to the second floor. After a brief search, they found the librarian, Peter Sturges, in the stacks. A spare man with equally spare hair, he slid a silver flask out from between two books, unscrewed the cap, and took a fast nip. He wiped his mouth and licked his fingers as he returned the flask to its hiding place, with none the wiser.

Or so he thought. Emily wrinkled her nose at such an appalling display. While on duty, too.

Mr. Sturges bristled like an offended porcupine when the lieutenant explained why they were there. "How *dare* you accuse me of theft," he cried.

"No one's accusing you of anything," Fleming said. "I just want to know where you were this morning around ten."

"I was in a staff meeting. A dozen library employees can account for my whereabouts."

The lieutenant apparently lacked the stamina or interest to interview those employees, so he took Sturges at his word and declared the investigation had come to an end.

"In my opinion, no crime's been committed," he said as they returned downstairs. "I firmly believe the old boy misplaced his book and forgot about it. He'll find his Darwin on his kitchen counter at home and kick himself for getting so riled up. Mark my words."

Emily tried to argue with him, but he suddenly recalled an urgent appointment and bolted, nearly running down a few more coeds on his way out the door.

Seamus picked Emily up at eight for their dinner at Luigi's. He held her chair, then took his own, looking nervous. A violinist came to their table and plucked out a romantic tune. Luigi himself brought them a bottle of his finest red wine, and gave Seamus a conspiratorial wink as he filled their glasses. He apologized for the lack of steak or veal on the menu, due to rationing, but promised the chef had come up with a delicious chicken scaloppini to tempt their taste buds.

After Luigi left, Seamus eyed Emily and cleared his throat. "Listen, Em, there's something I want to talk to you about." He tugged at his collar as if the launderer had put too much starch in it.

"I want to talk to you, too, Seamus. We need to get to the bottom of who stole that Darwin, even if Lieutenant Fleming won't."

"Uh, that's not what I had in mind."

"There are so many suspects." Emily snapped her napkin open and placed it across her lap. "Even Miss Wyler. She may have fooled the lieutenant with her dizzy dame act, but I suspect the secretary's a lot smarter than she lets on."

"Em, I—"

"And then there's that sticky substance on the dean's desk. What is it? A bit of Professor Siletsky's chocolate? Or drops of whiskey from the librarian's flask? The dean's teaching assistant *must* be interviewed. I'll do that tomorrow before I go into work. I'll find out what Miss Capra knows." Emily sipped her wine, then laughed. "Listen to me, running on like Tuppence Beresford on the trail of a criminal, without giving you a moment to speak. What did you want to say?"

Seamus flashed a rueful grin. "It can wait. I know better than to interrupt Detective Applegate when she's on the case."

Emily had to change buses at city hall and was running behind schedule by the time she got to the college the next morning. Few people were about and the tap of her heels on

206

the floor as she hurried down the hallway to Miss Capra's office echoed ominously.

She peered through the glass into Lavinia Wyler's cubbyhole as she passed. The lights were off, her typewriter neatly covered, and the stack of V-Mail on her desk gone. No one was in the teaching assistant's office either, though the door was open. Papers were strewn about the small desk, along with crumbs and blots of something dark and gooey.

"Hello?" Emily called, gazing up and down the empty corridor. That ominous sense of dread stole over her again.

A high-pitched squeal like someone stepping on a mouse erupted from the dean's office. Emily crept down the corridor and found the door ajar. Prickles of fear raced down her spine as she reached for the knob and stepped into the room.

She gasped. She found the source of the squeak. A dark-haired young woman she presumed to be Miss Capra stood by the desk, a ream of papers and the blood-soaked bust of Charles Darwin at her feet.

Right next to the body of Dean Albert Van Dyke.

Lieutenant Fleming led Miss Capra to a wooden bench outside the dean's office. The young woman sat, trembling from head to toe.

"Stay here. I'll get your statement later," Fleming said to her, then rounded on Emily. "This is a *real* crime now, Miss Applegate. Your help isn't needed. You can go."

He returned to the crime scene and shut the door in Emily's face, leaving her fighting the urge to hurl some profane words at him that would get a book banned in Boston.

There was no way on this green earth she'd do what he asked and leave. Not when she had a puzzle to figure out. Someone had murdered Albert Van Dyke, struck him over the head with the bust of Charles Darwin. Some sort of poetic justice in the killer's mind? Or just a convenient, easy-to-reach murder weapon?

After Emily called work to report she'd be late, expecting the library's persnickety new director to read her the riot act when she got in, she joined the still trembling Miss Capra on the bench. A petite and pretty young woman with large brown eyes and an overbite, she wore a pleated skirt and a flowered blouse blotched with the same dark, sticky substance Emily had seen on the teaching assistant's desk. And the dean's.

A piece of the puzzle clicked into place, but she needed more answers.

"I know you're upset," Emily said, with a comforting smile. "It might help you to calm your nerves if you talk about what happened."

Miss Capra opened and closed her mouth several times before she found her words. "I . . . I don't know. I came in early as I always do, went to give the dean the papers he asked me to type up yesterday, and . . . and . . ."

"And you found him dead. A terrible thing." She held the young woman in a steady gaze. "I suspect he was killed by someone he knew."

The girl let out another mouse squeak of alarm. "Surely you don't think *I* had anything to do with it."

If Emily had a nickel for each time the guilty party said that in the detective novels and radio mystery programs she and Seamus enjoyed so much, she would be a wealthy woman. But she doubted Miss Capra was the culprit. She appeared genuinely upset.

Emily shook her head. "Do you recall hearing the dean argue with anyone yesterday? Or the day before?"

"Who *didn't* he argue with? I hate to speak ill of the dead, but he was a difficult man. He fought with everyone."

"Anyone specific?"

"Professor Siletsky. I heard them, shortly before my meeting with the dean. They fought like cats and dogs for a good long time. The professor insisted he get a salary hike, despite the wage freeze. He threatened to take all the dean's paintings and rare books and throw them into a bonfire on the quad."

Bluff and bluster? Or was the professor actually capable of such a heinous act? "What about Mr. Sturges, the librarian? Or Miss Wyler?"

"Oh, he and Mr. Sturges were like bickering brothers. They seemed to enjoy sniping at one another. Like a game, you know? But the way he and Professor Siletsky argued, I expected them to come to blows." Miss Capra's trembling had stopped, and only some nervous leg jiggling betrayed her anxiety. "With Miss Wyler, the dean acted the righteous prude. Called her Hester Prynne and Allotment Annie because he didn't approve of her dating servicemen. I say, what's the harm in a date with a couple of boys going overseas? Not like she married them."

Emily straightened. Several more puzzle pieces clicked into place. "Did anyone mention the rare Darwin book the dean kept on his desk?"

Miss Capra's eyes went wide. "The book? What does the book have to do with anything?"

"Didn't you hear? Dean Van Dyke reported it stolen yesterday."

209

"Stolen?" The young woman gulped. "No. It wasn't stolen. It . . . it . . . " She pressed her lips together and said no more.

Emily's eyebrows rose. The puzzle was taking shape, but she still couldn't see the full picture.

Deep in thought, she sat on the bench for some time with Miss Capra, or Francine, as she'd insisted Emily call her. Several of Seamus's colleagues arrived to remove the dean's body and Seamus himself stopped by to offer Emily an affectionate hello.

Soon after, the number of police officials dwindled to just Seamus and Lieutenant Fleming, who called Francine into Van Dyke's office to make her statement. Emily followed on her heels, ignoring the lieutenant's glower.

"Now, Miss Capra," Fleming said. "Why don't you tell me exactly what you saw, and how you found yourself in a dead man's office so early in the day."

Francine's trembling began again. Emily escorted her to a chair. The lieutenant waited a whole three seconds for the young woman to catch her breath before repeating his question.

She rallied but had barely begun her tale of woe when the rapid tap of heels on the floor outside announced Lavinia Wyler's arrival.

"What's happened?" she asked, poking her head through the open door. "Why are you here?"

"I'm sorry, Miss Wyler," Lieutenant Fleming said in a mournful voice. "Your boss is dead."

"The dean . . . dead?" Her gaze flashed to the spot on the floor where Van Dyke had fallen. "I can't believe it. This is just awful. How could someone do such a thing to him?"

Emily tapped her toe. She'd seen bad actresses in her time, but this woman took the cake and every pie in the bakery.

"That's the question we're asking, Miss Wyler." Lieutenant Fleming offered a reassuring smile. "Don't fret, we'll get to the bottom of it. I know this is unpleasant, but do you have information on the dean's next of kin?"

She dabbed at dry eyes with a lacy handkerchief. "Yes. There's a number to contact in my desk. I'll get it."

"Wait," Emily called. She'd almost figured it out. "I have a question for you." The lieutenant aimed an unhappy look at her, but Seamus gave a nod, all the encouragement she needed. "How did you know someone had *done* something to the dean? Lieutenant Fleming only said he'd died. Not that he'd been murdered."

Now it was Miss Wyler's turn to tremble. "Uh, well, I assume that's the case, after his silly book had been stolen and all."

"But the Darwin wasn't stolen." Emily eyed Francine, perched on the edge of her chair. "Care to explain, Miss Capra?"

Francine's cheeks grew as red as fire. "I took it. I had a meeting with the dean yesterday morning. I forgot my notes and came back to get them after he stepped out. I was eating a jelly doughnut at the time and some of the jelly squirted out and got on the book. I tried to clean it up, but my sticky fingers only made more of a mess." She hung her head. "So, I took the book home, hoping to clean it off there."

Lieutenant Fleming groaned. Seamus looked from Francine to Emily and his lips quirked.

"There you have it," Emily said. "Though it pains me to think of the condition the book's cover must be in, we can consider the case of the stolen Darwin solved. As to the murder . . ." She turned to Miss Wyler. "Yesterday you said you were out around ten, mailing a letter. Which husband were you sending it to?"

"I don't know what you're talking about," Lavinia said.

"I think you do. I also think you killed Dean Van Dyke because he found out you're a bigamist."

Francine's mouth fell open. Seamus released a surprised—and impressed—snort. The lieutenant stared at Emily, working his jaw as if he chewed on a mouthful of glass.

"It took me a while to figure it out." Emily paced the room slowly, feeling like Hercule Poirot laying out the suspects and motivations at the conclusion of an Agatha Christie novel. "Francine said she overheard the dean call Miss Wyler an Allotment Annie in the most insulting manner. I'd heard that phrase before. In fact, I knew I'd read it somewhere. My library receives no fewer than six newspapers a day and a dozen magazines and periodicals every week. I read them all, especially the news about crimes and criminals. Somewhere in all those pages, I read about Allotment Annies. Women who marry multiple servicemen to collect the spouse's weekly allotment. A tidy sum of . . ." She stopped pacing and faced Lavinia. "What is the amount? Twenty dollars a week? Just enough for a wife to make ends meet with one husband overseas. But with five or six or seven husbands? You could live like a queen."

Lieutenant Fleming swung on Miss Wyler. "You're a bigamist?" He couldn't have sounded more shocked if she had revealed she was Mussolini himself.

"Yeah, so what, I'm a bigamist." Lavinia's sweet and befuddled demeanor turned brittle. "What of it? Nobody got hurt. None of the fellas know about the others, and you know the chances of them making it home are . . . Well, I may soon find myself a widow several times over."

The room fell deathly quiet as they all digested this callous declaration.

"The dean discovered what you were up to," Emily said, breaking the silence after a few moments. "He threatened to turn you in, so you killed him."

Lavinia held up her hands, palms up. "I had no choice. He called me in here last night before going home. He all but accused me of stealing his stupid book. I denied it, but he didn't believe me." She gave a bitter laugh. "The one thing I've ever been honest about in my life, and he thought I lied. He said he was onto my scheme. He'd seen the letters on my desk and figured it out. If I would stoop to tricking soldiers, he said, stealing his precious book would be child's play. He offered not to report me if I returned the book. I denied stealing it until I was blue in the face. Finally, I got so furious with his stubbornness, I grabbed one of those busts and conked him, just to shut him up."

"You did shut him up," the lieutenant said, his voice grim. "For good."

After Lieutenant Fleming marched Lavinia off to the police station to be formally charged, and Francine tearfully returned the sticky Darwin, Seamus drove Emily to her library. He parked at the curb, held the car door, and took her arm, leading her up the steps.

"You figured it out again, Em," he said, turning to her at the library's front door. "Nothing slips by you."

She ducked her head to hide the blush that warmed her face. The lieutenant had given her a grudging thank you,

213

but Seamus's respect and admiration was what mattered to her most.

"Except there's one clue you've completely missed."

"What?" Emily's gaze flew to his face. His blue eyes twinkled with mischief.

"Last night at dinner, I wasn't even remotely interested in talking about the book's theft."

"You weren't?"

"No. For someone as perceptive as Sherlock Holmes, you really missed this one." He dropped to one knee and took her hand. Emily gasped. A passing car tooted its horn. "Emily Louise Applegate, you don't have to investigate too deeply to discover I love you. I think it's time we make it official. Will you marry me?"

She grinned. "Oh, Seamus, you're right. The evidence was there all along, but I didn't put the clues together."

"Don't leave me in suspense. What's the answer to this mystery?"

Emily's heart soared. "Yes, Seamus. A resounding *yes.*"

Followed by a kiss to seal the deal. ❖

The Boss of Butler Square

Sharon Daynard

It was Mother's Day, May 14, 1972. Richard Nixon was president, *The Godfather* was number one at the box office and my husband, Gavin, owned Butler Square. Gavin was in the favor business. He collected, traded, and called them in like commodities on the stock market. He also collected insurance money from local businesses. On-time payments protected against property damage and bodily harm. Some called Gavin a street thug, others an animal, but everyone called him Mr. Kavanagh when they needed a favor.

Gavin drove a '71 Mulsanne Blue Chevelle SS, wore sharkskin suits Monday through Friday, and jeans on the weekends. He was every bit a respected businessman as Ted Shumsky, who owned the drugstore, and Delmar Jacques, who ran the gas station. Gavin conducted most of his business over whiskey at Moynihan's, except on Sundays. On Sundays, he took us to the eight o'clock Mass at St. Patrick's. He smoked Cuban cigars in the rectory and held audience while I attended the Ladies' Tea in the parish hall and the kids took catechism class.

Gavin Kavanagh made Ward Cleaver look like a deadbeat dad. He endured every dance recital, Christmas pageant, and PTA meeting. He coached Little League, chaperoned field trips and volunteered as a Cub Scout den leader. He put food on the table, clothes on our backs, and treated me like a queen. He brought me flowers every Saturday, called me his Irish Rose, and taught me how to fire a Colt Python .357 Magnum like every bullet was my last. And I taught myself to look past his bloodstained shirt cuffs, the late-night phone calls, and the police details parked across from our double-decker on Dexter Street.

It was drizzling that Mother's Day morning when Gavin left the house before Mass to grab a cup of coffee and the Sunday paper at the corner doughnut shop. Three weeks later, his bludgeoned body was pulled from the murky water of a granite quarry. When Gavin died, so did the phone calls and the police details. Widowed at twenty-nine, I took a pink-collar job behind the lunch counter at Woolworth's and lived in relative obscurity for thirty-nine years until late one night the phone rang and a frail, frightened voice whispered, "I need a favor."

I thought it was a crank call and hung up. It rang again.

"Please, Rose, it's Oona Carmody. Tell me you're still in contact with Gavin's associates."

"Associates?" Anyone Gavin once associated with had long since departed this world.

"I don't know what else to do." She cleared a sob from her throat. "Edmund's missing."

Oona Carmody was ninety at best. She lived alone in a Victorian eyesore with a blue parakeet named Sir

Edmund and any number of stray cats. The joke around Butler Square was she'd lost her virginity to Ben Franklin. The truth was, at least according to Gavin, she slept on a mattress stuffed with hundred-dollar bills sporting Franklin's portrait.

"One of your cats must have—"

"There's a ransom note, Rose. And a feather."

I tried telling Oona no one held dime-store parakeets for ransom, but she was on the verge of hysterics. Out of sheer pity for the woman, I agreed to meet in the morning.

I tried not to laugh as I read the ransom note out loud. " 'If you want to see the bird again, leave five large in a lunch bag taped to the underside of the cement bench outside the library.' Five large, Oona? Who talks that way? No self-respecting kidnapper would leave a ransom note. He'd make a phone call. A short one."

"Just do what he wants." Oona handed me the bag and broke down in tears.

Wishing I'd disconnected my phone instead of hanging up, I drove Gavin's old Chevelle to the dead drop and waited. Twenty minutes later, our friendly neighborhood mailman, Fred Garside, took a seat on the cement bench and snatched the bag. I floored the gas pedal, pinning him between the bench and the Chevelle.

Garside let out a wail that could peel paper from walls as he collapsed onto the car. One hand clutched the bag. The other pounded the hood in a pathetic display of pain.

He lifted his head and shot me a look of disbelief. "Are you insane!"

"Where's the bird?" I shouted.

"What bird?" he asked through a strangled sob.

217

I planted my left foot on the brake and revved the engine with my right. "The bird, Herb."

"It was an accident. I opened the cage and it flew out the front door."

I slammed the car into PARK, tore the bag from Garside's hand, and promised next time I saw him, he was going to beg me to put a bullet through his brain. I left him sniveling in a crumpled heap and drove to the nearest pet store.

I paid fifty dollars for an adult male blue parakeet and a birdcage. Another four hundred and fifty found their way into a donation jar for the local animal shelter. Maybe the bird was an exact match, maybe it wasn't. The fact that Oona was legally blind made it a moot point. If the bird didn't tweet quite the same or shied away from her, it could be chalked up to emotional trauma. Thirty minutes later, Sir Edmund and forty-five hundred dollars were reunited with Oona Carmody. I told her I'd taken five hundred dollars as my fee for kneecapping Edmund's kidnapper and the mail was going to be late that afternoon. Oona didn't have a problem with either.

Whispers of the Carmody Job, as it became known, circulated first among the AARP crowd and then trickled down to the rest of the community, growing to the point where you'd think I was Butler Square's own Vito Corleone. Suddenly my bingo cards down at the VFW were comped. Anything I ordered at the coffee shop was on the house. The paperboy hand-delivered the newspaper to my front stoop instead of flinging it into the bushes or nearest puddle. The mail was on time, the Chevelle breezed through state inspections, and Sophie Greenblatt from down the street magically found someone else's front lawn for her St. Bernard to do its business on.

Verna Mulvaney was the next to call asking for a favor. She'd paid a small fortune to have her house painted. The color was more than a shade off, the trim was sloppy, and the peonies along the foundation were trampled. The miserable paint job Verna could live with; the peonies she wanted replaced. Wally Duncan, the contractor, had stopped taking her calls. She called the police. She called the Better Business Bureau. She'd even called a lawyer. No one cared about the precious peonies her late husband planted forty years earlier on her birthday. One way or the other, Verna wanted the matter settled.

Wally was more than happy to drive out and give an estimate to paint my double-decker. After leveling his ladder with shims, he was even happier to condemn the gutters. While Wally was pulling leaves from them, I gave the ladder a shake. Wally was too busy exalting the wonders of seamless vinyl gutters with leaf guards to notice. I got his attention when I knocked the shims out from under the ladder with a sledgehammer I'd pulled from the Chevelle's trunk. Considering those shoddy gutters were able to support Wally Duncan's two hundred plus pounds, I figured I'd keep them.

I also figured it was a good time to bring up Verna Mulvaney's peonies. If Wally promised to replace them, I'd replace the ladder. Wally's response was less than cordial. It took a gust of wind for Wally to cave. Somehow, I never thought to use the shims. When Wally climbed on, the ladder fell over. He flailed and grabbed the wires running from the electric pole to the house. The paramedics assured me Wally was dead before he hit the driveway. Out of respect, I sent the Widow Duncan a potted peony to plant on Wally's grave.

Like Oona Carmody, Verna was tickled with the outcome.

219

So began my career in the favor business. Turned out I had a real knack for getting people to see things my way. Cheating husbands only needed to see the pruning shears in my hand to develop a new-found respect for the sanctity of marriage. Most times all I had to do was park outside someone's house in Gavin's old Chevelle for them to get the message. Other times it took a bit of finesse, a flair for the dramatic, and the message only a well-placed bullet could send. Picture windows and windshields could be replaced. Balls and brains were harder to come by.

And like Gavin, I didn't mind getting my hands dirty when needed. Of course, some favors were beyond my expertise or outside my comfort zone. I farmed out those favors. There was never a shortage of cash-strapped toughs looking to make a quick buck.

I will say, it was quite a boost to my sense of self-worth the first time I walked into Mitchell's Meat Market and asked for the manager's special in a plain white envelope. Every first of the month since, I've collected envelopes filled with cash from every mom-and-pop business in Butler Square with the exception of the fish market. Talk around town was it got a free pass because Gavin's cousin owned the place. Family had nothing to do with it. I'd developed an acute fish allergy in my forties. I couldn't even touch the stuff without breaking out in hives.

I've lost track of how many favors I've collected and how many I've called in. How many far-from-chance encounters I've had at the coffee shop with those in need of my services. But up until last week, no one had walked past the police detail outside my house and knocked on my door asking for tea.

I watched patiently as Deirdre Cleary folded and unfolded her linen napkin a good fifty times before depositing it on her lap. The ritual she performed stirring sugar into her tea was pretty much along the same lines.

"Aside from the tea, is there any particular reason you've come here today?" I asked.

Avoiding my question, Deirdre took a sip from the teacup and asked, "Is this Dublin Morning?"

It was Tetley, but I nodded just the same.

"Blueberry scones, lemon curd, shortbread, and wafers." Deirdre took inventory of the tea tray.

"Would a bit of Jameson help?" I offered.

She looked at me as if I'd sprouted horns. "It's ten-fifteen in the morning, Rose."

"Three fingers then?"

Deirdre nodded, took in a deep breath, and let it out in a shudder. "I've come asking a favor, Rose."

"Deidre, don't," I cautioned.

"He murdered my Thomas." She wept through a voice so small and tortured my heart ached.

"It was an accident, Deirdre." I reached for her hand but she shrank back. "Thomas shouldn't have been driving in that storm. He hit a patch of ice and—"

"I want Anthony Bonacorsi dead."

"It's only been a few months, Deirdre. Give it a little time; you'll adjust."

"I've done nothing but *adjust* these last five months." She spat out the word *adjust* like it was spoiled milk.

I handed her a tissue and listened as her story played out.

"We went to the bank asking for a twenty-five-thousand-dollar loan for a new roof and replacement

221

windows. The branch manager, Anthony Bonacorsi, wouldn't listen to what we wanted. He wanted us to take out a three-hundred-and-fifty-thousand-dollar home equity line of credit. He reasoned the rate was better, we'd have an emergency fund at our disposal should any of life's incidentals crop up, not to mention money for all the things we'd gone without. We'd have ten years to draw down on the loan, paying only the interest. After that, we'd have fifteen years to pay it off. He said we wouldn't have to worry about that. He'd rewrite the loan and it'd go back to interest only for another ten years. He even joked about the loan outliving us."

She paused long enough to drag the tissue across her tear-streaked cheeks. "It was like we'd hit the lottery. We took early retirements and Thomas bought that Cadillac he always wanted. We went to Ireland for our fiftieth anniversary. We took day trips to casinos, ate out more than we should have, went to the movies, the theater, and concerts. We rented a summer cottage on the Vineyard and a condo in Key West for the winter. For the first time in our lives, we put ourselves first. And then the repayment period began. The once more-than-manageable payments increased tenfold."

She took a drink of whiskey, swallowed hard, and shrugged. "We went to the bank just like Anthony Bonacorsi told us only to find our debt-to-income ratio no longer supported the loan. He actually smiled when he told us the good news was we had fifteen years to pay it off. Good news, Rose? Pay it off with what? Both our Social Security checks combined didn't come close to the monthly payment. We paid what we could but kept falling further and further behind. We could have sold the house, but Thomas wouldn't hear of it. When the bank threatened to foreclose, he took a part-time job bagging groceries. *Bagging groceries,*" she echoed in a sob.

"It was Anthony Bonacorsi's fault my Thomas was driving to work that day. I didn't even have enough money to give him a proper burial. When I brought a copy of Thomas's death certificate to the bank, Anthony Bonacorsi never offered his condolences. He handed me a promotional T-shirt and escorted me to the door."

"I'm so sorry, Deirdre," I consoled.

"He was more than happy to rewrite the loan after I paid it down with Thomas's life insurance. All that does is buy me another ten years before I find myself out on the streets."

"If it's a matter of money, Deirdre—"

"*Dúnmharú gan trua,*" she said, shredding the tissue onto her lap.

I couldn't remember the last time I'd heard anyone utter those words, but I knew what they meant—murder without pity. Maybe Anthony Bonacorsi deserved the Irish equivalent of sleeping with the fishes. Maybe he didn't. Gavin didn't make judgments; he took requests. He was in the business of granting favors, not saving souls. It wasn't always as black and white for me. I lay awake some nights worrying about the lives I meddled in and second-guessing the things I'd done. I could counsel, offer alternatives, but ultimately the decisions weren't mine.

"You're certain this is what you want?" I gave Deirdre's trembling hand a squeeze. "It'll stay with you the rest of your time in this world and surely follow you into the next."

She took a breath and released it in a raspy groan. "Dúnmharú gan trua."

I lowered my gaze, knowing full well Deirdre Cleary didn't deserve an eternity of paying for the favor she was asking. It might take a week, a month, or even a year, but eventually the intoxication that came along with the deed would wear off and Deirdre would succumb to sobriety and the awareness that no amount of penance and prayer would rid her of the act she'd set in motion.

"Nothing quick." Her voice took on a tone of brutal detachment. "I want him to see it coming. I want him to suffer. I want every minute of his miserable existence to feel like a never-ending hell. And I want to laugh, Rose. I want to laugh at his pain."

All I could do was nod.

"I want him poisoned, Rose."

"I don't know enough about poisons." I lied. I knew more than I'd ever admit. "They're too unpredictable. There are so many variables to—"

"A slow-acting poison with no antidote." Deirdre narrowed it down for me. "Every time I walk into that bank I want to see Anthony Bonacorsi a deeper shade of green. I want to ask him how he's feeling and offer a pout when he tells me he feels like death. I want the stench of his rotting soul to engulf him. I want it to linger for days before he figures it out."

"Dragging it out requires multiple doses, Deirdre. It's impossible."

"Please, Rose, I've no one else to turn to."

Bohemian Rhapsody was playing on the radio when I jockeyed the Chevelle across two spaces at the bank's front door marked NO PARKING. According to the dashboard clock, I was two hours late for the 9:30 appointment I'd booked with Anthony Bonacorsi. I blew a few puffs of breath into two latex surgical gloves, slid my hands inside, and covered them with white cotton gloves before leaving the car.

The bank was my last stop in a morning that had already been overwhelmed with errands. A trip to the farmers' market for fresh fruits and vegetables, the butcher shop for a corned beef brisket, the fish market for cod, and the bakery for a bag of day-old doughnuts.

I pulled a folding shopping cart from the trunk, loaded up my groceries, and wheeled it into the bank. A grin teased the corners of my mouth as I cut a path through every procrastinator in Butler Square who'd suddenly realized not only that the bank closed at noon on Saturdays, but Monday was a holiday.

The six chairs that made up the waiting area were already taken and the overflow spilled out into the lobby. Customers leaned up against the walls and counters clutching debit cards that didn't work, overdraft notices that had to be a mistake, and documents in need of notarizing. Children with sticky hands and runny noses ran in circles, scribbled in crayon on the tiled floor, and swung on the velvet ropes designed to corral patrons into an orderly traffic pattern. Babies bawled, people complained in stage whispers, and somewhere in the mix a yappy little dog barked out what sounded like Morse code.

"How nice of you to save me a seat," I said to no one in particular. Six people looked up at me. Four of them couldn't vacate their chairs fast enough. The other two were either out-of-towners or had a penchant for living dangerously.

I waited until almost noon to push my shopping cart into Anthony Bonacorsi's office. His desk was devoid of personal items. No knickknacks. No pictures of a loving wife and adoring little ones. Not even a potted plant that depended on him for its survival, just a pile of promotional T-shirts and a business card holder.

"Mrs. Kavanagh." He greeted me with a well-rehearsed smile. "I don't usually work Saturdays, but since you mentioned on the phone you'd be opening an account with a sizable deposit, I made an exception. Please, take a seat."

I looked down at the two upholstered chairs and waited until he sheepishly pulled one out for me and returned to his seat. "In the future, Mr. Bonacorsi, a gentleman stands when a lady enters the room."

"I, I . . ."

I let him swing in the breeze while I waited for an apology that never materialized beyond his stammer. "Along with opening an account, I'd like to rent a large safe-deposit box." I pulled a stack of savings bonds from my purse—an old five-thousand-dollar bond on top and two inches of card stock cut to size beneath, bound together with an elastic band. I made sure he got a good look at the bond before adding, "Last time I checked, these were worth over three-quarters of a million dollars."

"Really." He tugged at the cuffs of his starched white shirt and straightened his back, eyeing the stack. "Well then, we can open the account today and cash the bonds on Tuesday for deposit, if that's to your liking? Can I get you a cup of coffee? Tea, maybe?"

"The bonds are for the safe-deposit box. I'll be opening a Christmas Club today."

"But . . . ?" He looked from the bonds to me. "You said you'd be making a sizable deposit into an account."

226

"Did I? I meant I'd be making a sizeable deposit into a safe-deposit box. On second thought, forget about the club. I'll just rent the box."

He looked at me, the clock, mumbled something under his breath, and handed me a rental agreement and contract card.

"Read the agreement and bring the signed card back on Tuesday." He motioned to the door.

"I'll do it now." I smiled and pulled a retractable cobalt blue fountain pen with gold trim from my purse. "And I'll take that cup of tea."

"We're out."

I exhaled a sigh of disappointment. "I find I write so much slower when parched."

"Ice water with a slice of lemon, maybe?" he asked, heavy on the sarcasm.

"Cucumber." I scrunched up my nose and shoulders. "Two paper-thin slices with the peel removed. And a straw, a paper one." I coughed and motioned him to the door.

"Again, we're out."

If the Academy Awards included a category for Most Protracted Transaction, I would have taken home an Oscar. I read and reread every line of the three-page agreement, mulled over the terms, and asked so many hypothetical questions even I was getting annoyed. Finally, I signed my name. I made a face at the puddle of ink the pen left on the card, shrugged my shoulders, and inched it across the desk. And then there was the matter of paying for the box. I lost my place four times counting out fifty ones from the wad of cash I pulled from my purse. I pretended not to notice when Anthony Bonacorsi snatched up my fountain pen along with the cash.

"When you're done, Mr. Bonacorsi, I'd like to place the bonds in the box."

"Of course, you would." He looked at me as if I were fresh dog shit on the bottom of his best pair of shoes.

"Free T-shirts!" I squealed, grabbing one from his desk along with a business card.

My shopping cart clipped Anthony Bonacorsi's heels more times than could be considered accidental as I followed him to the vault. With all the fanfare of a funeral, he stabbed the master key into one of the safe-deposit box's locks, gave it a turn, and waited for me to do the same. Four exaggerated tries later, he handed me the box and tapped the face of his watch. "Make it quick. The branch closed twenty minutes ago."

With a shrug, I placed the aluminum box inside the cart and took my own sweet time wheeling it into a privacy room. Closing the door behind me, I placed the empty safe-deposit box on the small counter and said a silent prayer for Deirdre.

Ten minutes later, I peeled off my gloves, dropped them inside the box, and secured the lid. I used disinfectant towelettes to wipe down everything I came in contact with and disposed of them in the wastepaper barrel before returning the safe-deposit box to an agitated Anthony Bonacorsi. You did what you had to, I told myself, noticing the blue Rorschach bleeding through the breast pocket of his white linen shirt from the fountain pen.

I'd have to have been deaf not to hear the "Good riddance" he muttered under his breath as he unlocked the bank's front door and let me out. I should've returned the sentiment knowing come Wednesday his sense of smell will be a bit off. By next Saturday he'll swear something is wrong, but won't quite be able to put his finger on it. Give it another week and he'll be turning green at the gills. Every day it'll get worse. He'll lose his appetite, feel nauseated and lightheaded to the point where he'll be physically ill.

I parked Gavin's old Chevelle in the driveway of my double-decker on Dexter Street, and wheeled my shopping cart across the street to the unmarked police car. The cops were more than grateful for the bag of day-old doughnuts. I doubt they'll remember the gesture a few weeks from now when Anthony Bonacorsi figures out what I've done. By the time a sheriff obtains a court order, it'll have gotten so bad Anthony Bonacorsi will wish he were dead. When they finally open the safe-deposit box, I doubt Anthony Bonacorsi or anyone else present will miss the less-than-subtle message.

When the cops come pounding on my door demanding an explanation, I'll look mortified. On the verge of tears, I'll write a check for the box being drilled. For the life of me, I won't remember how the fish heads I'd bought for stock ended up wrapped in a bank T-shirt in the safe-deposit box along with Anthony Bonacorsi's business card, or why I still had the saving bonds I could've sworn I'd put inside it. I'll blame it all on a senior moment. I'll suddenly feel dizzy, my knees will threaten to buckle, and I'll need help getting to a chair. I'll chastise myself for getting old, let the cops see themselves out, and then wait for the next phone call or knock at my door, by someone in need of a favor.

But for now, I'll take a long, hot soak in the tub to wash the deed from my skin, before cooking a braised corned beef with colcannon and Brussels sprouts, and an apple cake for dinner with Deirdre. Granted, a simple shepherd's pie would have done, but the woman was a saint who up until now had never asked anyone for a favor.

I did Deirdre Cleary the biggest favor of her life today. I did everything she'd asked for short of leaving the mortal sin of murder on her soul. It might take awhile, but eventually she'll see it my way. ❖

The Gentleman Burglar

Leslie Wheeler

Lenox, Massachusetts, June 1901

Emily Grey peered up at the "cottage" looming above her. A leviathan of stone and shingles, three-storied with brooding, eyebrowed windows and turrets like devil's horns, it threatened to swallow her up like Jonah into the whale. And spew her out again when it discovered she wasn't the right kind of morsel? Squaring her shoulders, Emily rang the bell.

The butler frowned as he ushered her into a huge main hall. Could he tell at a glance that she didn't belong in this summer colony of the wealthy and powerful? She'd been invited to the weekend house party at Greenleigh only because a distant relative had a tenuous connection to the Four Hundred, as the elite of New York society were called. Or the butler might be frowning because, having missed the earlier train to Lenox, she was unfashionably late for a dinner that had begun at the fashionably late hour of eight?

"Shall I show you to your room, miss?" the butler inquired after he'd taken her wrap. Clearly, he expected her to retire there to repair her toilette after the journey on the cars.

"No, I would like to go in to dinner."

The butler's disapproving look deepened. "Very well."

On the threshold of the dining room, Emily hesitated. Dwarfed by the sheer size of Greenleigh from the outside, now she was dazzled by the scene that lay before her. Lit by a massive chandelier, the long table gleamed with silverware, fine china, and crystal set on white linen. Her hosts, Mr. and Mrs. Horace Schuyler, were seated at opposite ends, with more than a dozen guests—some known to Emily, others not—on either side. The ladies were resplendent in silk and lace, their Worth gowns from Paris a rainbow of color, in pleasing contrast to the black and white of the gentlemen's evening dress.

Emily touched the frayed lace at her throat. How shabby she must appear to these ladies in a gown that was neither from Paris, nor new, but a hand-me-down. She could only hope that her emerald necklace made up for some of the deficiencies in her appearance. The room had buzzed with conversation before the butler announced her arrival. Now it was silent, and all eyes were upon her.

"Delighted to see you, my dear," Mrs. Schuyler said with a tight smile. She nodded at a liveried footman, who showed Emily to her place at the table. Conversation resumed.

"Do you suppose he's come back?" Natalie Thornton, seated across from Emily, asked, picking up the thread of a previous discussion.

Emily's brow furrowed. "Who?"

"The Gentleman Burglar, of course!" Natalie replied with an impatient toss of her jet-black curls. "Haven't you heard the news?"

"No. I only just arrived."

"There was a burglary last night at Pinecrest," Robert, the Schuyler's elder son, informed Emily. "Jewelry belonging to the ladies in the house was stolen, as were various gentlemen's money and watches."

Fair, with blond hair and a pale wisp of a mustache, Robert was a Harvard graduate and a serious, scholarly sort. Emily had heard that the squint in his blue eyes stemmed from the amount of time he spent poring over old volumes.

"Oh dear." She fingered her emerald necklace nervously. "Why do you think it might be the Gentleman Burglar?" she asked Natalie. "Wasn't he arrested and sent to prison years ago?"

"The man who was arrested may not have been the real Gentleman Burglar," Harry Prince, seated two places down from Emily, chimed in. "It's also possible the current burglar is a copycat. According to several witnesses, he resembles the burglar of the past, in that he is more than six feet tall and wore a derby hat pulled down over his forehead, with a piece of black silk covering the lower part of his face. Most important of all, he spoke to the ladies in soft, soothing tones. They were so mesmerized by his voice and good manners that they willingly gave up their valuables, though one of the men put up a struggle."

"What fools those women were to let themselves be robbed just because the thief had a pleasing voice and appeared to be a gentleman," Natalie scoffed. "If it had been me, I should have fought him like Mrs. Field did the burglar of the nineties, rather than lose my darlings."

Natalie caressed the lustrous pearls that formed a wide collar around her neck. Then, her fingers traced the single strand of similarly lustrous pearls that dangled almost to her waist, before coming to rest on the diamond brooch above her left breast. She turned the brooch so that it caught the light and sparkled brilliantly.

"Bravo!" Harry Prince cried, raising his wine glass in a toast. "I admire your spirit, Miss Thornton."

"Thank you, Mr. Prince." Lowering her head, Natalie regarded him through the fringe of her dark lashes, a coy smile on her lips.

Emily's eyes darted from one to the other. "What did Mrs. Field do?"

"You don't know the story?" Harry twisted one end of his mustache in the manner of a stage villain, a part Emily thought he seemed well suited for with his dark hair and eyes, and swarthy complexion, rumored to come from the pirate blood in his ancestry.

"No."

"Mrs. Field lay in bed when the burglar entered her room. In his search for valuables, he bent over her and seized the watch she'd hidden under her pillow. To prevent him from making off with it, Mrs. Field grabbed him by the neck and clung to him. She continued to hold on, even though her feet left the ground as he stood, and he stuck the barrel of his gun into her forehead and threatened to shoot her."

Emily gasped. "B—but she could have been killed! Surely, no watch was worth that."

"It was to Mrs. Field," Harry said. "Fortunately for her, the thief didn't fire, but heaved her off and escaped through the rear door. Still, it cannot be denied that she showed remarkable courage."

Emily shook her head with disbelief. "I should never have done as she."

"Of course, you wouldn't, you little mouse," Natalie said.

Robert Schuyler threw Natalie a severe look. "In my opinion, Mrs. Field acted rashly by resisting. The sensible thing would have been to let him have the watch. After all, in cases like that, discretion is often the better part of valor." He concluded with an approving glance at Emily. She gave him a shy smile of gratitude.

"You *would* say that," Harry shot back.

Robert seemed about to retort, when his mother broke in. "What I don't understand is why the current burglar—whoever he is—chose Pinecrest over Greenleigh to rob. Did he mean to imply that our jewels are paste, our artwork copies, our coffers empty, when that is far from the case? And where else but at Greenleigh would you find a grandfather clock that not only strikes the hours and half hours, but chimes the quarter hours just like Big Ben. I feel quite insulted by—"

As if on cue, clock bells from somewhere in the house rang out the quarter hour. Mrs. Schuyler's ample bosom swelled with pride. Others at the table seemed embarrassed by the blatant boasting.

"Mother," Robert chided gently.

"That's enough about burglaries," Mr. Schuyler blustered from the other end of the table. "Let us talk about more pleasant subjects."

Although the discussion turned to happier topics, Emily barely touched her food. Her hands kept traveling to her necklace, as if to assure herself it was still there.

After dinner when Emily and the other guests had gathered in the drawing room, Harry Prince approached her, a glass of brandy in hand. "If I may speak frankly, Miss Grey, you don't look well. I hope it's not because of the burglary at Pinecrest. If so, rest assured the police have the matter well in hand. A nighttime watch has been set up around Lenox, in case the burglar is still in the vicinity. Which appears unlikely, given the fact that the injured parties have offered a reward of several hundred dollars for his arrest."

"Thank you for telling me," Emily said. "However, it doesn't put me entirely at ease. The burglar may still elude the police and strike again. And should he strike here at Greenleigh, my necklace would be his for the taking. I would be far too frightened to defend myself, even though I can ill afford to lose it. It's not only my most valuable possession, but a family heirloom, passed down to me by my great-great grandmother."

"I would hate to see you lose it then," Harry said. "But perhaps I can do something to prevent that."

Emily looked at him with surprise. "What would you do?"

Harry swirled the golden-brown liquid in his glass thoughtfully. "Why not give me the necklace for safekeeping?"

Emily's hand flew to her throat. She took a step backward, brushing against Robert Schuyler, standing nearby. "Give you the necklace? I—I'm not sure that would be wise."

"Why not?" Harry said, moving closer. "It's only for the weekend. Then, if the burglar does appear, I can fight him off."

Emily gazed up at him. He had to be at least six feet tall and towered over her. Nevertheless, she held her ground. "Thank you for the offer, but it's better if the necklace stays with me," she demurred. "I wouldn't want to put you in danger on my account."

Harry gave her a searching look. "Is that the real reason you don't want me to hold it for you?"

"What makes you think there's another reason?"

"It could be that you don't trust me," Harry said with a mischievous glint in his eyes.

"Well, I—" Emily began.

"Miss Grey is right not to trust you," Robert Schuyler intervened. "After all, you might use her precious necklace to pay your gambling debts."

Harry scowled. "Speak for yourself, Robert. Lady Luck hasn't exactly smiled on you lately."

Emily glanced from one man to the other. Both were tall and attractive, but of the two Robert was the taller, Harry the handsomer.

Robert's blue eyes narrowed as he stepped forward to answer for Emily. "Maybe not, but at least I'm able to make good my debts, whereas you—"

"Enough," Harry cut him off. "This conversation serves no purpose but to further alarm Miss Grey, who is already agitated. I was only trying to be helpful, but since my services aren't wanted, I'll seek more agreeable company." Downing his brandy, he sauntered off toward Natalie, who flashed her diamond brooch, as if signaling him to join her.

"Good riddance," Robert muttered at Harry's departing figure. Turning back to Emily, he said, "I'm sorry if I've alarmed you, but I felt you should be warned about him."

"I'm glad you did," Emily said. "I didn't feel comfortable letting him hold my necklace, and what you said about his gambling debts reinforces that. But what am I to do? If the burglar visits tonight, mouse that I am, I'll be easy prey. Whether he does or not, I won't sleep a wink. Maybe I should spend the night at the Curtis Hotel, or even take the late train back to the city."

"No, you mustn't leave," Robert said. "You'll be safe here at Greenleigh."

"How will you ensure that? Post guards around the house?"

Robert placed a finger on his upper lip while he considered this. "I have a better idea," he said finally. "Give me your necklace and I will lock it in our safe with the family valuables." He held out a hand, palm up, as if he expected Emily to surrender it on the spot.

As she had with Harry, Emily backed away. "No, if I'm to part with my most prized possession, I must see it placed in your safe with my own eyes."

"You mean you don't trust me either?" Robert looked abashed.

"I'm sorry, Robert, but I must see it secured in your safe," Emily insisted.

Robert sighed. "Very well."

Emily lay awake, listening to doors being opened and shut and goodnights exchanged, as the last of her fellow guests retired to their rooms. There was a tinkle of flirtatious laughter she recognized as coming from Natalie Thornton, followed by a deep chuckle from Harry Prince. Then it was quiet, the only sounds the occasional whisper of wind in the trees and the distant bark of a dog.

A watchdog? What a pity the dog at Greenleigh was too old and deaf to alert them to possible danger. Still, a watchman might be about. Emily arose and looked out the window. It was a clear June night with a nearly full moon and a generous sprinkling of stars. Her room was at the front of the house, so she could look down onto the drive and the road beyond. She caught a flicker of light among the trees on one side of the drive. A watchman's lantern? There was another flicker in a different spot, then another and another, each in a different location. Emily smiled. Fireflies never failed to delight her.

Returning to bed, she glanced at the clock on the bedside table, its face barely visible in the moonlight from the window. She thought it said half past eleven, but wasn't sure until she heard the much-vaunted grandfather clock, on the landing above the main staircase, strike the half hour.

As midnight approached, Emily became more and more uneasy. She sat bolt upright on the bed, every nerve straining. To calm herself, she began silently reciting Tennyson's "The Lady of Shalott," which she'd committed to memory as a girl. She'd reached the third stanza that began with "Four gray walls, and four gray towers/Overlook a space of flowers" when she heard muffled footsteps in the hall.

Who could it be? Another guest who like her was having a restless night or . . . ? Throwing on her dressing gown, she crept to the door. It creaked as she opened it. She froze, heart pounding. Peeking through the crack, she glimpsed the tall, shadowy figure of a man near the end of the hall. He stood with his back to her, so she couldn't make out who it was, but at least he couldn't see her either. After what seemed an eternity, the man disappeared around the corner.

Emily tiptoed down the hall after him. When she reached the corner, she stopped and peered around it, which gave her a view of the landing and the stairs below. The man was nowhere to be seen. Perhaps he'd crossed the landing and gone into the other wing. Then again, maybe there was no man; maybe what she'd seen was a figment of her overwrought imagination. She should return to her room. No, she couldn't rest until she found out who it was.

Emily passed swiftly across the landing, aided by the light from a large Tiffany window at the top of the stairs, and into the dim corridor beyond. Although she felt her way through the corridor, she nevertheless bumped into a small table with a decorative bowl on top. She grabbed table and bowl before they crashed to the floor. She stood stock-still, waiting for doors to open and alarmed guests to poke their heads out.

Nothing happened. Emily continued on, more slowly and carefully than before, until she came to another corridor veering off from the one she was on. Should she stay on the straight and narrow path, or explore this one? After various twists and turns, the second corridor brought her to a window that looked out on the gardens behind the house. To the left of the window, she spied a narrow door. Opening it, she saw a staircase leading up to the third floor, where the servants' quarters must be. Could the man she'd spotted have been a servant? Or was it some demon that had descended from its turret home to lead her astray?

Emily's spine tingled. Alone in the rear of this monstrous house with its maze of corridors, she was suddenly afraid. She should have never ventured so far from her room. At any moment the demon she'd trailed might leap out from the shadows and attack. She dashed back the way she'd come, stopping only when she reached the fork. Which way, oh, which way? Her head spun. She placed a hand on the wall to steady herself. When her brain finally stopped its frantic whirl, she realized that having turned left the first time, she needed to reverse directions.

Emily could have cried out with joy when she saw the landing above the main staircase. In a few moments, she'd be safely back in her room. Bells clanged. So loud they might have been fire bells in the night. But not loud enough to rouse whoever was snoring in the corridor beyond. The snores continued, uninterrupted. Was there a fire? Emily glanced around. No smoke billowed from anywhere in the house. No flames licked greedily at the furnishings.

Of course not, silly, Emily chided herself. The noise came from the grandfather clock chiming the quarter hour. Then she saw something that made her pulse race. In the great hall below, a pale strip of light flickered under the door to the library, where the safe was hidden behind a portrait of a dour-looking Schuyler ancestor! The figure she'd glimpsed earlier was no phantom, but a real person. Someone who probably shouldn't be there at this time of night.

Pulling herself together, Emily crept soundlessly down the stairs toward the library. Her eyes trained on the door, she didn't see the shadowy shape lying on the carpet a short distance away. The old deaf watchdog groaned when she tripped over him.

The library door swung open. A tall man in evening dress stood before her. Robert! Emily's mouth fell open with shock. He seemed just as surprised to see her.

"Miss Grey, what are you doing here?"

"I heard footsteps and feared it was an intruder."

Robert stared at her incredulously. "If it was an intruder, weren't you afraid of being harmed?"

Emily's gaze dropped to her slippered feet. "I guess I'm braver than I realized." Meeting his eyes again, she said, "Why are you in the library?"

"I—I couldn't sleep and came downstairs to fetch a book."

"From the safe?" Emily gestured toward the wall behind Robert, where the portrait had been moved, exposing the safe.

"I thought I might as well check it while I was here."

Emily clutched her throat, where her necklace had been. "Everything's still there, I hope."

"Oh yes, nothing's been taken. I'll put the portrait back in place." Turning away, he did so.

"Did you find your book?" Emily asked, following him into the room.

Robert made a cursory search of the shelves and a pile of books on the desk. "No, it doesn't seem to be here. I'll go for my walk now."

"You're going out? Is that why you're fully dressed?"

Robert adjusted his bow tie. "That's right. I decided that if I couldn't find my book I'd get some air. While I'm at it, I'll check the perimeters, in case that burglar fellow is lurking outside. One can't be too careful, you know."

"Of course. Don't let me stop you." Emily stepped aside to let him pass.

"After you, Miss Grey." Tipping his head slightly, Robert motioned toward the door. Emily passed into the entry hall, Robert in her wake. They stood for a moment regarding each other. Then Robert bade her good night and left the house. Emily went to a window by the front door.

Moonlight shone on Robert's tall figure as he strode down the drive. At a bend in the drive he turned and glanced back at the house. Then he vanished from sight.

Emily stood at her post, listening to the low rumble of the snorer upstairs. The grandfather clock struck midnight, then the quarter-hour chimes rang. When these had faded, and the only sound was that of the snorer, she left the window with a sigh.

The next morning, Emily was awakened by a commotion from below. Pulling on her dressing gown, she ran into the hall.

"My darlings are gone! My pearls and my diamond brooch!" Natalie Thornton's voice rose above those of other distraught women.

Emily hurried downstairs. "What happened? Did the burglar come during the night?"

"Yes!" Natalie cried.

"Into your room?" Emily demanded, wide eyed.

"No! Into the library, where the safe is. When I heard Robert had locked your emerald necklace there, I decided my darlings should go in also."

"My jewelry, too!" wailed another woman.

"And mine! And mine!" Others joined the chorus of dismay.

"It's all your fault!" Natalie stabbed an accusing finger at Emily. "If you hadn't made such a fuss about your stupid necklace, Robert wouldn't have put it in the safe, we wouldn't have followed suit, and none of this would have happened."

"My necklace is gone, too?" Emily's voice was somber.

"Of course!" Natalie flared. "Why should you be spared when the rest of us were robbed?"

"Ladies, please." Robert joined them, his face ashen. "If anyone's to blame, it's I. It never occurred to me that the burglar would try the safe, since that wasn't how he operated the other night at Pinecrest."

"Perhaps there were two separate burglars," Harry Prince suggested lightly. "Or the Pinecrest burglar decided to conduct his business here in a different manner. Which is a pity, because in so doing, he deprived Miss Thornton of the opportunity to demonstrate her valor in resisting him."

"You're taking this rather calmly." Natalie turned on him. "Weren't you robbed also?"

"Indeed, I was," Harry replied in the same light, careless tone. "But I've lost so many times at the gaming table, I've become philosophical."

Natalie glared at him, and seemed about to say more, when there was a loud knocking at the door, and the butler ushered in the police.

Refusing the porter's offer of help, Emily lugged her bags onto the last car of the late evening train to New York. She took a seat in the rear, though she could have sat anywhere. Except for one other passenger, she had the car to herself, her fellow travelers preferring the front cars. After a day of hand-wringing, tears, and recriminations at Greenleigh, combined with intense questioning by police, she was happy to be alone.

But not for long. After the conductor passed through the car to collect the tickets, the other passenger rose and approached her. "Excuse me, Miss, but is that place taken?" he asked politely, pointing to the space next to her. Emily shook her head.

She and her companion were silent on the short ride from Lenox to Stockbridge, then to Great Barrington. Once the train was under way again, and no other passengers had joined them in the car, he leaned toward Emily and said in a low voice, "So, my little mouse, are you ready to leave your hole now?"

Emily sighed. "If I must, Harry."

"Good. Then let me commend you on your performance last night and today. You played the damsel in distress to a tee."

"I wish I could say the same for you," Emily retorted.

"What's the matter? Wasn't I superb as the carefree, eminently eligible bachelor with an eye for the ladies?"

"Yes, but did you have to drink so much at dinner and afterward that you went to bed in a drunken stupor, completely missing the stroke-of-midnight signal to rob the safe? Wasn't it enough that I gave you the combination without having to do the job myself?"

"You could have roused me," Harry grumbled.

"And risked waking up the entire household? Even if I had awakened you, I couldn't be certain you were capable of staying upright, let alone committing a robbery."

Harry shifted uncomfortably in his seat. "All right, you've made your point and I apologize." Then stretching his long legs in a languid manner, he said, "But to quote the Bard: 'all's well that ends well.' "

"It didn't end well for Robert."

"No, but it was always our plan to set him up as the burglar. He knew the combination and personally deposited all the valuables in the safe. When you caught him in the library and told the police about it, he played right into our hands."

"I wonder if he would have made off with the contents of the safe if I hadn't surprised him," Emily said.

"We'll never know, will we?"

"I suppose not. Still, I can't help feeling a tad sorry he was arrested."

"I wouldn't worry about him," Harry said. "He's sure to get off and once he's free, he and his family will be telling thrilling tales about the burglary to their dying days. His mother won't feel slighted anymore, and Robert will have better success with the ladies, who, as we all know, prefer dashing fellows like me to serious, studious types like him. In my opinion, we've done the Schuylers a great favor."

"You *would* say that, you old pirate." Emily gave him a playful peck on the cheek. He leaned in for more. She smiled. "Later, Harry, later." ❖

By the Book

Tilia Klebenov Jacobs

Officer, I had no way of knowing that book was stolen. And why on earth did you arrest Zarita? She's just a kid going through a rough patch. Say, would you mind taking off these handcuffs?

Well, how about loosening them, then?

(You always were a piece of work, Kevin.)

What? Nothing.

Very well, then, here's how it happened. Or should I say, "went sideways"?

All right, then, I won't. But first things first. "Stolen" is, I think, a bit harsh. "Misplaced" might be better. I found it on the shelf when I was making my display of this year's banned books.

Oh, yes, it's something I do every spring. Everything goes on that big table by the library doors, all cross-indexed by Supreme Court decisions, and every book gets a darling little tag explaining where it was banned and why. I started doing it a year or two after you graduated.

And, of course, I was using the White List, you know, from PURE.

Oh, Kevin, you know PURE. It stands for Parents United for Responsible Education. They're that group that tried to get the legislature to put cameras in every classroom so they could monitor the teachers. As I recall, they didn't want the science teachers teaching evolution or the history teachers discussing slavery, and they were seriously miffed about any number of things in the English Department. I believe your mother is a founding member. How is she, by the way?

Well, you can tell her how much I love the White List. It's my go-to for literary depravity, though I must say I was a little disappointed that *A Wrinkle in Time* didn't make the cut this year. Still, that made room for *Beloved* in the top ten. One of these years we really ought to have a betting pool on the rankings. Such fun!

Yes, Kevin, this is entirely relevant.

I pulled *Harry Potter and the Philosopher's Stone* off the shelf—it clocked in at number sixty-three this year—and right away I saw that something was off. The label on the spine was misnumbered, for one thing, and then there was the title. The American version is *Sorcerer's Stone*, you see, so this had to be either Canadian or British. It certainly didn't belong to the school library. Then I opened it up to check the copyright, and gosh all hemlock if it wasn't a first edition! Can you imagine? I was shaking like Jell-O in a high wind.

What do you mean, what's the big deal?

Kevin, dear, a first edition of *Harry Potter and the Philosopher's Stone* can be worth well over a hundred thousand dollars if it's in good condition, and this one was.

Well, Kevin, I'm not surprised you don't know the value of a book.

I mean that not too many people know how truly valuable first editions can be. Why? What did you think I meant?

But there was more. The flyleaf was inscribed, "To Monica from Luis. You are my magic." Isn't that lovely? So naturally I knew right away whose it was. I tell you, I felt like Miss Marple.

Why, Kevin, you remember Monica. Monica Rubio? She was a year or two ahead of you.

Well, that's odd, because I distinctly remember that you asked her to prom. But of course, by the time prom season rolled around you two had split and she was seeing Luis. Honestly, I never thought he was the right fellow for her, but after you left I guess she was lonely. Well, they had one of those tempestuous, on-again, off-again romances, and a few years after graduation they got married, and then a few years after *that* they welcomed lovely little Zarita. She's a junior this year. Such a sweet kid. She works at the library Tuesdays and Thursdays after school, and just before I found the *Harry Potter* book, she'd texted me to say she was running late because she had a meeting with her AP US History teacher. APUSH, the kids call it. Honestly, if she'd been on time I suppose none of this would have happened, because I'd just have given her the book to take home to her mother. But late she was, so I pulled out the student directory and called Monica. She put me on speaker, which turned out to be very unfortunate because Luis heard me too. Next thing you know, there's an unholy amount of barking and bawling at the other end of the line, and the phone went dead. I guess they jumped into their respective cars and came tearing over here.

Well, of course my first thought was for Zarita, because I was afraid they'd all three arrive at the same time. She's been so miserable over her parents' divorcing. You remember what that's like, don't you, Kevin? Everything you thought was solid just explodes under your feet. But even with all that chaos at home, she's never missed a day of work or showed up late without letting me know first.

Well, wouldn't you know, just then she walked in, still carrying that leaden tome they use for APUSH. *American Pageant*, it's called. Do you know how much that thing weighs? I have to shelve the extras, and it gives me back spasms every fall. Well, when Zarita saw the copy of *Harry Potter* on my desk, she went as white as that banned book list. That's when I knew she was somehow responsible. So I asked her, and she told me all about it. Basically, she was hoping that if she took it hostage, so to speak, she could force Monica and Luis to talk things out. And because she'd just read "The Purloined Letter" in English class, she concluded the library was the best place to stash it.

Well, dear, I didn't say it was a very *good* plan. But children of divorcing parents don't always make the best decisions, as I'm sure you'll agree. And in any case, I still don't see why you arrested her. It's hardly stealing if the book comes from her house, is it? You'd be hard pressed to make a legal case, it seems to me.

Kevin. I'd be happy to read whatever this is you're shoving under my nose, but it's very difficult with handcuffs on, and in any case I need my reading glasses. So if you could just kindly—

Ah, that's much better. Those things really do pinch, don't they? You know, I'm half-tempted to rub my wrists the way the perps do on TV shows. Now, where are my glasses? Let's see what this says.

"Purported equitable ownership of the house as well as the contents thereunto appertaining, notwithstanding the condition of divorce immediately sought, agreed to, and ongoing, resulting in inter alia, replevin, trespass to chattels, conspiracy to commit trespass to chattels . . ."

Kevin, dear, you don't have any idea what this means, do you?

(No, you don't. I saw your verbal scores.)

I saw. Yes, I saw the point you're trying to make. Ownership is ownership, and property is property, yes? Zarita shouldn't have taken the book. Even when your parents are breaking down every atom of their household in the midst of the implosion of their marriage, stealing is stealing.

Perhaps. But in this case, I think there's a little more to it than that.

Well, the larger point is that right now there's a girl sitting in your cruiser, bawling her eyes out. She's a nice kid in a rotten situation. Why ruin her life?

Besides, prom is next weekend. Remember how important that was to you, even though Monica went with Luis? Now, *that* was a prom to remember. Heavens, the gym looked so lovely. And of course, that was also the night Luis's car exploded.

I'm not surprised you remember it, dear, seeing as it was you who reported it. Or anyway, you were just about to when we ran into each other, almost literally as I recall. I'd chaperoned enough proms by that point to know the best make-out spots, so I was doing a sweep of the hallways when you came tearing round that corner. You said there was a car fire in the school parking lot, and you were looking for a phone to call 911. I remember thinking you must have gotten dangerously close to it because you simply *reeked* of lighter fluid. So I called, and by the time I was off the phone word must have gotten out because the gym was empty and everyone was out in the parking lot placing bets on which tire was going to detonate first. Heavens, Luis was in a *state*, especially when the air bags deployed. And melted. They looked just like enormous marshmallows, if you recall, though the smell was something else entirely. You know, I've often thought that night cemented his and Monica's relationship, because she was right there, comforting him through his grief and rage.

And of course your mother was there too, seeing as she was also a chaperone. I think she was even more upset than Luis. She kept raving about kids today, and how the flames of the car were a portent of the eternal fire that would surely await whoever was responsible. I thought that was a bit histrionic, to be honest, and I guess you did, too, to judge by the look on your face. You looked positively ill.

Where was I? Oh, yes—Zarita had just told me about nicking the book, when Monica and Luis arrived. The next few seconds were like being inside a hornet's nest someone's just kicked. Zarita was crying and saying, "You care more about that book than you do about me!" and both her parents were scrabbling for it. It was still on my desk where I'd left it, not knowing any better. Luis got to it first and held it out of Monica's reach. He was shouting, "I gave this to my wife, and you're not my wife!" I could tell he was going to rip it to petals, and I guess Monica could too because she was sobbing and saying, "Don't—it's her college fund!" Well, Luis either didn't hear or didn't care, because he grabbed a handful of pages. That's when Monica lunged—for him or the book I don't know, because Luis shoved her pretty hard. She fell backward onto Zarita, and both of them hit the table and knocked over the display, and next thing you know, they'd disappeared under a pile of depraved literature. I thought that would give Luis pause, but instead he started kicking at whatever bits of Monica that he could still see. It was pretty clear to me that he wasn't going to stop at anything, so I grabbed *The American Pageant* and clonked him with it.

That's right, Zarita's history textbook. Luis didn't lose consciousness, no matter what he might have told you, but he did drop the *Harry Potter* book, and he did stop attacking his wife. That makes it a win, in my opinion. Plus, it's the best use *American Pageant* has ever been put to, if you want my thoughts on the matter. That is one monster of a book—almost seven pounds! Fortunately, I work out. I'm at high risk for osteoporosis, what with my age and family history, so weight-bearing exercise is—

Oh, yes, well. The next thing that happened was you walked into the library, swinging open both doors like Burt Lancaster in some old Western, and clapped me and Zarita in irons.

So here we are. My question is, what happens next?

Oh, I don't mean for me, dear. I mean for Zarita. Her parents are frantic about her. It's probably the first thing they've agreed on in years. You certainly do have a knack for pushing those two together.

Yes, you could take her downtown to some nasty holding cell, and you could keep her overnight, and you could have her appear before a judge tomorrow. But what good would that do?

Kevin. Look at me.

Don't you think a confused, unhappy kid with difficult parents might deserve a second chance?

Kevin? Are you all right?

Yes, I'm fine. You can see that, can't you? I'm sure Zarita will be too, eventually.

Of course. Naturally, you needed to sort everything out. No, no hard feelings whatsoever.

I'll just be getting back to work now. And please do say hello to your mother for me. You know, I don't think I've spoken to her since the night of your prom. ❖

The Beauport Incident

Christine Bagley

Coming out of Gloucester Harbor, the boat passed Hammond Castle, a gloomy medieval structure made of rough granite. Scarlett remembered when she and Sarah had toured it years ago. The gory image in the dining room of St. Romanus having his tongue cut out was jarring. What kind of weirdo hangs a gruesome painting where he eats?

A cool day for August, the sky was anemic, glum and colorless. Whether it was the weather, or the anniversary of Sarah's death, Scarlett was in a somber mood. She'd hoped being out on the water would help but it only provoked sadness and loss.

Interrupting her thoughts, Captain Sanford's gravelly voice came over the loud speaker. "Okay, everybody, got our first sighting on your left: a humpback we call Spoon."

Scarlett looked to where a crowd had gathered. A gigantic, black mammal breached the water, its immensity and grace breathtaking. While everyone watched and snapped pictures, she figured it was a good time to use the bathroom.

When she came out, she froze.

A tall man with graying hair was lifting a small woman's body, and rolling it over the railing into the water. No one else was in sight. Scarlett backed into the bathroom and dialed 911 but couldn't get a signal. Sitting on the toilet, she put her head between her knees, shaking like a branch in a hurricane. Still distraught from Sarah's drowning, she'd just seen another woman about to drown twenty feet away. Raising the toilet seat, she threw up her lobster roll then leaned against the wall for support. From her backpack, she pulled out a bottle of water and popped a Xanax.

She knew she should tell the captain so he could call the authorities but she was afraid to go outside again. A few minutes later someone knocked on the door.

Was it him? Had he seen her? "In a minute," she said, trying to sound normal.

Ten minutes passed before she cracked the door and peeked out. He was gone. Cautiously, she made her way to the stairs, spotting him sitting in the galley reading a newspaper as if nothing had happened. What the . . . ?

On the point of hysteria, she raced upstairs to the bridge, falling down at the top. "Are you all right?" asked Captain Stanford.

"No! My name is Scarlett O'Hara, and I just saw a man throw his wife overboard."

"Your name is what?"

She'd had this reaction all her life, but was that all the guy could say? "Scarlett O'Hara. I just saw a man throw his wife overboard. No one else was around but me—but I know what I saw."

"What man?"

"He's sitting in the galley downstairs. A tall man with a navy windbreaker. Gray hair. His wife was petite with black hair, wearing a green sweater."

"You sure?"

Raising her voice, she said, "Of course, I'm sure! Why would I make something like that up?" She'd hoped the Xanax would have kicked in by now but she still felt panicky.

"I realize this must be upsetting for you but let's just try to keep calm, shall we?"

Gritting her teeth, she said, "I will keep calm when I see you stop this boat and start searching for the man's wife."

The captain broke out in a cold sweat, and wiped his face with a handkerchief.

"How do you know it was his wife?"

"I just assumed."

"Like you assumed he threw her overboard?"

Now she was yelling. "What is wrong with you? And why aren't you stopping this boat?"

"Because this is a very serious accusation, Miss O'Hara."

Scarlett watched as he slowly picked up the mic.

"Two weeks from retirement and now this," he muttered, his hand shaking. Clearing his throat, he said, "All staff report to the captain immediately."

Minutes later, five staffers appeared and Captain Sanford told them to look for a tall man with gray hair and a navy windbreaker.

"What's happening?" asked a staffer wearing a navy T-shirt with the *Whistling Whale I* logo.

"We think a woman might have gone overboard."

"You mean *thrown*," said Scarlett.

"Holy shit!" said the only female staffer.

"Holly. Keep your voice down," said the captain. "We don't want to alarm the passengers unnecessarily."

"*Unnecessarily?*" Scarlett hollered.

"Please, Miss O'Hara. We will locate this man and question him, and I will contact the Coast Guard."

Scarlett stamped her foot. "Stop the boat! What if she's out there flailing for her life?"

"I'm following standard safety procedures." But he still didn't stop the boat.

Startled, Scarlett watched the man she'd seen saunter up to the captain. A staffer smiled behind him like he'd just won the Big Tuna prize.

"Oh no. It's Mr. Beauport," said Holly.

"Leo, what's this about?"

The captain's eyes widened and his face turned bright red. He wiped his forehead. "Dear lord. Mr. Beauport, I'm so sorry, but this lady here says she saw you toss a woman overboard about fifteen minutes ago." He turned to Scarlett and asked, "Is this the man you saw, Miss O'Hara?"

"Yes."

"What?" asked Beauport. "What woman? I'm by myself enjoying my first day off in years."

"That's what this lady here alleges."

Turning to Scarlett, Beauport said, "Who the hell are you?"

Scarlett tried to appear confident, but her stomach was roiling like a storm at sea. "My name is Scarlett O'Hara, and I saw you lift a woman and throw her into the water. I was coming out of the bathroom when it happened.

"Scarlett O'Hara, huh?" Beauport gave her the once-over as if she was wearing a For Sale sign. "If that's true, which it's certainly not, why didn't you try to stop him?"

Scarlett glanced at the captain, who raised his eyebrows in a *Yeah, why didn't you?*

"Because, I was afraid you'd throw me over too."

"Miss O'Hara, this here is Harold Beauport, a well-known man in our community."

Scarlett was seething inside. Why was he defending Beauport? "Captain Sanford, are you going to stop the boat instead of standing there like a flagpole?"

Sanford closed his eyes and took a deep breath. He looked at Harold Beauport. Finally, he stopped the boat and radioed the Coast Guard. Another twenty minutes went by before they pulled up. Three uniformed guardsmen boarded the boat, and Scarlett hoped their leader wasn't going to give her a hard time too.

"Chief Petty Officer Rhys McGowan, Search and Rescue," said the senior officer, extending his hand to Sanford. His cap, with the silver and gold insignia, was pulled down to the top of his eyes. Scarlett judged him to be in his midfifties and very fit.

"Captain Leo Sanford, sir. This is Scarlett O'Hara, who claims this man, Mr. Harold Beauport, threw his wife overboard. Mr. Beauport says he was alone on the boat." Sanford exhaled loudly as if he'd just delivered the Gettysburg Address.

"When?"

" 'Bout thirty minutes ago."

"What exactly did you see, Miss O'Hara?"

"Wait—you believe her?" asked Beauport, stepping forward.

McGowan ignored him. "Miss O'Hara?"

"I saw Mr. Beauport lift a small woman with a green sweater up over the railing, and toss her into the water. I was so scared I backed into the bathroom. When I came out, he was gone."

Officer McGowan studied her for a long time, as Scarlett's expression pleaded with him to believe her. Her father often stared at her the same way to see if she was lying.

"Do you remember what else the woman was wearing?"

"White pants."

"Is there anything else—any small detail helps."

"She had black hair in a ponytail."

"Captain Sanford, any chance you recall a woman with that description?"

"Can't say I do, sir. But there's probably thirty people on the boat today."

"This is preposterous!" said Beauport at the top of his voice.

Officer McGowan continued. "How tall would you say she was?"

"She was petite, maybe my height."

"Weight?"

Scarlett shrugged. "A hundred ten?"

"Pocketbook?" continued Officer McGowan.

She paused. "Yes, a pink shoulder bag."

He turned to Harold Beauport. "What were you doing at the time, Mr. Beauport?"

Beauport got in McGowan's face. "Do you know who I am?"

"Mr. Beauport, I asked what you were doing at the time."

Beauport's right temple throbbed as he answered in a monotone. "I was standing at the bow. The captain announced a humpback portside. I turned but stayed put. No one was with me. I don't know what this lady is talking about."

"Miss O'Hara, can you remember any identifying landmarks near the area where you saw the woman fall in the water?"

"There was a small island with two lighthouses."

Both McGowan and Sanford said at the same time, "Thacher Island."

Turning to Sanford, McGowan said, "Turn the boat around and head back to Gloucester Harbor ASAP."

"This is outrageous!" said Beauport. "So help me God I'll have your job for this, McGowan."

"And get a list of the passengers to confirm the names match the people on board," McGowan added.

"Yessir."

Next, McGowan instructed his men to escort the boat back to the harbor. "Miss O'Hara, please come with me."

"Gladly," she said, rushing forward.

Holly Wilson had been a staffer on the *Whistling Whale I* for four years while raising her son. A single mom, she became pregnant right out of college. She'd known Scarlett O'Hara from Endicott College; everyone did because of her name. Holly felt bad for Scarlett because she'd lost her parents in a plane crash in her junior year. She'd moved in with an aunt, who hadn't even shown up for Scarlett's graduation. The only person Holly ever saw her with was Sarah Caulfield, who'd drowned last year. Holly heard Scarlett had a breakdown after Sarah's death, and took a leave of absence from her job as a teacher at Seaford Elementary.

She could tell Scarlett didn't recognize her but then they hadn't been close. Seeing her again, accusing Harold Beauport of murder, had made Holly question Scarlett's mental state. But why would she lie? Especially where a man like Harold Beauport was concerned.

When Rhys and Scarlett boarded the lifeboat, Rhys introduced her to the rest of the crew.

"What will they do about Harold Beauport?" Scarlett asked.

"He'll be questioned by the police and held until we find some evidence."

"What if we don't find any evidence?"

"Then it's your word against Beauport's."

"Oh great."

"What?"

"A year ago today, I was questioned about another drowning."

McGowan kept silent as the boat bumped and battled its way over the water. Scarlett had not talked about Sarah's death since it happened. Yet today, she felt the need to tell McGowan.

"I was with my friend who'd been challenged by this jock to jump off Xander's Quarry. She took him up on it, even when I begged her not to do it." Scarlett's voice broke, and she wiped her nose with the back of her hand. "She'd always been a daredevil especially with guys, you know? But then she just sprang into the air, freefalling into the pit like a cormorant. She hit a rock, and she never came back up." Scarlett shook her head. "There was nothing I could do." And then she burst out crying.

McGowan passed her a handkerchief. "I'm so sorry. I did read about it."

After a while she continued. "The police questioned me, and I was so hysterical they recommended a psychiatrist. I learned some ways to control my anxiety, and the doctor put me on medication. Now, here I am again, a witness to another drowning, and I'm probably not going to save her either."

"That's a whole lot of guilt you're hauling around," said McGowan.

Scarlett shrugged. "I can't help it. Anyway, why do you believe my story instead of Beauport's?"

"Instinct. And I know Harold Beauport."

"Meaning?"

"He's been avoiding jail time for years with expensive lawyers. He's nothing but a rich man's crook."

"Does Sanford know that?"

McGowan frowned. "Of course, but Harold Beauport owns Sanford's boat, *Whistling Whale I*. He also owns *II* and *III*."

"So even if Sanford smelled a rat, he might not say anything. Could he be in on it?"

"No. He's no Einstein but I don't see him covering for Beauport."

"How long can someone last in there?" she asked, tilting her head toward the ocean.

"Depends on the temperature of the water, how well she can swim, dehydration. How long before you reported the incident to Captain Sanford?" he asked.

"About ten minutes, maybe more. I'm not sure how long I hid in the bathroom."

"Then she's been in the water for approximately an hour. And the water temp right now is sixty-three degrees."

"Is that good?"

"Hard to say. She could have been pulled out to sea with the current. Most people lost at sea stay lost. Did you look in the water after you came out of the bathroom?"

"No. I ran right upstairs to the bridge."

It was comforting to Scarlett that McGowan took her seriously. He was very professional and respectful, and she trusted him. Again, she was reminded of her father's calm and knowing manner. They stopped talking while she considered the odds of the woman's survival.

The boat slowed as they reached Thacher Island.

"Is this where you saw Beauport throw the woman overboard?"

"Yes."

"Was she struggling?"

"She seemed to go over pretty easily. Why?"

"He might have drugged her." He stared at Thacher Island then back toward Rockport several times. "Petty Officer Johnson, call the station and get a couple of Jayhawks to fly over the area."

"Yessir."

They circumnavigated the immediate area, then widened the range. McGowan radioed Captain Sanford and asked if he'd matched the names with those who bought tickets. Sanford said he hadn't had time as he was too busy calming his passengers down.

"Have you asked if anyone saw a small dark-haired woman wearing a green sweater?"

"Ah . . . no sir, I didn't."

"Do it now, Captain," he said. Then he called the Coast Guard Command Center in Boston, which he kept in touch with for the next few hours.

"How long will you search?" Scarlett asked.

"Until we've exhausted every possibility. Most people are recovered within the first twenty-four hours unless they're dragged under and carried out to sea."

Scarlett shivered and McGowan handed her a blanket. She hoped that a green sweater or a pink pocketbook would turn up, anything that would prove what she saw was real. They looked up as two Jayhawks flew overhead, circling the island and vicinity. At one point, the orange and white helicopters hovered, and Scarlett thought they'd found something, but they moved on and her hopes took a dive.

A short time later, McGowan received a call and looked at her while he listened. "Will do," he said and hung up.

"The police want to talk to you," he said. "Be prepared." He contacted the Coast Guard Station and asked for a search and rescue replacement right away.

"Oh God, not again. Do I need a lawyer?"

"I doubt it. There's no body and no evidence of a crime. Beauport could sue you for slander but I think he'll just want it to go away."

Scarlett thought of taking another Xanax but didn't want to appear groggy during the questioning.

"Do you want me to go with you?"

She couldn't believe how nice he was. "Why would you do that, sir?"

"Because I've known those guys for years, and I don't want to see you drilled needlessly. And you don't have to call me sir. Call me Rhys."

"I would really like that . . . Rhys." She felt like a china doll, fragile and easily breakable. Lowering her head, she tried not to cry.

Holly checked the boat for any belongings left behind, when she spotted something shiny where Scarlett said she saw Mr. Beauport and that woman. Checking behind a cleat, she fished out a tiny anklet with the name *Sonia* engraved on a sliver of gold. Had it belonged to the woman who drowned? Holly bit her lower lip. Captain Sanford worked for Harold Beauport. If she showed the anklet to the captain, would he realize it might be evidence against Mr. Beauport? Would he turn it in to the police, or would he give it to Mr. Beauport? Holly needed her job. She had a small son to raise with no help from an absent father. Unsure what to do, she put the anklet in her pocket and quickly left the boat.

At the police station, Scarlett was introduced to Sergeant Mike Foster, who remembered her from Sarah's drowning. "Another drowning, Scarlett?" he asked.

"Easy, Mike. I believe her," said Rhys. "I'm waiting for more info from Sanford."

"You'll wait till Christmas for that good-for-nothing."

"Where's Beauport?"

"He's in a cell but I'll have to release him once the ambulance chaser shows up."

"What's he saying?" Scarlett asked.

Sergeant Foster looked at Rhys, and Rhys looked at Scarlett.

"That you're a mental case and belong in a nuthouse," said the sergeant.

"Figures," said Rhys.

"You saw Mr. Beauport throw a woman overboard on Sanford's boat, and there were no witnesses, correct?" asked the sergeant.

"Yes."

"Are you still seeing a psychiatrist, Scarlett?"

"Yes."

"That shouldn't make a difference, Mike," said Rhys. "Being a witness to her best friend's death would affect anyone."

Foster paused and glanced at both of them. "Okay. No body, no evidence yet, no witnesses, and a denial of the crime by the accused. What do we do with that, Rhys?"

"Don't know there's anything you can do right now."

"You still live in Gloucester, Scarlett?"

"Yes."

"Well, we may have more questions. If anything turns up, Rhys, let me know. Beauport's a son of a bitch, so keep an eye on her."

On the way to her car, Scarlett asked, "Since everyone knows Beauport's an SOB why haven't they made a point to lock him up?"

"Because he's got money, and buys his way through everything. From what I hear, he's also got his own gang of longshoremen to do his dirty work."

"What exactly was Beauport accused of?"

"For one, embezzling a client's money in West Palm Beach. The rumor was Beauport and the son split the money, but no one could prove it.

"Then he was accused of a hit-and-run that paralyzed a woman. A witness saw the accident and identified Beauport's Jag, but coincidentally Beauport reported the car stolen and they never found it.

"He's also been accused of assault, bribery, and a slew of other crimes."

"Do you think he'll come after me?"

"I doubt it but I asked Mike to get a cruiser over to your place for the next few weeks. Don't worry too much. Beauport doesn't need any more negative publicity than he already has."

"When this is over, I'm moving away. My life here is ruined."

"I hear you. But just remember, 'The only way round is through.' "

"Thoreau?"

"Frost."

"Ah." Scarlett liked that she'd learned a little more about Rhys McGowan. "I'm thinking you've had a few hard hits yourself?"

"Yep. Maybe I'll tell you some day."

She hoped that meant they were becoming friends. God knows she needed one.

"I've been thinking we should revisit Thacher Island on foot," he said. "It's a small island and maybe we can find evidence that this woman existed. What are you doing tomorrow morning?"

Her face brightened. "Going to Thacher Island."

The next day, they took Rhys's small Whaler out to sea. Scarlett's face burned from a salty wind while her red hair trailed behind her like a lit torch. Why would Beauport throw a woman overboard? And who the heck was she? Nearing Hammond Castle, Scarlett asked Rhys if he'd ever been there.

"I took a Boy Scout troop there once," and then he chuckled.

"What's so funny?"

"Guess who's chairman of the Hammond Castle Foundation and Trust?"

"No."

"Yep. Harold Beauport."

On Thacher Island, they split up. Scarlett wore Rhys's Coast Guard jacket, but she was still cold from a sharp wind that felt like a slap. She scoured for anything green or pink, an elastic hair band, a sandal or sneaker, but she couldn't find one scrap of evidence to substantiate her claim. And neither could Rhys.

Scarlett was beyond despondent and for the first time began to doubt what she saw. Her head was pounding like a war drum, and she felt on the verge of a meltdown.

Sensing her mood, McGowan said, "Look, for whatever it's worth, I believe Harold Beauport threw that woman overboard. I don't know who she was, or what happened to her, but I believe what you said."

"Thank you for that."

That night Scarlett lay in bed going over and over the incident in her mind. She fell asleep and dreamed of a woman in a green sweater floating face up, bloated, with eyes wide open and staring at her. Scarlett sat up in terror unsure if she'd dreamed it or if it was real. Then she wondered if she could have imagined Beauport throwing that woman overboard. Some kind of visual delusion or side effect from her medication?

She googled Xanax and learned that in some cases there were side effects of hallucination and delirium. Was she one of those cases? What if it was all in her head, or posttraumatic stress from Sarah's drowning?

She looked out the window of her apartment. As promised, a cruiser was parked out front. Although she was trembling and filled with self-doubt, she realized her word would mean nothing ever again, to her or anyone else, if she couldn't prove Beauport's guilt. Could she really let it go?

Holly knew she should turn the anklet in to the police, but what if it didn't even belong to the woman who'd drowned? Yet, if she did nothing, Scarlett's accusation would be dismissed and she'd probably lose her job. Hadn't she had enough sorrow in her life? Holly took the anklet from inside a roll of socks, and stared at it. Who was Sonia?

While her son napped, Holly googled Harold Beauport, scrolling through a dozen photos, and stopping at one of Anthony Beauport's wedding, with Harold as his best man. She looked closely at Anthony's bride, a petite dark-haired woman. Then she read through the announcement and found the bride's full name, biting so hard on her bottom lip she tasted blood.

> Mr. Anthony Beauport is the youngest
> son of Benjamin Sewell Beauport,
> and the grandson of Josiah Beauport,
> the Gloucester shipping magnate.
> Mrs. Beauport is the former Sonia Villas
> of Mar del Plata, Argentina. His
> brother, Harold Beauport, was best man.

Holly didn't need to read more. She printed the announcement, grabbed the anklet, and left the house.

Scarlett was surprised when she answered the door and saw the woman standing there.

"I'm sorry to disturb you, Scarlett. My name is—"

"Holly from the whale watch."

"Yes. I also graduated from Endicott with you."

"I thought you looked familiar. Please, come in."

Holly sat down and folded her hands. "The reason why I've come is that I think I have some evidence that will help prove your accusation against Mr. Beauport."

"*What?*"

Holly handed her the anklet and told her to look closely at the name. Then she pulled out the wedding announcement.

"Where did you find this?"

"Behind the cleat where you said Mr. Beauport threw that woman overboard. I thought you could give it to that Coast Guard guy or the police."

Scarlett jumped up and hugged her. "I thought I was going crazy. I owe you one, Holly."

"Maybe some time we could have coffee?" asked Holly.

Scarlett hugged her again, whispering, "Absolutely."

That night, Scarlett called Rhys. Two days later, she called Harold Beauport.

"Who is this?"

"Scarlett O'Hara, your favorite heroine."

"What the hell do you want?"

"I have something that might interest you."

"What's that?"

"An anklet with the name *Sonia* engraved on it."

Scarlett heard the quick intake of his breath.

"I'd like to make a deal," she said. "I need money, and you could use a get-out-of-jail-free card. I'm sure you don't want the police to see what I found. Especially since Sonia Villas was your brother's wife."

There was a long pause. Finally, "When and where?"

Hammond Castle was closed for repairs, but Beauport told Scarlett the door at the end of the drawbridge would be unlocked. Scarlett thought it was as good a place as any to meet a creep.

The Castle stood stark against a moonlit sky, its towers reaching high over the rocky coastline, the surf pounding in concert with her heart.

A full moon cast shadows over a tall figure in the Great Hall. "Caught me in a fish net, eh, Miss O'Hara?" Beauport's voice echoed. "A little conniver just like your namesake."

"My mother always told me that when I was little." Scarlett curtsied, and in her best southern accent said, "I do declare you are a black-hearted varmint, Mr. Harold Beauport."

"Cut the drama and give me the anklet."

She held her hands behind her back. "Not until you tell me why you threw that woman overboard. You at least owe me that."

"I owe you nothing, you little bitch."

"I must say, Mr. Beauport, it was a brilliant plan. You are an absolute genius at getting what you want. All that money, beautiful estate, status in the community, and an expert crime dodger. I could learn a few tricks from you. Actually, we'd make a great team."

"Well, I suppose you're curious."

Beauport's ego got the best of him. "Okay fine. Mother died, then father passed away and me and my brother, Anthony, inherited everything. But poor Tony died when his brakes failed rounding a corner out in Big Sur, and the bulk of the estate came to me."

"I assume you had a hand in your brother's death?"

"Of course, I mean I have people."

Scarlett could tell he was enjoying himself.

"Sonia contested the will of course, gold digger that she was. Hired some big New York lawyer. My investments went belly up and I borrowed money from the wrong people. What can I say?"

"So, you got rid of her."

Beauport smiled. "Yes. Always tie up the loose ends, Miss O'Hara."

"How did you get her on the boat? That was a smooth trick."

"Not really. I told her I wanted to settle my brother's estate—that she clearly deserved more money. Oh, she came right away. I took her to dinner, gave her some old photos of Tony, wrote her a check she'd never cash. Then I invited her on the whale watch. My boat, friendly day on the water, and all that. I waited for the right time and over she went."

"Was Captain Sanford in on it?"

"Sanford? Hell no! He couldn't run a two-car funeral. Now give me the damn anklet."

Scarlett passed him a small bag, and he looked inside. But instead of passing her the $20K she'd requested, he pulled out a gun. "You really didn't think I'd allow you to blackmail me, did you?"

"Hold it right there, Beauport!" yelled Rhys, as Sergeant Foster and three policemen entered the Great Hall, and arrested Harold Beauport. Smiling, Scarlett carefully removed the wires from her chest.

"Are you okay?" Rhys asked.

"Oh yes," she said, feeling a happiness she hadn't felt since before Sarah passed away. "What's going to happen to him?"

And just like Clark Gable, Rhys said, "Frankly my dear, I don't give a damn."

"How long have you been waiting to say that," said Scarlett, grinning. ❖

Framed

Hans Copek

A small town near Berlin, Germany, October 1930
"It's me, Sommer!" I shouted from the front door, to let Winkler know that I'd arrived. No answer. Not a soul in the office. On a Saturday, the staff would have gone home at one o'clock, but the door had been left unlocked. I looked around. The rolltop desks were closed. The ashtrays hadn't been emptied.

Once more, "Hello?"

The sound of a gunshot echoed through the empty building. From upstairs. The crash of furniture was followed by a heavy thump.

I raced up the steps. The door to my former office stood ajar. I smelled gunpowder. Where was Winkler? Crumpled behind the desk, next to the upturned chair. Brains were splattered; blood was still oozing on the new rug— probably not even paid for. The back of his skull blown away. A nauseating sight. I gagged. Why didn't he have the decency to go into the bathroom to do away with himself? He couldn't do anything right.

275

A large pistol lay inches from his hand. It looked familiar. Could that be my old Luger? I was about to pick it up when I heard the rumble of heavy boots clomping up the staircase. Two policemen busted through the door, pointing their revolvers at me.

"Hands up!"

"No, no. I can explain. I was about to call you." With a sigh, I raised my arms.

"All clear, Herr Kommissar," the older officer shouted over his shoulder.

A man in a business suit stepped in and walked over to where Winkler had fallen.

"Did you come to arrest Herr Winkler?" I asked him. "We're all too late. I heard the shot when I . . . he shot himself just a few minutes ago."

The commissar took one look at the prone body behind the desk, and snapped, "You are under arrest."

The policemen holstered their weapons. One of them yanked my arms behind my back, and before I could make another move, I felt handcuffs snap around my wrists.

"Wait! You got this all wrong. Winkler was dead when I got here."

The commissar paid no attention to me.

"Take him away."

The officers grabbed my arms, hustled me down the stairs, and stuffed me into the back seat of a car. The younger stayed with me; the other ran back into the building. A few gawkers were peering into the car. I turned my head away, only to see a woman pressing her face against the window from the other side. Sliding down in my seat didn't work; those heavy steel cuffs poking into my back made that maneuver much too painful.

Word would be out in no time. Herr Sommer has

been taken into custody. I had never felt so humiliated. When I tried to talk to my watcher, he merely shook his head. A grunt was all I got out of him. Minutes later, his comrade got behind the wheel. It was getting dark. An ambulance arrived. I saw more police trotting to the crime scene. The crowd of the curious stood three deep as we drove off.

At the station I had to empty my pockets. The desk sergeant used a *Kopierstift*, an indelible pencil, to enter everything on a form with two sheets of carbon paper: a gold pocket watch, a billfold containing four ten-mark notes; a coin purse containing eight marks and twenty-six pfennigs; a Pelikan fountain pen, an etui with three cigars, and my Borsalino hat. I was allowed to keep my handkerchief, but had to surrender my necktie, stickpin, and my suspenders. I signed the original and the two copies. The policeman kept all three. Then I had to dunk all my fingertips in black ink, and roll their prints on a sheet of paper. Very messy. I was treated like a common criminal.

When I requested a lawyer, I was told that wouldn't be possible until Monday morning during regular business hours. I asked that my landlady be notified. No phone? We'll send an officer around in the morning. What would they tell her, I wondered. "Herr Sommer has been detained on suspicion of having murdered Herr Winkler." Ridiculous.

And Jenny, now a widow? Someone would have to ring her doorbell and inform her that her husband was dead. A suspect in custody.

Two men in prison-guard uniforms marched me across the street to the jail adjacent to the courthouse. Cell Number 34 had a bunk bed for two inmates, a desk, a chair, and a porcelain toilet without a wooden seat. Way up, near the ceiling, was a tiny window, unreachable unless you brought a trampoline. Three sturdy rods of iron drove home the message: "You are behind bars."

Later that evening, a slider in the cell door was pushed aside, and an invisible person handed me a plate with sandwiches and a glass of seltzer water.

My new domicile had been cool when I came in. It turned frigid during the night. Since the upper bunk was not occupied, I helped myself to the extra blanket, which reeked of disinfectant. The hard wooden slats hurt my back. Sleep did not come.

I tried to reconstruct today's events. No, yesterday's. The distant church bells having chimed four times, followed by two deep bongs, told me that I was still awake at two o'clock on Sunday.

Winkler had sent me a note, asking me to come to the office at five o'clock. *There had been promising developments*, he wrote. I went.

I wasn't more than five minutes late. The only light in the office came from a green-shaded desk lamp in Winkler's office. No, not his office anymore; he had moved upstairs when I left the company. It was now the accountant's desk. Strange. Had Bohnenzahl worked late? He was supposed to be on his deathbed.

Then I heard the shot. Winkler was dead. No surprise. It was not his first attempt at suicide, merely his first successful one. He had been hinting there was only one way to avoid the consequences of his company's failure, his mountain of debts, the pressure from the bank. I also knew that desperation had driven my former partner to commit fraud. He might be indicted any moment. Lately, I heard rumors that he was blaming *me* for his troubles.

Why were three policemen on the scene within minutes? There was no other explanation but that Winkler had tricked me. As long as he was going to die, he was going to take me with him—by way of the executioner's axe.

It was still dark outside when a guard woke me up and led me to a different cell. Same gray walls, same carbolic acid stench. Lunch was no longer passed through a hole in the door. A man in striped prisoner garb ladled out soup into my tin bowl.

On Monday afternoon, the attorney who had handled the sale of my share in the *Bammer Sarg und Kistenfabrik* came to see me. Bail had been denied because homicide was a capital crime. The lawyer declared that he would not handle my case. That saved me from having to fire him.

Where to find a new lawyer? I did not know many people in this town. I came here two years ago, after my father died. He had left me the majority share in the coffin-and-crate enterprise.

Almost fifty years old, I've been a lifelong bachelor. Soon after I arrived, I befriended a rich widow and, after a couple of months, moved in with her. (That her married daughter is no longer talking to her isn't my concern. In fact, it makes life a lot easier.)

Since I was held in *Untersuchungshaft*, investigative detention, I enjoyed certain privileges, like I didn't have to wear a prison uniform. In addition to seeing a lawyer as often as needed, I could receive a visitor once a week. My landlady came at the first chance. She suggested that I hire one of the best defense attorneys from Berlin. I didn't have the money, at least nothing that could be turned into quick cash. And the insurance company wouldn't pay if I were convicted. My landlady was willing to advance me five thousand marks. Her price? Marriage if acquitted; sole beneficiary in my will if convicted. I agreed. (Wills can always be changed.)

I never slept well. The dread of the unjustified murder charge would never leave my mind. Most of the time I felt chest pains. They came and went. Sometimes they stretched into my arms. I begged that I be taken to the hospital. The warden only scoffed. "Stop malingering. All you want is a warmer room, a softer bed, and better food. We can't afford to have a policeman sit in front of your hospital room twenty-four hours a day."

I couldn't be sure I would get off, but I balked at the thought of thinking of my landlady as my fiancée. She came once a week. In early December she brought a tin of cookies. She had baked them herself. The tin had a small Christmas tree painted on it. When I opened the lid, I got a whiff that reminded me more of a public restroom urinal than the traditional *Lebkuchen*. I thanked her and that evening I handed the present to one of the guards. He probably fed them to his dog. I shuddered at the prospect of this woman cooking my lunch for the rest of my life.

A week later, I met my new lawyer in the visitors' room.

"The trial date has been set for Wednesday, the twenty-eighth of January," he told me.

"Here?"

"No, murder is a matter for the Provincial Court, the *Landgericht*, in Potsdam."

"Will there be a jury?" I asked him.

"No, we'll face a panel of three judges. Much more expedient. They'll be done in less than two days."

My lawyer and I sat at the long ends of a wooden table, close enough to hear each other, far enough not to pass anything. On a chair against the wall, a guard saw to it that all the rules were observed. Not that I expected the lawyer to push a lollipop in my direction.

His name was Friedrich Wilhelm Schuester, doctor of jurisprudence. He insisted on being addressed as *Herr Doktor*. His potbelly, adorned with a gold watch chain, kept him some extra inches from the edge of the table. Florid hamster cheeks rolled over a stiff celluloid collar. His gray mustache ended where his dueling scar began. He sported the same brushed-up hairdo as our Reich President Hindenburg. Schuester could have posed for a cartoon of a fat, smug Prussian bureaucrat. I didn't like the man. In fact, I never cared for *any* Prussians. I was from Stuttgart in the South.

Schuester fished some paperwork from his briefcase and stuck a pince-nez on his wine-red nose. "I'm trying to have the charges reduced to manslaughter. We won't get anywhere with self-defense."

"How often do I have to tell you that I didn't kill this schmuck?"

"Telling the judge that you didn't do it has never worked as a good defense." He gave me a long look. "Yours is a weak case. You were the only person in the room. Your fingerprints were all over the pistol."

"Of course, they were. This gun at one time belonged to me. I had it stashed away somewhere in the office, and had forgotten all about it when I left the company."

"Did you pick it up?"

"Good Lord, no. The arrival of the bulls kept me from doing so."

Schuester looked up. "Let me think about this."

He kept fidgeting with the impressive stack of paper, mumbling under his breath. How could my defense lawyer have bought into the police's idea that I was guilty?

"What did you just say?" My mind had been wandering.

"I won't see you again before the holidays, not until the New Year."

Dr. Schuester nodded toward the guard, who held the door for him.

"Merry Christmas," I shouted after him. "*Sau Preuss,*" I mumbled under my breath, Prussian pig.

One of the judicial minions led me back to my cell. I stretched out on my bunk with two wool blankets wrapped around my shoulders. I was shivering. An hour ago, I had been sweating. My potato soup from the lunch tray sat untouched. At six o'clock they would bring the usual evening fare, two slices of rye with either salami or liverwurst. For days, I hadn't been able to keep my food down. I still wore the suit I had on when they brought me in. Without my suspenders, I had a hard time keeping my pants up. And now another five weeks until the end of January in this stink hole. I should have become used to it, but the smell hit me anew every time I came back from the visitors' room. If I was acquitted, I planned to sue the state for false imprisonment. Make that *when* I was acquitted. Think positively!

A terrifying thought kept nagging me. Whereas Winkler knew all about the technical side of the business, accounting practices were riddles to him. I, on the other hand, had studied finance. This allowed me to keep three sets of books: one for the tax authorities, another to show the bank, and the true one for myself. No need to rehash the details. But about a year ago, the bankruptcy of our largest customer left us in a hole; it was time to bail. It was not my fault that Winkler agreed to pay me in full. It left the company underfunded. The well-timed bonus I paid to Bohnenzahl, the accountant, kept him quiet. Unfortunately, he had to come back for more "loan" requests due to his deteriorating health. I considered it a real blessing if a merciful death were to relieve him of his suffering before my trial. Financial matters should not spill over into the homicide case. I didn't think it necessary to burden Dr. Schuester with this subject.

On a frosty January morning, the day before the trial, I climbed into the Green Minna, the nickname for a vehicle used to transport prisoners. The padlocked compartment was unheated. My teeth were chattering. The only light came through narrow slits near the top. The glass in one of them had a chip missing. It sent more cold air whistling down on me. The wooden bench was hard. For kilometers on end, each cobblestone sent jolts though my spine up to my aching head. The dread of the tribunal roiled my guts. Barely going twice the speed of a horse-drawn tumbrel, it took us two and a half hours to reach the courthouse in Potsdam. I never felt more miserable in my life. Clearly, this ride had to be punishment enough for every foul deed I had committed in my life—starting with pinching a cookie from my sister's plate when I was three. The one thing that I should *not* have to suffer was the indictment that had landed me on this truck.

At eight o'clock the next morning, two prison guards barged into my private suite—without knocking first, of course—just as I was finishing my business on the throne. One of them carried a bowl of water. I saw steam rising from it. Naturally, guards need not observe such niceties as to introduce themselves, but I had no trouble making up names for them: Ratface and Bullneck. Ratface treated me to a haircut and a shave courtesy of the State. For the first time in two months, I saw my face in a mirror. My hair had turned white. Bullneck unwrapped a package. It contained a clean shirt, my necktie, and most importantly, my suspenders. It finally freed my left hand from holding up my trousers. I must have lost twenty pounds during my confinement.

The two men kept up a merry banter, discussing the finer points of decapitation by axe versus guillotine. Ratface asked me whether I had an opinion on the English way of execution, to wit: the drop where your neck is broken by the hangman's knot. He wished it could be used here because the henchmen didn't have to hose away all that gore. Their talk made me lose my appetite. When a third officer brought breakfast, consisting of two rolls and a hard-boiled egg, I couldn't touch it. I sipped hot coffee from a tin cup. The two ghouls then marched me through a dark tunnel to the courtroom. Axe or guillotine? Or, the rest of my life locked up, with a murderer for a cellmate? Or, if acquitted, trapped into matrimony. I would know in a day or two. My knees were wobbly.

We entered through a door that led directly into a balustraded enclosure. I looked around. To my left, at the head of the hall, I saw the judges' bench with three tall chairs behind it. The bench extended around the bend to under the windows opposite my dock. The prosecutor's seat was on the same level as the judges. Not a good sign. Dressed in a shiny black cassock, the *Staatsanwalt* was already there, giving the impression of being busy by flipping through his files.

A policeman sat down on an extra chair behind me. I greeted Schuester, who stood at a desk in front of my box.

He too wore a black robe over his formal cutaway. "Don't worry about a thing," Schuester assured me.

Hah, I worried plenty. So much in fact that I felt those stabs of pain in my chest again. What if Schuester's gambit didn't work? I scanned the visitors' ranks. My landlady had made the trip to Potsdam. I did not catch her eye. Hell and damnation. I had to gulp. Sitting near the front was Bohnenzahl, the accountant. Looking much too hale, he had a stupid grin on his face, and gave me a thumbs-up sign. The last person I wanted to see . . . alive.

The room fell silent when punctually at nine o'clock the three judges emerged from a door behind the bench, all of them in black robes. The face of the principal judge resembled a medieval woodcut, chiseled into oak with a dull blade. This image was heightened by his equally middle-agey beret, like a huge black cupcake. He might as well have carried a scythe and a lantern. Expect no mercy from this man.

After the usual preliminaries, the prosecutor stood up, removed a monocle from his eye, twirled it on a black string, stuck out his chest, and cleared his throat. In a deep baritone he addressed the bench.

"The State charges the defendant with murder. We will prove our case."

Not satisfied with this perfectly adequate statement, he continued, while stabbing his finger in my direction at regular intervals. This gasbag was eager to show off his rich vocabulary: *cold-blooded, heinous, fiendish, greedy, treacherous, obvious, irrefutable, premeditated.* At long last, he concluded his peroration: "A cut-and-dried case. The defendant is guilty of murder with malice aforethought."

Some performance! He looked about the room as if he expected applause. I almost believed him myself.

The presiding judge directed the defense to state its case. Dr. Schuester explained why the defendant's fingerprints showed up on the Luger. "This weapon had once been my *mandant's* property. Like all officers, he was permitted to keep his sidearm when he was mustered out of the Kaiser's army in 1919. He had never bothered to register the weapon, and it became the property of the deceased, together with the rest of the company's inventory. *Au contraire*, it might have been highly suspicious had my *mandant's* fingerprints *not* been on the pistol. Even the dumbest of killers would have wiped off his prints."

Dr. Schuester went on for awhile and summed up. "My *mandant* is innocent of the charge. This was not a homicide. The deceased died by his own hand."

The first witness was sworn in. He was the plainclothes officer who came storming in seconds after I had discovered the bloody mess that had been Winkler. Prompted by the prosecutor, he reiterated that this was a cut-and-dried case. The accused had been caught red-handed.

Then it was Schuester's turn. "Herr Kommissar, you keep saying 'you caught my *mandant* red-handed.' Does this mean you were present at the moment of the shooting?"

"No, we entered the room while the accused was standing over his victim. The smell of gunpowder was in the air, and the dead man's blood was still fresh."

"That's not my idea of red-handed." Schuester shook his head, and went on. "How come you and two armed officers arrived on the scene so promptly?"

"We had a call from Herr Winkler that the accused was in his office threatening to shoot him."

Just as I thought.

But Schuester didn't let this chance slip by. "You wouldn't have an idea when the call came in?"

"Of course we do. At 16:51." The commissar didn't even have to consult his notes.

"Nine minutes to five. I can just imagine what was said," sneered my lawyer. "I have a gentleman here pointing a gun at me. Would it be convenient to send a gendarme around to remove him? In fifteen to twenty minutes? Very good. Thanks, officer. That will be greatly appreciated."

Laughter from the spectator benches. The detective looked flustered.

Schuester went on. "It so happens that Herr Winkler had asked my *mandant* to call on him at five o'clock. He remembers being five minutes late. Immediately after announcing his arrival, he heard a gunshot upstairs."

"You won't be able to substantiate this convenient bit of timing." The commissar had recovered his composure. "Also, his fingerprints were recovered from the weapon."

"Apparently, this satisfied you. And you didn't think to conduct further tests?" Schuester kept at it.

"We caught the defendant red-handed."

"Yes, I see you're fond of this phrase. Speaking of hands, I have here the complete handprints of my *mandant*. The only prints that interest me are the ones of the tip and middle link of Herr Sommer's right index finger. You might call it the trigger finger. Did you take an impression of what was on the trigger?"

"I'm sure," the commissar stammered. "We caught him red—"

"Enough of that," thundered the judge. "Answer counsel's question. Did you test the trigger for prints?"

The detective turned toward the spectator seats. His assistant shrugged his shoulders.

"Do we have personnel on hand to retest the weapon for prints?" Old Oakface addressed the gallery.

"Yes, sir, we can do this." I heard a voice from the back of the room. A policeman stepped to the front and lifted the cloth with the pistol on it from the exhibits table.

"I would like to witness this." Schuester stood up.

"Agreed," said the presiding judge. "Counsel may attend the test. Adjourned till two o'clock this afternoon." He banged his gavel and he and his two associates exited stage right.

I relished the sight of the commissar mopping his forehead. Then the policeman took me by the arm and turned me over to the prison detail. At lunchtime they brought in a bowl of pea soup. The best food I'd had in months. Alas, I could not keep it down. My nerves were shredded.

At five minutes before two, Bullneck and Ratface led me back to the courtroom.

I saw Schuester across the room, talking to my landlady. Everyone rose when the judges returned. Schuester hustled back to his station. The fingerprint man was sworn in.

"What did you find out?" asked the presiding judge.

"The print on the trigger of the Luger pistol is not consistent with the handprint of the defendant."

"Meaning?"

"Although the print was slightly smudged, the trigger could not have been pulled by the defendant."

Shouts and clapping of hands from the visitors' benches.

We won. My Berlin lawyer is a genius.

Dr. Schuester turned around, a big smile on his face. I stretched out my hand to . . . oh, my chest . . . a fiery stab of pain . . . in my chest . . . my knees buckled . . . I felt the policeman grasp my arm. . . .

Darkness.

On the next day, on page three, the *Berliner Morgenpost* carried this notice:

Potsdam: Tragedy in Courtroom. Carl S., accused of having shot to death his former business partner, was acquitted of the charge. At the very moment when the presiding judge ordered him released, Carl S. collapsed. He was rushed by ambulance to St. Josef Hospital where he was pronounced dead on arrival. ❖

One Week in Royal Rajasthan

Judith Green

W hat you need to drive in India," the driver sang out, "is a good horn and good brakes. And good luck." He took one hand off the wheel to touch the little statue of Ganesh, the elephant-headed god, attached to the dashboard.

"Mr. Singh! A cow!" shrieked an all-too-familiar voice from the back of the bus.

Beside her, Margery's husband sighed. "Why can't that woman just close her eyes?"

As the cow shambled onto the roadway, Mr. Singh yanked on the wheel. The bus swerved out around the cow—and into the lane of an enormous truck, its hood painted with orange flowers, its bed stacked high with slabs of marble. Yellow tassels danced around its windshield as the truck roared toward them.

"Mr. Singh! Sheep!" Lillian cried.

The bus skirted the flock of sheep, dodged a motorbike carrying an entire family—Dad, Mom, in a flapping sari with a baby in her arms, and two small boys on the handlebars—then passed a camel, which ambled along pulling a two-wheeled cart while its driver chatted on his phone. At the last possible moment, Mr. Singh pulled the bus back into its own lane, and the truck rumbled past in a blast of diesel smoke.

"Did you *see* that?" Lillian's indignant voice was pitched so everyone on the bus could hear her. "We missed that truck by *inches*!"

"Mr. Singh is an excellent driver." The young tour guide leaned across the aisle toward Margery and Tom, soft brown eyes wide and earnest. "He drives this route every week."

"How about you, Param?" Margery cringed as another truck came at them. "How many times have you done this trip?"

"Truth to tell, this is my very first tour."

"But you sound—"

"So American?" Param smiled sheepishly. "In my previous employment, I made telephone calls for an American bank. To urge clients to borrow on their credit cards for home improvements. Put on an addition, build a garage—"

"On their credit cards? That's expensive!"

"Exactly. But many clients agreed to it. I chose the name Walter, to make myself sound older, and I told the clients I was calling from Omaha. It seemed to reassure them. Have you been there?"

"Um, no. We're from Maine."

"At least, in my new position, I can work in the daytime," Param said, as the bus lurched to a stop. He leapt up, microphone in hand. "And here we are, my friends, arriving in Agra, for the thrill of a lifetime!"

Oh, yes. The Taj Mahal. The instant Mr. Singh set the step in place, Margery hopped off the bus and danced with impatience while the rest of the group clambered down. In two days, they'd already become so familiar. First the Sedgewicks, a pleasant seventy-ish couple from Ontario, then the Browns—parents and grown children and a daughter-in-law, a traveling family reunion—then Tricia and Bill from California, followed quickly by Josh and Jess, who were on their honeymoon, and who, judging by their shining faces, thought the Taj Mahal had been built expressly for them. A long pause meant that poor old Gerald Fournier was hobbling his way to the front of the bus in his bright red 49ers jacket, leaning on his four-pronged cane. And right behind him, breathing down the poor guy's neck, came Lillian Hanks.

Margery watched Lillian descend the steps, her well-lipsticked mouth curved in a courtly smile, her bottle-blond hair cascading over her shoulders in a style much too young for her, and that great rock of a diamond twinkling on her hand. She accepted Mr. Singh's fingertips to steady herself, then swept by him without even a nod, and sashayed after Gerald. "Oh, do be careful," she called. "The pavement is *so* uneven."

Forget Lillian, Margery told herself as she and Tom passed through the turnstile and then through the grand doorway. For before them, seeming to float above the reflecting pool, exquisitely white among its delicate minarets, more beautiful than she could ever have imagined, was the Taj Mahal.

"It's lovely," said a voice beside her. Margery turned to see Gerald standing still, gazing at the distant building, his face rapt.

"My poor wife," he said. "It was the one great desire of her life to see the Taj Mahal." Gerald started along the reflecting pool, and Tom and Margery fell into step beside him. "I said I'd take her," he went on, "but I had my restaurants to run—always too busy to get away. And when I finally retired five years ago, she'd already been diagnosed with cancer. She fought so hard."

"That's a tough one," Tom murmured.

Margery patted Gerald's arm. "I'm sorry."

He stared up at the building. "God, I miss her." And he pulled off his shoes and, leaning on his cane, climbed alone up the steps.

They let him go. While Tom untied his sneakers, Margery slipped out of her sandals and savored the feel of the marble smooth and cool beneath her feet.

Until the shriek from behind her: "Didn't you bring socks? It's not sanitary."

Margery flinched. "Um, no, Lillian. I'm fine. I was brought up on a farm." After running barefoot in the cow pasture, what was a little pigeon poop?

"I'm a nurse, you know. I've come prepared!" Lillian dug in her huge leather purse and brought out a pair of thick, white socks. "I wear them at each shrine, and then throw them away."

A nurse? In diamond earrings and a ring so heavy she practically needed a wheelbarrow? Oh, never mind Lillian. Above her, Margery could see the intricate tracery of semiprecious stones set into the vast, snowy-white walls. Ah—The Taj Mahal!

Lillian bent to pull on her socks. "I'm not walking barefoot in this place."

The bus jolted through a construction zone where, along the roadway, women hacked at the ground with pickaxes, or carried trays of sand and rock on their heads, their saris fluttering orange and yellow and fuchsia. Beyond them, carefully tended crops stretched to the horizon.

In the back of the bus, Gerald's eyes were closed behind his old-fashioned half-glasses, while in the seat behind him Lillian leaned across the aisle, deep in conversation with Tricia and Bill. Josh was nuzzling Jess's neck, and most of the rest of the gang were lost in their phones. *Come on,* Margery wanted to call. *We're in India! Look at the scenery, people.*

The bus pulled into the forecourt of an ancient mansion covered in ivy. A doorman stepped forward, resplendent in tunic and turban, palms pressed together in greeting. "Namaste," he said, and led the group into the hotel's courtyard, where a young woman in a scarlet sari waited to dot their foreheads with paint, and pour out tiny cups of tea.

Gerald hobbled by, poking at the flagstones with his cane, followed by Josh and Jess with their backpacks. Next came Lillian . . . and the turbaned doorman juggling five or six enormous baby-blue suitcases. "Man," Bill said, "Lillian doesn't just have luggage. She has a flotilla."

"Have you seen her diamond?" Tricia asked Margery. "It's *huge.* And yes, it's real—the way it catches the light."

Margery glanced down at her own ring. The tiny diamond chip had been all Tom could afford on his teacher's salary. "But isn't Lillian a nurse?"

"Yes, she started as a nurse," Tricia said. "Then she married one of her patients. When he died—"

"Or she bumped him off?" Tom muttered.

Tricia glanced at him, then leaned forward conspiratorially. "And then she made a killing on the stock market."

"Specifically with some really smart purchases of a new tech stock," Bill said. "She offered to give me a few tips."

"Ssh!" Tricia whispered. "That's our little secret. Now, I saw Gerald talking to you at the Taj Mahal. What's *his* story?"

"Well. . . " Margery paused. "He, um, he lost his wife."

"Oh, no. Another rich old widower." Tricia chortled. "Lillian could be set for life."

Margery was relieved when Param bustled up with their room keys. "This is actually a private home," he explained as he led her and Tom up a flight of stairs. "It has belonged to a Jain family for generations, but now they live in one section and let out the rest."

Even compared to the luxurious hotel where they'd stayed in New Delhi, their room was incredible. The sweep of space, the high ceilings and antique woodwork, a bathtub carved of jade-colored marble. "This is beautiful," Margery said. "I'll never want to leave."

She wandered to the open window. A warm breeze sighed by her, fragrant with flowers, as she peered out over the garden below, where bushes were bursting with pink blossoms and tiny birds fluttered about. At home in Maine, it was still winter, the colors limited to white snow and the dark green of pines.

A shriek of laughter drew her eyes to a swimming pool set just inside the tawny stone wall that surrounded the mansion. Lillian, in a bathing suit that left little to the imagination, was splashing about in the water. Gerald sat in a deck chair, watching her.

Margery looked out over the wall, beyond the sparkling water of the pool. A man walked along a row of dusty, knee-high plants with a huge clay pot, bending to dribble water onto the roots of one plant, straightening up under his burden, moving to the next plant, bending again. The man's shadow moved with him, sharp and dark under the setting sun.

"Tom, can you do me a favor?" Gerald asked as he left the buffet table. Leaning on his cane, he set down a plate loaded with lamb stew and dumplings and heaps of mysterious vegetables, then dug into the pocket of his 49ers jacket and pulled out his phone. "I need a photo for my grandchildren. Otherwise they'll never believe I ate all this spicy stuff."

"Sure." Tom lifted the camera and took several shots, while Gerald held up the plate, topped with a huge grin.

"Isn't he the cutest thing?" Jess murmured from behind Margery.

"No, you are," Josh told her, managing to nuzzle her neck without dropping his plate.

"Anyway," Jess said, "we have a great plan. Lillian is going to help us with some investments."

Josh put his arm around Jess and pulled her close. "We don't want to miss this chance. Like Lillian says: a down payment on a house—we could think about starting a family."

Margery blinked. House? Family? Lillian knew how to work 'em.

The next morning, as they loaded onto the bus, Lillian leaned across the aisle toward Margery. "He made me take them off."

"What?" Margery stared at her. "Who?"

"Param." Lillian nodded toward the guide. "He said it wasn't safe for me to wear my sparklies."

By now, Tricia had turned in her seat. "What's happened?"

Lillian held up her hand, now empty of the gigantic rock, and drew back her hair to show plain gold studs in her earlobes instead of the great fall of diamonds. "Param said it wasn't safe for me on the streets." She stuck out her ruby-red lower lip in a pout.

"Well, your jewelry will be fine in your luggage," Tricia assured her. "Mr. Singh never leaves the bus while we're touring."

"Oh, no," Lillian said. "You just can't trust—" She glanced meaningfully toward the turbaned doorman. "Them," she concluded. "So I hid my sparklies in a sock and stuffed the sock in with my dirty laundry."

She thinks a sock is a great hiding place? Margery thought. *And this woman is giving financial advice?*

Gerald came hobbling down the aisle, grasping the seat backs for support. He settled into a seat near the back, and Lillian jumped up to go sit next to him.

"Gerald had better watch out," Tricia said. "Lillian's gonna stuff *him* into a sock."

"Welcome to Jaipur," Param said into his microphone as he clung to a seatback to keep himself upright in the aisle, "the pink city."

Boxy pink-stucco houses jostled for space up the hillside topped by a colossal fort. The bus maneuvered through narrow streets straight out of a movie set, while bright yellow three-wheeled *tuk-tuks* darted in and out of the crush of traffic.

"Here we are at the citadel," Param announced. "You will enter the fortress like maharajas—on elephants."

And there they were: a line of elephants with brightly decorated howdahs on their backs, shifting their gargantuan feet as they waited for passengers.

Lillian climbed the mounting block and settled herself regally in the howdah of the first elephant in line, and Gerald scrambled in beside her. The elephant's driver handed Gerald his cane, then slipped up onto the elephant's neck, and they were off, lumbering up the steep roadway into the citadel. "Whee!" Lillian screeched.

"Okay, then," Margery said. "I wasn't sure poor Gerald would be able to get up on that elephant, but–"

"I think our Lillian inspires him," Mrs. Sedgewick cut in. "And Harold and I were fortunate to meet her on this trip, too. We have a little nest egg, but it's not doing much, if you know what I mean. But Lillian is going to put us in touch with her investment firm."

"But–" Margery paused. "We hardly know Lillian."

"Of course we do," Mrs. Sedgewick said. "Why, we've spent every day with her for almost a whole week."

"But—"

Now the Sedgewicks were onto their elephant and gone, and Param was urging Margery and Tom to climb aboard the next one. In moments, the elephant heaved forward, and they bobbed and swayed and lurched along in a marvelous rolling motion, and with the great warm beast beneath them she and Tom sat high above the roadway like kings—for the moment—of the whole world.

Back in Delhi. The farewell dinner. Conversation was loud and cheerful as people passed email addresses jotted on napkins, and promised to keep in touch.

Lillian sat next to Gerald, and she was radiant. Gerald leaned close, peering at her over his half-glasses, and whispered something in her ear. She laughed and swung her head so that the diamond earrings flashed. The big ring, too, was back on her hand, here in the safety of the hotel.

"I do believe Lillian and Gerald have become a—a couple," Mrs. Sedgewick told Margery. "Did you know he owned a whole string of restaurants? A good catch for our Lillian."

At the far end of the table, Param stood up, hand raised for silence. "I want to thank you all. You've been a wonderful group. But we're not done yet. Tomorrow we see the Red Fort—and yes, we'll visit the bazaar, in case you have any room left in your suitcases."

The group laughed on cue, but Param hurried on. "In the morning, please put your luggage outside your room for the porters to put into storage here at the hotel until your evening flights. As usual, please ensure that your suitcases are locked. Breakfast will be at eight o'clock, and—"

Suddenly Gerald staggered to his feet and grabbed the back of his chair for balance. "I think I'll turn in," he gasped.

Lillian leapt up. "Gerald! Are you all right?"

"Just tired," he whispered. Leaning heavily on his cane, he stepped away from the table.

"I'll go with you," Lillian said firmly, "and see to it that you're properly settled in." At that moment, she certainly sounded like a nurse—and looked like one, as she escorted Gerald toward the elevator, one arm held protectively around him.

There was a momentary silence around the table. Then Bill spoke up. "Well, that's *one* way to get a woman into your bed."

"Or the other way around." Tricia grinned.

"Tom," Margery whispered, "we've got to do something."

Tom patted her hand. "Gerald is an adult."

At breakfast, it appeared that things had moved along during the night. Lillian was glowing, and Gerald strutted about like the cock of the walk, obviously pleased with himself.

"He's asked me to marry him!" Lillian announced to Tricia in the hotel lobby, in a stage whisper that probably carried out into the street.

"Well, well, well," Tricia cooed.

"Are your suitcases properly locked and checked in for storage?" Param called. "Then let's get on the bus. Next stop, the Red Fort."

Lillian pirouetted away and gave her hand—once again devoid of diamond—to Gerald, who led her toward the bus with all the tenderness proper to a lover.

The bazaar bustled with sellers and buyers, and handicrafts galore, while overloaded motorcycles and *tuk-tuks* squeezed through the throngs of people.

Margery and Tom were standing in front of a booth, inhaling the aromas of turmeric, cumin, cardamon that rose from enormous open sacks of colorful spices, when Tricia grabbed Margery's elbow. "Look! Do you see what they're buying over there?"

Tricia pointed to the next stall, where Lillian stood swathed in a blue-and-gold sari embroidered with gold spangles while Gerald stood by, beaming. "I'll bet that's a wedding sari! Isn't that sweet? Let's go see—"

At that moment, Lillian's shriek surmounted all the hubbub of the bazaar: "Gerald!"

Gerald leaned over his cane, coughing miserably. "I just need to sit down, is all," he wheezed.

"The bus is right over there, under that tree," Tricia called. "Let's get him over there."

One on either side of him, Lillian and Tom walked Gerald slowly back to the bus, trailed by Tricia and Margery. Mr. Singh was dozing in his seat, but he quickly opened the door at Lillian's no-nonsense rap, and helped Gerald up the steps. Lillian and Tricia disappeared into the bus after them.

But a moment later, the two women reappeared. "Gerald's just tired," Tricia whispered to Tom and Margery as Lillian hurried away. "I think he and Lillian had quite a night of it," she added with a wink. "The driver said he'd look after Gerald. C'mon, we've only got an hour left—and Lillian wants that wedding sari!"

Long before the hour was up, the group congealed around the bus. Tricia appeared, arms laden with purchases. "How's ol' Gerald doing? Going to survive until his wedding day?"

Margery peered into the bus. "I don't see him. He must've rallied and gone off with Lillian."

"That old fart'll have fun trying to keep up with her," Tricia said, then clamped her mouth shut as Lillian emerged from the crowd in a flurry of fat shopping bags.

Lillian hopped onto the bus. And hopped off again. "Where is Gerald?" she demanded.

Mr. Singh leaned forward from his seat. "He went back to the hotel, madam. He wanted to get a drink in the restaurant, so I called a *tuk-tuk* for him. He said he will meet you there."

Lillian's brow creased. "Well, then, let's get going," she commanded. "We're all here, aren't we? There's no reason to wait. Let's go now."

301

The group obediently climbed onto the bus. As Param took a quick head count, Mr. Singh pulled into traffic. Lillian sat forward in her seat as if urging the bus to go faster.

"Oh, Tom, do you suppose Gerald's all right?" Margery whispered. "All this talk about a wedding. Maybe he got cold feet."

"Or maybe he went back to the hotel for a drink," Tom said.

At the hotel, Gerald was not in the restaurant. Nor in the lobby.

As the porters bustled about rolling the luggage out of the storage area, and accepting tips, Lillian stood in the middle of her battery of baby-blue suitcases, wringing her hands. "Where is Gerald?" She was working up to screech mode again. "Where is Gerald?"

"Now, now, he's here somewhere. Look, there are his glasses," Mrs. Sedgewick said, pointing to the familiar half-glasses lying on a table next to a fat couch. "He's probably just in the loo. Shall I help you put your purchases into your suitcases while you're waiting for him?"

Lillian looked down at the parcels she had dumped on the floor. "I can do it," she snapped. "And I'll feel better with my sparklies on."

She unlocked the largest suitcase and pulled out a white sock. Paused. Pulled out another, and another, dropping them in a heap on the floor. She felt around in the corners of the suitcase. "My diamonds! Where are my diamonds?"

"Are you sure you put them in this suitcase?" Tricia asked.

"Yes! I put them right in here," she said, grabbing for the first sock. "They were all wrapped up in my extra cash. And I put the sock in this suitcase. Gerald was right there—he can tell you. As soon as I came out of the shower and got dressed, he helped me lock the suitcases. The diamonds and the money were never out of my sight except when—"

She stopped. Realization began to dawn on her face.

"Where is Gerald?" Lillian looked around her. "Param, where is Gerald?"

"I just checked at the desk," Param said. "They say he was here a moment ago, ordering a *tuk-tuk*."

Lillian's voice rose. "A *tuk-tuk*? To the airport?"

"Ah, no." Param looked away. "They think he was headed to one of the train stations."

A porter approached bearing Gerald's four-pronged cane across the palms of both hands. "Madam, are you the nurse? I was to give this to you. The gentleman said to say thank you, he is feeling much better."

"Feeling much– No!" Lillian shrieked. "No! He couldn't. No!"

Margery turned away, toward the door. A flash of red. She waited just a beat–to give him a head start, then shouted. "Look!" she called. "There he goes!"

The rest of the group dashed toward the hotel window in time to see the familiar 49ers jacket disappear into the crush of people and vehicles on the street. With Lillian in hot pursuit. ❖

Women's Night Out

Susan Oleksiw

W ell, here we are." Mandy pulled up in front of the small cabin, her smile warming as she took in the beach and lake.

"It's just as you described it," Adele said. "So adorable." Her gold necklace glinted in the afternoon sun as she pushed a streaked blonde curl away from her eyes. "I'm so looking forward to this."

The cabin was more than adorable to Mandy. Here she learned to swim at age four, and to dive soon thereafter from a makeshift raft. She chased frogs in the lake, fished for supper, and learned the constellations.

Mandy and Adele unpacked the SUV, ferrying in the supplies. Adele slid a box of groceries onto the kitchen table. She pulled out a carton of milk and reached for the refrigerator handle, pushing the carton onto the top shelf. Mandy paused to nod in approval while unloading a box of food items Adele had thoughtfully prepared.

"Shall I unpack?" Adele raised an eyebrow in query before pulling her suitcase down the hall and into a guest room.

"Tonight, fresh bass," Mandy announced when Adele returned.

"From the lake?" Adele asked.

"From the lake for sure, but not caught by us." Mandy turned to the window. "You know, we have time for a trip around this side of the lake before supper. It stays light much longer up here. Whaddya say?"

"Sounds great. Oh, do you have a washing machine? I made a mess at the diner." Adele plucked at the front of her sweater and made a face.

"In the cellar. Right there." Mandy nodded to a door in the paneled wall. "It's next to the water heater. If it's not on, just throw the switch."

"Great." Adele pulled off the sweater and headed down the stairs.

Mandy loved the woods but she also loved her creature comforts. A washer-dryer combo and a new propane-fired furnace with safety features meant she and her husband could spend more time up here in the winter. She stacked the now empty containers on the porch, shelved more items in the refrigerator, and left her suitcase in the main bedroom.

"All set?" Mandy said when Adele reappeared.

The two women filed out of the house to the nearby shed.

"Now, first of all," Mandy began, "kayaking isn't hard, but you do have to follow certain safety rules." She worked her way through her spiel, answering Adele's questions one by one in great detail. Adele took it all in. "So, this is your first time?"

"My very first," Adele said. "I canoed as a teenager but I never tried this."

"Jake and I go out regularly." When they first met, she knew at once he was outdoorsy, which mattered to her. She couldn't imagine either of them falling for someone who didn't love sports and getting outside, which made the last few weeks feel very strange.

"The lake is calm too," Mandy added. "Makes it easy for your first time." She passed the handle of a kayak cart to Adele, and took hold of the other one. "Let's go." The women walked their kayaks down to the water's edge.

"How did you get started on this?" Adele asked.

"Through the club. I used to canoe all the time, and then tried kayaking a few years ago."

"Where we met?"

"The very same."

Mandy and Adele belonged to the Women's Night Out, a congenial group who met once a month. Each member set up an event, and everyone else went along whether it was one of their interests or not. Adele had been a member for only a month, but Mandy joined years ago. She'd been sky diving, deep sea diving, to a strip club, a motorcycle race, a shooting range, a macrame class, learned how a detective does his job, taken cooking classes, attended the ballet and a boxing match, taken a class on Know Your Rights, and more.

"How did you get into it?" Adele asked.

"A friend of my mother's. How did you find us?" Mandy dropped the handle and secured the wheels, so the cart didn't roll into the water while they were out.

"Someone in your husband's office mentioned it and it sounded like fun."

"Oh, it is," Mandy said. "I've never regretted joining. I've learned so much." She helped Adele launch her kayak and then launched her own. "Now, this is my plan. We can work our way out to the island, circle it and return. The moon will be coming up soon so we'll be able to paddle back in the moonlight. Then we'll have dinner. And tomorrow we'll do the whole lake. It's really gorgeous now, with all the leaves turning. How does that sound?"

"Sounds like a plan," Adele said. "I like a walk before dinner. Will I have time?"

"Oh sure."

"Great. I usually find a place where I can sit and meditate. No need to come with me if you'd like to rest. You did all the driving. Sound okay?"

"Sounds like a plan. Let's go."

Mandy watched her guest drop a tentative paddle into the water.

"Remember, if we get separated and you're not sure where you are, just head for the shore, and follow it till you come to the cabin. If it's dark, look for a porch light and paddle for that. There's another cabin not far from my place and they're here year-round. But don't worry. It's a beautiful time to be on the water—clear, warm, calm." Adele waved to indicate she understood, and Mandy moved ahead of her, leading the way to the small island not far off shore. Sunset was in less than an hour and moonrise soon thereafter.

The fall colors were at their peak, and Mandy stayed her paddle to admire the golds and reds and oranges. In the summer, her favorite time was moonrise, when she paddled along the silver reflection on the water, wrapped in the warmth of a still night up country. Most people were off the water by then, throwing another burger on the grill, opening another beer. She could hear them, their voices and laughter threading the air and drifting across the still surface of the lake. Tonight, few cabins were occupied. Less than a mile up from her place was a shingled house where lived an older couple, recently retired, who spent long evenings on the porch, a single light blazing through the trees. Like a beacon, it guided her path on many a night.

She first met the old man when he was trying to pull tree limbs out of the water. She spotted him from the middle of the lake when she went out, and noticed he was still there, hands on hips, glaring at the stubborn branch, when she returned. When he gave in, releasing the rope, the rotting limb fell back, sinking below the surface. That was last fall when the stream that flowed past the house filled with rain water rushing into the lake, creating a current that could sweep a paddler right into the strainers, the tangle of branches and debris hidden below the surface.

Ahead of her floated an empty aluminum can. Mandy called out to Adele, pointed to the can and to other sites on the lake, indicating she'd head over to collect the litter. Adele waved acknowledgment and continued on her languid way, seemingly confident in her new skill. Mandy picked up the can and paddled deeper into the lake, sweeping her hands through water though there was little to collect. Behind her, dusk thickened on the land and crept down to the shore.

Mandy let the kayak drift till she glimpsed the porch light glimmering through the trees. She was too far away to see clearly, but sound carried well at this hour. The older couple was inside now, with the television blaring, spewing out the sounds of laughter and applause.

The first thing she'd noticed about Adele was her strength. The woman didn't crush her fingers in a handshake, nor prove her might by lifting a chair over a cubicle wall. It was the sight of her muscles in a sleeveless blouse, and the muscular curvature of her calves. Jake had recently commented on the new employee's muscle definition, unusual in a woman, he thought. That caught Mandy's attention, but the changes in his mood over the following weeks kindled something else—suspicion. And Adele's behavior today confirmed her worst fears. She knew where the handle for the refrigerator was, concealed within the pine board; she knew the layout of the cabin; she left out onions from the foods she prepared for the weekend, a nod to an allergy Mandy never mentioned. Mandy's thoughts circled back to Jake's edginess over the last few weeks—since just after Adele arrived in the office. There was no point in Mandy waiting to see where all of this would go—it had already gone and arrived. Her husband was having an affair.

Mandy turned the kayak toward shore. Time to get her supper started. Adele would spot the porch light and paddle to it, then turn along the shore to continue down to Mandy and Jake's cabin.

In the cabin Mandy laid a fire in the fireplace and stuffed in newspaper and kindling. All at once she felt tired, exhausted. And why not? For weeks she'd been wound like a catapult, wanting to scream at Jake and scratch out Adele's eyes. Instead, she brought her rival here to confront her. She rubbed her hand over her forehead. A headache was building up, a sure sign of the stress she'd been under. The fire struggled to catch, and she reached for the poker to stir the newspaper. The poker fell from her loose grip. She felt sick. Maybe a breath of fresh air would help.

On the porch, leaning on the railing, she gulped in the cool evening air and immediately felt better. Her cell buzzed and she saw Jake's number. She punched on.

"Hey, babe." He sounded exhausted.

She hadn't expected him to call and wasn't ready to talk, but he seemed not to notice.

"It's good to hear your voice. Today was a wreck. Wally came in to tell me the project will be late because Cindi, his wife, has asked for a divorce and he's so upset he can't focus. The entire office has been gossiping about him and his affair with Adele. Oh, is she there? She can't hear this, can she?"

"No, she's out kayaking." Wally and Adele?

"It's taken me weeks to figure out what's going on. I finally tracked down one of her former bosses—people hop all over the place in high-tech—and got the whole sordid story. Adele moves from job to job because she has to. She gets everyone thinking she's having an affair with someone in the office, wrecks the marriage, and then gets fired. She's got a knack for ferreting out personal information and then convincing people that she's intimate with the guy. She also gets vindictive. She tried to ruin her last employer. She's pathological!"

"Wally? The guy with the cowlick who blinks all the time?"

"That's him. Cindi got a dose of gossip almost every day and finally collapsed, hysterical. I had to shut it down, telling the staff I'd fire the next one to spread the dirt. But I had no way to prove it was all made up and Cindi was beside herself. That's why I've been making all these calls into Adele's history. I had to tell her this week we were letting her go. She's wrecked half a dozen marriages with her lies. Everyone in the office is like a zombie with her around. You know, it would almost be funny if it weren't so awful. Wally as the office Lothario. He's sick over Cindi wanting a divorce and he has no idea why."

"Oh, Jake, that's awful. Listen, I gotta go. Call you back."

Mandy punched off. Jake must have been next on Adele's list of victims. She learned everything she could about Jake and the cabin, befriended Mandy, and set her up for a girls' weekend. Adele was out there now, just about ready to hit the strainers, lured there by the porch light on the only other occupied cabin in the area. Mandy had set her up to paddle into the most dangerous part of the lake, a sure trap for someone so unfamiliar with the water. All because of her own immature possessiveness. But Adele wasn't having an affair with Jake. All of a sudden, revenge didn't look so good. How could she have been so stupid?

Mandy dragged her kayak into the water and paddled hard up to the neighbors' cottage. Ahead, she caught sight of something moving toward her. Peering into the darkness, she heard Adele's kayak scraping against wood and Adele trying to fight it by paddling harder. The current from the stream caught her and she went over, splashing and struggling. Mandy grounded her kayak into the overhanging grasses, and dove into the deep. She slithered through the murky water to the branches, a network of slimy, rotting wood that refused to give way over the years, and instead seemed to grow deadlier with every season.

Adele was exactly where Mandy imagined she would end up, snagged on a twisted limb, her gold necklace caught, holding her down even if she'd had enough sense to leave the kayak and swim upward. Mandy yanked and broke the clasp on the cheap necklace, wrapped her arms around the half-conscious woman, and hauled her up to the surface. Adele's gasping cough was the most-welcome sound Mandy had ever heard. She pulled the woman to the shore and heaved her onto the grassy edge. On shore herself, she dragged Adele onto higher ground and rolled her onto her side, pushing the water from her lungs.

"What's going on out here?" The neighbor stood on the porch peering into the dark. "Anyone hurt out here?"

"It's me, Mr. Corwin. We need an ambulance."

"Say no more. I'll call 'em." A moment later he returned, reporting they were on their way.

"What happened?" Adele asked when she could breathe.

"You got caught on a limb." Mandy thought it best to leave the explanation at that. She was ashamed of herself, her cruel and blind attempt to lure someone into danger all because of adolescent jealousy.

"You saved me?" Adele looked perplexed. "I'm so sorry."

"Sorry?" Mandy was about to ask Adele what she meant when she was startled by a sudden flash of light—an explosion sent flames shooting up over the trees. Smoke billowed toward them, filled Mandy's nostrils and throat, and made her choke.

It couldn't be her cabin. That was impossible—all those safety features. She stared at the glowing arc of fire stretching across the sky, and remembered the just-laid fire that wouldn't hold a flame, how tired and achy she felt and then how quickly she recovered once outside, where she talked to Jake on her cell, Adele's trip to the cellar to use the washing machine located right next to the propane furnace, Jake's firing Adele earlier in the week. Mandy listened to the other woman coughing, still gasping for breath, telling her how sorry she was and how wonderful Mandy was, the best friend she'd ever had.

Mandy watched her cabin burn, waiting patiently for the police to arrive. ❖

Contributors' Notes

Jason Allison was born and raised in the Bronx, and spent two decades with the New York City Police Department. He was primarily a homicide detective, and ended his career as part of an elite federal task force. His fiction has been featured in the lit-noir journal *Rock and a Hard Place,* and previously shortlisted for the Al Blanchard award. He has consulted for numerous authors and presented to members of the Mystery Writers of America and attendees of ThrillerFest. He can be reached at jason-allison.com.

Christine Bagley's work appears in both crime anthologies and literary journals. She holds an MFA in Creative Writing from Lesley University, and was a fiction contributor to the Bread Loaf Writers Conference. From 2011-2019, she taught writing and presentation skills to Harvard Medical School foreign national physicians and scientists, and is the former editor of the *Medical Services Review* for Massachusetts General Hospital, and *Eye Contact* for the Schepens Eye Research Institute. Bagley's short stories have appeared in *Briar Cliff Review, Bryant Literary Review,* multiple publications in *Best New England Crime Stories* anthologies, and *Untoward Magazine.* christinebagley.com

Jeannette de Beauvoir is an award-winning author of both mystery and historical fiction as well as a published poet. She finds the concept of place—the spaces in which stories are set—endlessly fascinating, and has set mystery series in Provincetown, Boston, and Montréal; in this story she travels to New Hampshire. She lives and works in a small cottage in Provincetown, where, allegedly, Elizabeth Taylor once slept. More at jeannettedebeauvoir.com.

John R. Clark grew up in Union, Maine, on a poultry farm overlooking Sennebec Lake. He draws on his experience in mental health, the public library field, and over forty years of sobriety to create stories, most with a Maine flavor. His YA anthology *Hardscrabble Kids—Semi Magical Tales of Maine* will be published this summer. His short stories have appeared in numerous anthologies. When not writing, he reviews books, as well as reading to his three grandchildren.

Bruce Robert Coffin is the award-winning author of the Detective Byron Mysteries. Winner of Killer Nashville's Silver Falchion Awards for Best Procedural and for Best Investigator, and the Maine Literary Award for Best Crime Fiction Novel, Bruce was also a finalist for the Agatha Award for Best Contemporary Novel. His short fiction appears in a number of anthologies, including *Best American Mystery Stories 2016.* brucerobertcoffin.com

Hans Copek's short stories are often inspired by family events he either witnessed or has been told about. In reality they didn't always involve mayhem but he found it fun to allow morbid thoughts free reign. He credits his association with Sisters in Crime and Mystery Writers of America for his development as a writer, as well as weekly sessions with his writers'group. His eighteen-year involvement with the New England Crime Bake conference earned him their first lifetime achievement award.

Sharon Daynard's writing runs the gamut from light and quirky to downright dark and troubling. Her short stories have been published in magazines and anthologies in the U.S. and Canada. "The Boss of Butler Square" received Honorable Mention for the 2019 Al Blanchard Award and her fifty-one-word flash "Widows Peak" was short-listed for a 2004 Derringer Award. She's crossed paths with a serial killer, testified before grand juries, and taken lie detector tests. Her debut novel, *Murder Points North*, puts a humorous spin on murder. She is a member of the New England chapter of Sisters in Crime.

a.l. Dawson honed his fiction writing skills at Grub Street Writers' workshops. His short stories "Sacred Ground" and "The Keeper" were published in 2020 in *Aphelion*. "The Crossing" was published in *Bloodroot: Best New England Crime Stories 2021*. In 2022 his nonfiction writing has been published in *Mother Jones* magazine. Dawson received a BA from Duke University, a Post Graduate Diploma in African Studies from the University of Edinburgh, and a doctorate in Education from the University of Massachusetts, Boston.

Trish Esden lives in northern Vermont. She's the author of the Scandal Mountain Antiques Mysteries series, which explores the secretive and adrenaline-charged underbelly of the antique and art world. As Pat Esden, she writes contemporary fantasy novels set in New England. Her short fiction has appeared in a number of venues.

Kate Flora's fascination with people's criminal tendencies began in the Maine attorney general's office. Deadbeat dads, people who hurt their kids, and employers' discrimination aroused her curiosity about human behavior. The author of twenty-four books and many short stories, Flora's been a finalist for the Edgar, Agatha, Anthony, and Derringer awards. She won the Public Safety Writers Association Award for nonfiction and twice won the Maine Literary Award for crime fiction. Her most recent Thea Kozak mystery is *Death Sends a Message*; her most recent Joe Burgess is *A World of Deceit*. Her crime story collection is *Careful What You Wish For*.

Judith Green is the sixth generation of her family to live on her hillside in rural western Maine. As Adult Education Director for her eleven-town school district, she wrote twenty-five high-interest/low-level books for adult students for several publishers, including novels and short stories in every genre. Her mystery stories have appeared in multiple anthologies. "A Good, Safe Place," published in Level Best's *Thin Ice*, was nominated for an Edgar.

Tilia Klebenov Jacobs is the bestselling author of three novels and numerous short stories. She is a judge in San Francisco's Soul-Making Keats Literary Competition, a reviewer for IndieReader.com, and a board member of Mystery Writers of America-New England. HarperCollins describes her as one of "crime fiction's top authors." Tilia has taught students in middle school, high school, college, and prison. She lives near Boston with her husband, two children, and a pleasantly neurotic standard poodle.

Kathryn Marple Kalb writing as Nikki Knight describes herself as an Author/Anchor/Mom, not in that order. An award-winning weekend anchor at 1010 WINS Radio in New York, she writes short stories and novels, including *Live, Local, and Dead,* a Vermont Radio Mystery, from Crooked Lane, and as Kathleen Marple Kalb, the Ella Shane Historical Mysteries, for Kensington. Her short stories are in several anthologies, and she was a 2022 Derringer Award finalist. She, her husband, and son live in a Connecticut house owned by their cat.

Avram Lavinsky, writer and recovering musician, writes character-driven novels, short stories, and creative nonfiction. He has placed in the Writers of the Future contest and was a recent semifinalist in *Ruminate Magazine*'s VanderMey Prize competition. His work has appeared in, or been accepted by, *Boston Literary Magazine, San Antonio Review, Mystery Tribune,* and *Savage Planets.* He has also earned starred reviews from the industry's toughest critics, his three teenage sons, although not often.

Cheryl Marceau spent her childhood moving around the United States, Canada, the Caribbean, and the Marshall Islands, finally settling in the Boston area as an adult. She held senior leadership roles in the corporate world but always had a passion for writing and especially for crime fiction. She published her first short story in 2010 and has since had stories selected for a number of anthologies including those by Level Best and Malice Domestic. Cheryl is a member of Mystery Writers of America, Sisters in Crime, and the Historical Novel Society.

Edith Maxwell is the Agatha Award-winning author of the Quaker Midwife Mysteries, the Local Foods Mysteries, and short crime fiction. As Maddie Day she pens the Country Store Mysteries, the Cozy Capers Book Group Mysteries, and the Cece Barton Mysteries. A past president of Sisters in Crime New England, she's a lifetime member of Sisters in Crime and a member of Mystery Writers of America. Maxwell lives with her beau north of Boston, where she writes, gardens, cooks, and wastes time on Facebook. Find her (and Maddie) at EdithMaxwell.com, wickedauthors.com, Mystery Lovers' Kitchen, and on social media.

Ruth M. McCarty's short mysteries have appeared in Level Best Books anthologies, *Blunt Flash Trauma*, *Flash Bang Mysteries*, *Mystery Most Edible*, *A Plot for Any Occasion*, and *Over My Dead Body!* She won the 2009 Derringer Award given by the Short Mystery Fiction Society for her story "No Flowers for Stacey." She is a former editor at Level Best Books, and a member of Sisters in Crime and Mystery Writers of America.

Susan Oleksiw is the author of the Mellingham series, set in a New England coastal town, featuring Chief of Police Joe Silva, and the Anita Ray series, set in a South Indian tourist resort, following the adventures of an Indian American photographer living at her aunt's tourist hotel. The most recent title is *In Sita's Shadow*. Susan's numerous short stories have appeared in *Alfred Hitchcock Mystery Magazine* and numerous anthologies. A co-founder of Level Best Books, she later co-founded Crime Spell Books, which is continuing the publication of the annual anthology of Best New England Crime Stories. She lives outside Boston. https://www.susanoleksiw.com

Robin Hazard Ray is a crime fiction writer, historian, and essayist. She leads tours at Mount Auburn Cemetery in

Cambridge and Watertown, MA, and helps tend the courtyard garden at the Isabella Stewart Gardner Museum. Her short stories have twice been awarded Honorable Mention for the Al Blanchard Award sponsored by the New England Crime Bake Conference. Her first historical mystery novel based at Mount Auburn, *The Strangers' Tomb*, will soon be joined by the second in the Murder in the Cemetery series, *The Soldiers' Rest*. She lives in Somerville, MA, with her husband, David, and two black cats.

Stephen D. Rogers is the author of *Shot to Death* and more than eight hundred shorter works. His website, www.StephenDRogers.com, includes a list of new and upcoming titles as well as other timely information.

Janet Raye Stevens is a mom, reader, tea-drinker (okay, tea guzzler), and weaver of smart, stealthily romantic tales. A Derringer Award finalist and RWA Golden Heart and Daphne du Maurier Award winner, Janet writes mystery, time travel, paranormal, and the occasional Christmas romance with humor, heart, and a dash of suspense. She lives with her family in Massachusetts. Connect with Janet at janetrayestevens.com.

Leslie Wheeler is the award-winning author of two mystery series: the Berkshire Hilltown Mysteries and the Miranda Lewis Living History Mysteries. Her latest release is *Wolf Bog*, the third book in the Berkshire Hilltown series. Her short crime fiction has appeared in numerous anthologies including the Best New England Crime Stories anthologies, published by Level Best Books, where she was a co-editor/publisher for six years, and now by Crime Spell Books, where she holds the same position. She divides her time between Cambridge, Massachusetts, and the Berkshires, where she writes in a house overlooking a pond. http://www.lesliewheeler.com

Made in the USA
Middletown, DE
07 October 2022

12130452R00196